WINDY CITY BLUES

Also published in Large Print
from G.K. Hall by Sara Paretsky:

Guardian Angel
Burn Marks
Blood Shot
Bitter Medicine
Killing Orders
Deadlock
Indemnity Only

Edited by Sara Paretsky:
A Woman's Eye

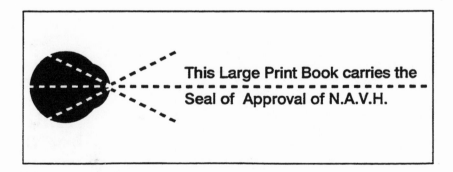

This Large Print Book carries the
Seal of Approval of N.A.V.H.

WINDY CITY BLUES

V.I. WARSHAWSKI STORIES

SARA PARETSKY

G.K. Hall & Co.
Thorndike, Maine

Published in 1996 by arrangement with Delacorte Press, an imprint of Dell Publishing Group, Inc.

G.K. Hall Large Print Core Collection.

The text of this Large Print edition is unabridged.
Other aspects of the book may vary from the original edition.

Set in 16 pt. News Plantin.

Printed in the United States on permanent paper.

Library of Congress Cataloging in Publication Data

Paretsky, Sara.
  Windy City blues / Sara Paretsky.
    p. cm.
  "V.I. Warshawski stories."
  ISBN 0-7838-1561-1 (lg. print : hc)
  ISBN 0-7838-1562-X (lg. print : lsc)
  1. Warshawski, V. I. (Fictitious character) — Fiction.
  2. Private investigators — Illinois — Chicago — Fiction.
  3. Women detectives — Illinois — Chicago — Fiction.
  4. Detective and mystery stories, American. 5. Chicago
  (Ill.) — Fiction. 6. Large type books. I. Title.
  [PS3566.A647W56 1996]
  813'.54—dc20   95-36362

For Isabel, always Agnes's
star pupil

Thanks to: Diana Haskell, Mena de Mario, Sarah Neely, Susan Ritter, and Mary Wylie for technical advice for "Grace Notes."

Thanks to Betty Nicholas, for essential technical advice and connections for "Strung Out."

Thanks to Dr. Robert Kirschner, for figuring out the murder method in "Settled Score."

CONTENTS

AUTHOR'S NOTE

These stories were written over a period of thirteen years, beginning with "The Takamoku *Joseki*" (1982) and ending with "Grace Notes" (1995), created especially for this collection. For that reason some details about V.I.'s life will appear inconsistent — sometimes she's driving an Omega, sometimes her Trans Am. She bought the Trans Am in 1990, at the end of the novel *Burn Marks*. Her dog, Peppy, became part of her life in 1988, at the conclusion of *Bitter Medicine*. The story "The Maltese Cat" was originally written in 1990, during the Bush-Quayle administration.

I sometimes write short stories when I am trying to understand a question that doesn't seem to merit a whole novel. That was true of "Settled Score," where I was wrestling with the issue of personal responsibility. Unusual settings suggest other stories: I once swam for a corporate competition (where I was so slow the other swimmers were eating dinner by the time I covered two laps); the starting gun and all of us diving at once turned into "At the Old Swimming Hole." However, in "The Maltese Cat," I simply wanted to pay my own particular homage to the great master of the hard-boiled detective.

Sara Paretsky
Chicago, June 1995

INTRODUCTION

A Walk on the Wild Side: Touring Chicago with V. I. Warshawski

A lone heron spreads its wings and rises from the marsh. It circles briefly, then heads south, disappearing in the shrouding mist. A handful of purple-necked ducks continues to nibble at delicacies in the fetid water. Their families have come here for millennia, breaking the journey from Canada to the Amazon at what we new-comers think of as the south side of Chicago.

The patch of marsh where they rest is small, about half a square mile. It's the sole remains of the wetlands which used to cover the twenty-five miles from Whiting, Indiana, north to Mc-Cormick Place, the monstrous convention center that squats next to Lake Michigan. Only fifty years ago much of this area, including the eight-lane highway that connects the south side with the Loop, was still under water. The marsh has been filled in with everything from cyanide to slag, with a lot of garbage to give it body.

The locals call the remaining bit of swamp Dead Stick Pond from the eponymous rotting wood which dots it. It appears on no city maps. It is so obscure that Chicago police officers stationed ten blocks away at the Port of Chicago haven't heard of it. Nor have officials at the local Chicago Park District office. To find it you have to know a native.

I'm not native to this neighborhood, nor even to this city. I first saw Chicago at two on a June morning in 1966. I was coming from a small town in eastern Kansas to do summer service work here for the Presbytery of Chicago — volunteer work in a time of great hope, great excitement, a time when we thought change possible, when we believed that if we poured enough energy, enough goodwill into the terrible problems of our country we could change those problems for good.

The vastness of the city at night was overwhelming. Red flares glowed against a yellow sky, followed by mile on mile of unbending lights: street lamps, neon signs, traffic lights, flashing police blues — lights that didn't illuminate but threw shadows, and made the city seem a monster, ready to devour the unwary.

The eye with which I see Chicago is always half cocked for alienation and despair, because for me the city is a dangerous place where both states are only just below the surface. When I fly in at night over the sprawl of lights, the feeling of tininess, of one lone unknown being, recurs. I have to scan the landscape trying to pick out the landmarks of the south side that tell me I have a home here, friends, a lover, a life of warmth.

Chicagoans find their own particular warmth where all city dwellers do — in their home neighborhood. My city holds seventy-seven separate neighborhoods, each with its own special ethnic or racial makeup, each with its own shopping area, library, police station, and schools. Adults, even those who've migrated to the suburbs, identify themselves with the neighborhoods of their childhood: an Irish-American secretary of mine from South Shore used to spit when she talked about Irish staff from west side communities. She wouldn't even pass along messages from them.

Northsiders don't go south; southsiders seldom venture even as far as the Loop, unless their jobs take them there. Chicago has two baseball teams to accommodate these parochial needs. The Cubs play at Wrigley Field five miles north of the Loop; the White Sox are at Comiskey Park, the same distance south of it. (Chicago's financial district is called the Loop because of the elevated train tracks that circle it.)

A southsider, I am often sharply criticized at south side events for being a Cubs fan. I have to explain that my allegiance dates from that summer of 1966, when I helped run an inner-city program for children. The Cubs, now sold out even in losing seasons, were then in such desperate need of an audience that they gave free tickets to our kids on Thursdays. The Sox didn't, so I became a Cubs fan. One thing all Chicagoans

11

understand is loyalty, especially loyalty to someone who has bribed you. For years the definition of an honest Chicago politician has been one who stays bought — so my explanation passes muster.

It was hard to get the kids on the train to go north. Although they lived four blocks from the el most had never ridden it, most had never been downtown, even to look at the fabled Christmas windows at Marshall Field (once a Chicago landmark, now a colonial property of a Minneapolis conglomerate) and none of them had ever been north. When they found that they weren't going to be killed going to and from Wrigley Field they started looking forward to the games.

Of all Chicago neighborhoods the most interesting to me are those on the far southeast side, where Dead Stick Pond fights for survival beneath the rusting sheds of the old steel mills. The whole history of the city is contained in four small neighborhoods there — South Chicago, South Deering, Pullman, and the East Side.

To see the true south side, drive south on I-94, the Dan Ryan Expressway, away from the Gold Coast with its pricey restaurants and shops. The route passes first Jackson Street, where members of Chicago's Greek community operate restaurants, then Cermak Road which which leads to Chinatown, then nods at 59th Street, which borders the world-renowned University of Chicago — my neighborhood — on its way to the very end of the city.

At 95th Street, where the expressway splits, offering the driver the choice between Memphis and Indiana, go east on I-94 toward Indiana. At 103rd Street the air becomes acrid. Even with the windows up and the heater or cooler turned off your nose stings and your eyes tear. Although the steel mills are dead and a third of the south side is out of work, enough heavy industry still exists to produce quite a stench in this old manufacturing corridor.

Out the window to your left a hillock dotted with methane flares stretches the mile from 103rd to 110th streets. This is the City of Chicago landfill, where we Chicagoans send our garbage. It's almost full, and the question of where to dump next is just one of the pressures on Dead Stick Pond. The flares keep the garbage from exploding as the bacteria devouring our refuse produce methane. (When landfill runs under a road, as it does here, exploding methane can destroy large sections of highway.)

You'll also see grain elevators poking up behind the garbage mountain, and, startlingly, the smokestacks from oceangoing freighters. The landfill and factories hide a network of waterways from the road.

At 130th Street, twenty miles southeast of the Water Tower where tourists and Chicagoans both like to shop, you finally leave the expressway and head east into the heart of the industrial zone. On a weekday yours may be the only car among the semis that compete with barges and trains

13

to supply the factories and haul their finished products.

One Hundred Thirtieth passes Metron, one of Chicago's few surviving steel mills, Medusa Cement, and the Scrap Corporation of Chicago — with a mountain of scrap iron to prove it. At Torrence Avenue you run into the giant Ford Assembly Plant, their largest in the world. There you turn north again, crossing the Calumet River on an old counterweight vertical lift bridge. Immediately beyond is 122nd Street, a narrow, badly paved industrial thoroughfare. Turn left under the Welded Tube Company billboard and follow the semis west.

Under a sky purple-pink with smog, marsh grasses and cattails tower above the cars. Despite a century of dumping that has filled the ground water with more carcinogens than the EPA can classify, the grasses flourish. If you are a bird-watcher, and patient, you can find meadowlarks and other prairie natives here.

After a mile 122nd Street intersects with a gravel track, Stony Island. To the right it goes up to the CID landfill. To the left it runs next to Dead Stick Pond until both of them dead-end at Lake Calumet. Medusa Cement is busy digging at the south end of the marsh; on the west the Feralloy Corporation buildings loom; to the east major construction is underway.

Conflicting signs tacked to the trees proclaim the area both a clean-water project and warn trespassers of hazardous wastes. Despite warning signs, on a good day you can find anything from a pair of boots to a bedstead dumped in Dead Stick Pond.

Fish have been returning to the Calumet River and its tributaries since passage of the Clean Water Act in the seventies, but the ones that make their way into the pond show up with massive tumors and rotted fins. The phosphates in the water further cut the amount of oxygen that can penetrate the surface. Even so, wild birds continue to land here on their migratory routes. And Chicagoans so poor they live in shanties without running water catch their dinners in the marsh. Their shacks dot unmarked trails in the swamps. The inhabitants have a high mortality rate from esophageal and stomach cancers because of the pollutants in their well water. The half-feral dogs around their homes make it hard for any social welfare agent to get a clear idea of their living situation.

By this point in your tour you are either cold and tired or hot and thirsty. Either way you would probably like to relax over the native drink — a shot and a beer. The ideal place to do so is Sonny's Inn a few miles north.

Retrace your route to Torrence Avenue, and go left, or north. From 117th to 103rd Street, almost two miles, you can see the remains of Wisconsin Steel. Once one of the world's largest producers, it has been bankrupt and gone half a decade now.

At 97th Torrence becomes Colfax. Ride it up to 95th, where you'll turn right and drive three blocks to Commercial Avenue, the main drag in South Chicago. Two blocks north to 91st Street and you'll find Sonny's Inn just across the railroad tracks.

The little bungalows that line the route are well kept up for the most part, although a few look pretty hopeless. Even though almost 50 percent of the population is out of work they still take pride in their homes and yards. And the Steel City and South Chicago banks, which hold most of their home mortgages, refinance them time and again. In themselves these banks make an amazing tourist attraction: what other big city in the world can boast of banks so committed to their community that they carry their customers through a prolonged period of trouble?

It is the gallantry of this old neighborhood that made me take it for the home of my detective, V. I. Warshawski. The gallantry, on the one hand, and the racial and ethnic mix that turned it into a volatile soup on the other. South Chicago was traditionally the first stop for new immigrants in Chicago. The mills, running three shifts a day, provided jobs for the unskilled and illiterate. The neighborhood has been home to Irish, Polish, Bohemian, Yugoslav, African, and most recently Hispanic Americans. As each new wave of immigrants arrived, the previous ones, with a fragile toehold on the American dream of universal prosperity, would fight to keep the newcomers out. The public schools were frequent arenas for real fights. Girls on South Chicago's streets either acquired boyfriends to protect them, or were carefully watched day and night by their parents, or learned the basics of street fighting to protect themselves. Even though V.I. grew up under the watchful eye of her mother, her father wanted her to be able to look after herself: as a police officer he knew better than most parents what dangers faced a girl who couldn't fight for herself.

So V.I. came of age under the shadow of the mills, with weekend treks to Dead Stick Pond to watch the herons feed. She certainly knows Sonny's Inn. Sonny's has stood through all the waves of ethnic and racial change. It is a throwback to the days of the late great Mayor Daley. His icons hang on the walls and stand on shelves — signed photos of him with the original Sonny, signed photos of him with President Kennedy, campaign stickers, yellowing newspaper articles. A set of antlers over the bar obscures some of the memorabilia.

If you go at lunchtime on a weekday your dining companions will represent a complete cross section of the south side — every racial and ethnic group the city can boast, and most of the neighborhood occupations. You can get a drink and a sandwich for under five dollars. And if you do decide to go native and ask for a shot and a beer — that's rye and a draw. Don't call attention to yourself by asking for brand-name whiskeys.

South Chicago doesn't top the city's list of neighborhoods eligible for limited street and sidewalk repair funds. You may notice places where pavements have collapsed. If you look into the holes you'll see cobblestones five feet down. Because the landfill a century ago didn't hold back the underlying marshes, the city jacked itself up and built another layer over the top. South Chicago is one of the few places where the original substratum remains.

If you happen to stay at the Palmer House downtown you might like to know that it is the only surviving building from the lower city. Not wanting to dismantle his pride and joy Mr. Palmer raised the whole building up on stilts so that the new, higher State Street could be paved in front.

With your shot and your Polish dog under your belt you're ready now for more sight-seeing. Driving west two miles to Stony Island and four blocks south to 95th Street you're now in the Pullman Historic Landmark District. George Pullman, who made his fortune inventing and manufacturing the Pullman car, built almost two thousand houses to form a model village in 1880. The area was supposed to be a showcase for workers, partly to keep union agitation low. The houses were built in the federal style from clay bricks dug out of nearby Lake Calumet. The Pullman Company operated all the village stores and provided all services.

Unfortunately the houses rapidly became too expensive for the working population to own. Discontent with the company over that and other matters came to a head during the depression of the 1890s, when many workers lost their jobs.

The scene of violent confrontations, Pullman lost a court battle with its workers over the right to own and operate the town. When the company pulled out the neighborhood went through numerous economic and ethnic upheavals, but in 1970 was designated a national landmark. Since then people have been renovating these beautiful old homes.

Clay from the Calumet made better bricks than any available today. One of the crimes Pullman residents have to guard against is loss of brick garages — people go on vacation and come home to find their garages have been dismantled brick by brick and carted off to become part of some house under construction in a remote neighborhood.

Instead of taking the expressway north, you should slide out of the south side the back way, going east to Buffalo Street, past the National Shrine to St. Jude, the Catholic patron of hopeless or difficult cases. Drive north on Buffalo, and suddenly you find it's turned into US highway 41. It twists and turns a bit for the next two miles, but the US 41 signs are easy to follow.

At 79th Street you'll see the last of the USX works on your right, and suddenly you're out of the industrial zone, back in quiet residential streets. At the corner of 71st Street and South Shore Drive stands the old South Shore Country Club. It was once the meeting place of the wealthy and powerful who lived in the area. One of the late Mayor Daley's daughters was married here.

The private beach and golf course have been taken over by the Chicago Park District, police horses now occupy the stables, and the natives are the ones swinging clubs on the green. The clubhouse is a community center now, a beautiful place, worth a side stop.

Beyond the country club Lake Michigan springs into view. You might pull off at La Rabida children's hospital half a mile up the road to climb the rocks overlooking the lake. From this vantage point, looking south you can see the industrial quag you just visited. To the north the skyline made famous by Skidmore, Edward Durrel Stone, Bud Goldberg, and their friends is silhouetted against the sky.

Back in your car return to US 41. Soon it becomes an eight-lane highway that takes you the quick way to the Loop. Lake Michigan will be your companion the rest of your journey, spewing foam against the rocks — a barricade put up by men hoping to tame the water. It is not a tame lake, though. Underneath the asphalt lies the marsh, home to herons for twenty-five thousand years. The lake may yet reclaim it.

Grace Notes

I

GABRIELLA SESTIERI
OF PITIGLIANO.
Anyone with knowledge of her
whereabouts should contact the office of Malcolm Ranier.

I WAS READING the *Herald-Star* at breakfast
when the notice jumped out at me from the personal section. I put my coffee down with extreme
care, as if I were in a dream and all my actions
moved with the slowness of dream time. I shut
the paper with the same slow motion, then opened
it again. The notice was still there. I spelled out
the headline letter by letter, in case my unconscious mind had substituted one name for another,
but the text remained the same. There could not
be more than one Gabriella Sestieri from Pitigliano. My mother, who died of cancer in 1968
at the age of forty-six.

"Who could want her all these years later?"
I said aloud.

21

Peppy, the golden retriever I share with my downstairs neighbor, raised a sympathetic eyebrow. We had just come back from a run on a dreary November morning and she was waiting hopefully for toast.

"It can't be her father." His mind had cracked after six months in a German concentration camp, and he refused to acknowledge Gabriella's death when my father wrote to inform him of it. I'd had to translate the letter, in which he said he was too old to travel but wished Gabriella well on her concert tour. Anyway, if he was alive still he'd be almost a hundred.

Maybe Gabriella's brother Italo was searching for her: he had disappeared in the maelstrom of the war, but Gabriella always hoped he survived. Or her first voice teacher, Francesca Salvini, whom Gabriella longed to see again, to explain why she had never fulfilled Salvini's hopes for her professional career. As Gabriella lay in her final bed in Jackson Park Hospital with tubes ringing her wasted body, her last messages had been for me and for Salvini. This morning it dawned on me for the first time how hurtful my father must have found that. He adored my mother, but for him she had only the quiet fondness of an old friend.

I realized my hands around the newspaper were wet with sweat, that paper and print were clinging to my palms. With an embarrassed laugh I put the paper down and washed off the ink under the kitchen tap. It was ludicrous to spin my mind with conjectures when all I had to do was phone Malcolm Ranier. I went to the living room and pawed through the papers on the piano for the phone book. Ranier seemed to be a lawyer with offices on La Salle Street, at the north end where the pricey new buildings stand.

His was apparently a solo practice. The woman who answered the phone assured me she was Mr. Ranier's assistant and conversant with all his files. Mr. Ranier couldn't speak with me himself now, because he was in conference. Or court. Or the john.

"I'm calling about the notice in this morning's paper, wanting to know the whereabouts of Gabriella Sestieri."

"What is your name, please, and your relationship with Mrs. Sestieri?" The assistant left out the second syllable so that the name came out as "Sistery."

"I'll be glad to tell you that if you tell me why you're trying to find her."

"I'm afraid I can't give out confidential client business over the phone. But if you tell me your name and what you know about Mrs. Sestieri we'll get back to you when we've discussed the matter with our client."

I thought we could keep this conversation going all day. "The person you're looking for may not be the same one I know, and I don't want to violate a family's privacy. But I'll be in a meeting on La Salle Street this morning; I can stop by to discuss the matter with Mr. Ranier."

The woman finally decided that Mr. Ranier had ten minutes free at twelve-thirty. I gave her my name and hung up. Sitting at the piano, I crashed out chords, as if the sound could bury the wildness of my feelings. I never could remember whether I knew how ill my mother was the last six months of her life. Had she told me and I couldn't — or didn't wish to — comprehend it? Or had she decided to shelter me from the knowledge? Gabriella usually made me face bad news, but perhaps not the worst of all possible news, our final separation.

Why did I never work on my singing? It was one thing I could have done for her. I didn't have a Voice, as Gabriella put it, but I had a serviceable contralto, and of course she insisted I acquire some musicianship. I stood up and began working on a few vocal stretches, then suddenly became wild with the desire to find my mother's music, the old exercise books she had me learn from.

I burrowed through the hall closet for the trunk that held her books. I finally found it in the farthest corner, under a carton holding my old case files, a baseball bat, a box of clothes I no longer wore but couldn't bring myself to give away. . . . I sat on the closet floor in misery, with a sense of having buried her so deep I couldn't find her.

Peppy's whimpering pulled me back to the present. She had followed me into the closet and was pushing her nose into my arm. I fondled her ears.

At length it occurred to me that if someone was trying to find my mother I'd need documents to prove the relationship. I got up from the floor and pulled the trunk into the hall. On top lay her black silk concert gown: I'd forgotten wrapping that in tissue and storing it. In the end I found my parents' marriage license and Gabriella's death certificate tucked into the score of *Don Giovanni.*

When I returned the score to the trunk another old envelope floated out. I picked it up and recognized Mr. Fortieri's spiky writing. Carlo Fortieri repaired musical instruments and sold, or at least used to sell music. He was the person Gabriella went to for Italian conversation, musical conversation, advice. He still sometimes tuned my own piano out of affection for her.

When Gabriella met him, he'd been a widower for years, also with one child, also a girl. Gabriella thought I ought to play with her while she sang or discussed music with Mr. Fortieri, but Barbara was ten years or so my senior and we'd never had much to say to each other.

I pulled out the yellowed paper. It was written in Italian, and hard for me to decipher, but apparently dated from 1965.

Addressing her as *"Cara signora Warshawski,"* Mr. Fortieri sent his regrets that she was forced to cancel her May 14 concert. "I shall, of course, respect your wishes and not reveal the nature of your indisposition to anyone else. And, *cara signora,* you should know by now that I regard

25

any confidence of yours as a sacred trust: you need not fear an indiscretion." It was signed with his full name.

I wondered now if he'd been my mother's lover. My stomach tightened, as it does when you think of your parents stepping outside their prescribed roles, and I folded the paper back into the envelope. Fifteen years ago the same notion must have prompted me to put his letter inside *Don Giovanni*. For want of a better idea I stuck it back in the score and returned everything to the trunk. I needed to rummage through a different carton to find my own birth certificate, and it was getting too late in the morning for me to indulge in nostalgia.

II

Malcolm Ranier's office overlooked the Chicago River and all the new glass and marble flanking it. It was a spectacular view — if you squinted to shut out the burnt-out waste of Chicago's west side that lay beyond. I arrived just at twelve-thirty, dressed in my one good suit, black, with a white crepe-de-chine blouse. I looked feminine, but austere — or at least that was my intention.

Ranier's assistant-cum-receptionist was buried in Danielle Steel. When I handed her my card, she marked her page without haste and took the card into an inner office. After a ten-minute wait to let me understand his importance, Ranier came out to greet me in person. He was a soft round man of about sixty, with gray eyes that lay like pebbles above an apparently jovial smile.

"Ms. Warshawski. Good of you to stop by. I understand you can help us with our inquiry into Mrs. Sestieri." He gave my mother's name a genuine Italian lilt, but his voice was as hard as his eyes.

"Hold my calls, Cindy." He put a hand on the nape of my neck to steer me into his office.

Before we'd shut the door Cindy was reabsorbed into Danielle. I moved away from the hand — I didn't want grease on my five-hundred-dollar jacket — and went to admire a bronze nymph on a shelf at the window.

"Beautiful, isn't it." Ranier might have been commenting on the weather. "One of my clients brought it from France."

"It looks as though it should be in a museum."

A call to the bar association before I left my apartment told me he was an import-export lawyer. Various imports seemed to have attached themselves to him on their way into the country. The room was dominated by a slab of rose marble, presumably a work table, but several antique chairs were also worth a second glance. A marquetry credenza stood against the far wall. The Modigliani above it was probably an original.

"Coffee, Ms." — he glanced at my card again — "Warshawski?"

"No, thank you. I understand you're very busy,

27

and so am I. So let's talk about Gabriella Sestieri."

"*D'accordo.*" He motioned me to one of the spindly antiques near the marble slab. "You know where she is?"

The chair didn't look as though it could support my hundred and forty pounds, but when Ranier perched on a similar one I sat, with a wariness that made me think he had them to keep people deliberately off balance. I leaned back and crossed my legs. The woman at ease.

"I'd like to make sure we're talking about the same person. And that I know why you want to find her."

A smile crossed his full lips, again not touching the slate chips of his eyes. "We could fence all day, Ms. Warshawski, but as you say, time is valuable to us both. The Gabriella Sestieri I seek was born in Pitigliano on October thirtieth, 1921. She left Italy sometime early in 1941, no one knows exactly when, but she was last heard of in Siena that February. And there's some belief she came to Chicago. As to why I want to find her, a relative of hers, now in Florence, but from the Pitigliano family, is interested in locating her. My specialty is import-export law, particularly with Italy: I'm no expert in finding missing persons, but I agreed to assist as a favor to a client. The relative — Mrs. Sestieri's relative — has a professional connection to my client. And now it is your turn, Ms. Warshawski."

"Ms. Sestieri died in March 1968." My blood was racing; I was pleased to hear my voice come

28

out without a tremor. "She married a Chicago police officer in April 1942. They had one child. Me."

"And your father? Officer Warshawski?"

"Died in 1979. Now may I have the name of my mother's relative? I've known only one member of her family, my grandmother's sister who lives here in Chicago, and am eager to find others." Actually, if they bore any resemblance to my embittered Aunt Rosa I'd just as soon not meet the remaining Verazi clan.

"You were cautious, Ms. Warshawski, so you will forgive my caution: do you have proof of your identity?"

"You make it sound as though treasure awaits the missing heir, Mr. Ranier." I pulled out the copies of my legal documents and handed them over. "Who or what is looking for my mother?"

Ranier ignored my question. He studied the documents briefly, then put them on the marble slab while condoling me on losing my parents. His voice had the same soft flat cadence as when he'd discussed the nymph.

"You've no doubt remained close to your grandmother's sister? If she's the person who brought your mother to Chicago it might be helpful for me to have her name and address."

"My aunt is a difficult woman to be close to, but I can check with her, to see if she doesn't mind my giving you her name and address."

"And the rest of your mother's family?"

I held out my hands, empty. "I don't know

any of them. I don't even know how many there are. Who is my mystery relative? What does he — she — want?"

He paused, looking at the file in his hands. "I actually don't know. I ran the ad merely as a favor to my client. But I'll pass your name and address along, Ms. Warshawski, and when he's been in touch with the person I'm sure you'll hear."

This runaround was starting to irritate me. "You're a heck of a poker player, Mr. Ranier. But you know as well as I that you're lying like a rug."

I spoke lightly, smiling as I got to my feet and crossed to the door, snatching my documents from the marble slab as I passed. For once his feelings reached his eyes, turning the slate to molten rock. As I waited for the elevator I wondered if answering that ad meant I was going to be sucker-punched.

Over dinner that night with Dr. Lotty Herschel I went through my conversation with Ranier, trying to sort out my confused feelings. Trying, too, to figure out who in Gabriella's family might want to find her, if the inquiry was genuine.

"They surely know she's dead," Lotty said.

"That's what I thought at first, but it's not that simple. See, my grandmother converted to Judaism when she married Nonno Mattia — sorry, that's Gabriella's father — Grandpa Matthias — Gabriella usually spoke Italian to me. Anyway,

30

my grandmother died in Auschwitz when the Italian Jews were rounded up in 1944. Then, my grandfather didn't go back to Pitigliano, the little town they were from, after he was liberated — the Jewish community there had been decimated and he didn't have any family left. So he was sent to a Jewish-run sanatorium in Turin, but Gabriella only found that out after years of writing letters to relief agencies."

I stared into my wineglass, as though the claret could reveal the secrets of my family. "There was one cousin she was really close to, from the Christian side of her family, named Frederica. Frederica had a baby out of wedlock the year before Gabriella came to Chicago, and got sent away in disgrace. After the war Gabriella kept trying to find her, but Frederica's family wouldn't forward the letters — they really didn't want to be in touch with her. Gabriella might have saved enough money to go back to Italy to look for herself, but then she started to be ill. She had a miscarriage the summer of sixty-five and bled and bled. Tony and I thought she was dying then."

My voice trailed away as I thought of that hot unhappy summer, the summer the city burst into riot-spawned flames and my mother lay in the stifling front bedroom oozing blood. She and Tony had one of their infrequent fights. I'd been on my paper route and they didn't hear me come in. He wanted her to sell something which she said wasn't hers to dispose of.

"And your life," my father shouted. "You can give that away as a gift? Even if she was still alive —" He broke off then, seeing me, and neither of them talked about the matter again, at least when I was around to hear.

Lotty squeezed my hand. "What about your aunt, great-aunt in Melrose Park? She might have told her siblings, don't you think? Was she close to any of them?"

I grimaced. "I can't imagine Rosa being close to anyone. See, she was the last child, and Gabriella's grandmother died giving birth to her. So some cousins adopted her, and when they emigrated in the twenties Rosa came to Chicago with them. She didn't really feel like she was part of the Verazi family. I know it seems strange, but with all the uprootings the war caused, and all the disconnections, it's possible that the main part of Gabriella's mother's family didn't know what became of her."

Lotty nodded, her face twisted in sympathy; much of her family had been destroyed in those death camps also. "There wasn't a schism when your grandmother converted?"

I shrugged. "I don't know. It's frustrating to think how little I know about those people. Gabriella says — said — the Verazis weren't crazy about it, and they didn't get together much except for weddings or funerals — except for the one cousin. But Pitigliano was a Jewish cultural center before the war and Nonno was considered a real catch. I guess he was rich until the Fascists con-

32

fiscated his property." Fantasies of reparations danced through my head.

"Not too likely," Lotty said. "You're imagining someone overcome with guilt sixty years after the fact coming to make you a present of some land?"

I blushed. "Factory, actually: the Sestieris were harness makers who switched to automobile interiors in the twenties. I suppose if the place is even still standing, it's part of Fiat or Mercedes. You know, all day long I've been swinging between wild fantasies — about Nonno's factory, or Gabriella's brother surfacing — and then I start getting terrified, wondering if it's all some kind of terrible trap. Although who'd want to trap me, or why, is beyond me. I know this Malcolm Ranier knows. It would be so easy —"

"No! Not to set your mind at rest, not to prove you can bypass the security of a modern high rise — for no reason whatsoever are you to break into that man's office."

"Oh, very well." I tried not to sound like a sulky child denied a treat.

"You promise, Victoria?" Lotty sounded ferocious.

I held up my right hand. "On my honor, I promise not to break into his office."

III

It was six days later that the phone call came to my office. A young man, with an Italian accent so thick that his English was almost incomprehensible, called up and gaily asked if I was his "Cousin Vittoria."

"Parliamo italiano," I suggested, and the gaiety in his voice increased as he switched thankfully to his own language.

He was my cousin Ludovico, the great-great-grandson of our mutual Verazi ancestors, he had arrived in Chicago from Milan only last night, terribly excited at finding someone from his mother's family, thrilled that I knew Italian, my accent was quite good, really, only a tinge of America in it, could we get together, any place, he would find me — just name the time as long as it was soon.

I couldn't help laughing as the words tumbled out, although I had to ask him to slow down and repeat. It had been a long time since I'd spoken Italian, and it took time for my mind to adjust. Ludovico was staying at the Garibaldi, a small hotel on the fringe of the Gold Coast, and would be thrilled if I met him there for a drink at six. Oh, yes, his last name — that was Verazi, the same as our great-grandfather.

I bustled through my business with greater efficiency than usual so that I had time to run the dogs and change before meeting him. I laughed at myself for dressing with care, in a pantsuit of crushed lavender velvet which could take me dancing if the evening ended that way, but no self-mockery could suppress my excitement. I'd been an only child with one cousin from each of my parents' families as my only relations. My cousin Boom-Boom, whom I adored, had been dead these ten years and more, while Rosa's son Albert was such a mass of twisted fears that I preferred not to be around him. Now I was meeting a whole new family.

I tap-danced around the dog in my excitement. Peppy gave me a long-suffering look and demanded that I return her to my downstairs neighbor: Mitch, her son, had stopped there on our way home from running.

"You look slick, doll," Mr. Contreras told me, torn between approval and jealousy. "New date?"

"New cousin." I continued to tap-dance in the hall outside his door. "Yep. The mystery relative finally surfaced. Ludovico Verazi."

"You be careful, doll," the old man said severely. "Plenty of con artists out there to pretend they're your cousins, you know, and next thing — phht."

"What'll he con me out of? my dirty laundry?" I planted a kiss on his nose and danced down the sidewalk to my car.

Three men were waiting in the Garibaldi's small lobby, but I knew my cousin at once. His hair

35

was amber, instead of black, but his face was my mother's, from the high rounded forehead to his wide sensuous mouth. He leapt up at my approach, seized my hands, and kissed me in the European style — sort of touching the air beside each ear.

"Bellissima!" Still holding my hands he stepped back to scrutinize me. My astonishment must have been written large on my face, because he laughed a little guiltily.

"I know it, I know it, I should have told you of the resemblance, but I didn't realize it was *so* strong: the only picture I've seen of Cousin Gabriella is a stage photo from 1940 when she starred in Jommelli's *Iphigenia."*

"Jommelli!" I interrupted. "I thought it was Gluck!"

"No, no, *cugina,* Jommelli. Surely Gabriella knew what she sang?" Laughing happily he moved to the armchair where he'd been sitting and took up a brown leather case. He pulled out a handful of papers and thumbed through them, then extracted a yellowing photograph for me to examine.

It was my mother, dressed as Iphigenia for her one stage role, the one that gave me my middle name. She was made up, her dark hair in an elaborate coil, but she looked absurdly young, like a little girl playing dress-up. At the bottom of the picture was the name of the studio, in Siena where she had sung, and on the back someone had lettered, *"Gabriella Sestieri fa la parte d'Iphigenia nella produzione d'Iphigenia da Jom-*

melli." The resemblance to Ludovico was clear, despite the blurring of time and cosmetics to the lines of her face. I felt a stab of jealousy: I inherited her olive skin, but my face is my father's.

"You know this photograph?" Ludovico asked.

I shook my head. "She left Italy in such a hurry: all she brought with her were some Venetian wineglasses that had been a wedding present to Nonna Laura. I never saw her onstage."

"I've made you sad, cousin Vittoria, by no means my intention. Perhaps you would like to keep this photograph?"

"I would, very much. Now — a drink? Or dinner?"

He laughed again. "I have been in America only twenty-four hours, not long enough to be accustomed to dinner in the middle of the afternoon. So — a drink, by all means. Take me to a typical American bar."

I collected my Trans Am from the doorman and drove down to the Golden Glow, the bar at the south end of the Loop owned by my friend Sal Barthele. My appearance with a good-looking stranger caused a stir among the regulars — as I'd hoped. Murray Ryerson, an investigative reporter whose relationship with me is compounded of friendship, competition, and a disastrous romantic episode, put down his beer with a snap and came over to our table. Sal Barthele emerged from her famous mahogany horseshoe bar. Under cover of Murray's greetings and Ludovico's accented English she muttered, "Girl, you are strutting. You look indecent! Anyway, isn't this cradle snatching? Boy looks *young!*"

I was glad the glow from the Tiffany table lamps was too dim for her to see me blushing. In the car coming over I had been calculating degrees of consanguinity and decided that as second cousins we were eugenically safe; I was embarrassed to show it so obviously. Anyway, he was only seven years younger than me.

"My newfound cousin," I said, too abruptly. "Ludovico Verazi — Sal Barthele, owner of the Glow."

Ludovico shook her hand. "So, you are an old friend of this cousin of mine. You know her more than I do — give me ideas about her character."

"Dangerous," Murray said. "She breaks men in her soup like crackers."

"Only if they're crackers to begin with," I snapped, annoyed to be presented to my cousin in such a light.

"Crackers to begin with?" Ludovico asked.

"Slang — *gergo* — for *'pazzo,'*" I explained. "Also a cracker is an oaf — a *cretino.*"

Murray put an arm around me. "Ah, Vic — the sparkle in your eyes lights a fire in my heart."

"It's just the third beer, Murray — that's heartburn," Sal put in. "Ludovico, what do you drink — whiskey, like your cousin? Or something nice and Italian like Campari?"

"Whiskey before dinner, Cousin Vittoria? No, no, by the time you eat you have no — no tasting sensation. For me, Signora, a glass of wine please."

Later over dinner at Filigree we became "Vic" and "Vico" — "Please, Veek, no one is calling me 'Ludovico' since the time I am a little boy in trouble —" And later still, after two bottles of Barolo, he asked me how much I knew about the Verazi family.

"*Niente,*" I said. "I don't even know how many brothers and sisters Gabriella's mother had. Or where you come into the picture. Or where I do, for that matter."

His eyebrows shot up in surprise. "So your mother was never in touch with her own family after she moved here?"

I told him what I'd told Lotty, about the war, my grandmother's estrangement from her family, and Gabriella's depression on learning of her cousin Frederica's death.

"But I am the grandson of that naughty Frederica, that girl who would have a baby with no father." Vico shouted in such excitement that the wait staff rushed over to make sure he wasn't choking to death. "This is remarkable, Vic, this is amazing, that the one person in our family *your* mother is close to turns out to be *my* grandmother.

"Ah, it was sad, very sad, what happened to her. The family is moved to Florence during the war, my grandmother has a baby, maybe the father is a partisan, my grandmother was the one person in the family to be supporting the partisans. My great-grandparents, they are very

39

prudish, they say, this is a disgrace, never mind there is a war on and much bigger disgraces are happening all the time, so — poof! — off goes this naughty Frederica with her baby to Milano. And the baby becomes my mother, but she and my grandmother both die when I am ten, so these most respectable Verazi cousins, finally they decide the war is over, the grandson is after all far enough removed from the taint of original sin, they come fetch me and raise me with all due respectability in Florence."

He broke off to order a cognac. I took another espresso: somehow after forty I no longer can manage the amount of alcohol I used to. I'd only drunk half of one of the bottles of wine.

"So how did you learn about Gabriella? And why did you want to try to find her?"

"Well, *cara cugina,* it is wonderful to meet you, but I have a confession I must make: it was in the hopes of finding — something — that I am coming to Chicago looking for my cousin Gabriella."

"What kind of something?"

"You say you know nothing about our great-grandmother, Claudia Fortezza? So you are not knowing even that she is in a small way a composer?"

I couldn't believe Gabriella never mentioned such a thing. If she didn't know about it, the rift with the Verazis must have been more severe than she led me to believe. "But maybe that explains why she was given early musical training,"

I added aloud. "You know my mother was a quite gifted singer. Although, alas, she never had the professional career she should have."

"Yes, yes, she trained with Francesca Salvini. I know all about that! Salvini was an important teacher, even in a little town like Pitigliano people came from Siena and Florence to train with her, and she had a connection to the Siena Opera. But anyway, Vic, I am wanting to collect Claudia Fortezza's music. The work of women composers is coming into vogue. I can find an ensemble to perform it, maybe to record it, so I am hoping Gabriella, too, has some of this music."

I shook my head. "I don't think so. I kept all her music in a trunk, and I don't think there's anything from that period."

"But you don't know definitely, do you, so maybe we can look together." He was leaning across the table, his voice vibrating with urgency.

I moved backward, the strength of his feelings making me uneasy. "I suppose so."

"Then let us pay the bill and go."

"Now? But, Vico, it's almost midnight. If it's been there all this while it will still be there in the morning."

"Ah: I am being the cracker, I see." We had been speaking in Italian all evening, but for this mangled idiom Vico switched to English. *"Mi scusi, cara cugina:* I have been so engaged in my hunt, through the papers of old aunts, through attics in Pitigliano, in used bookstores in Florence, that I forget not everyone shares my enthusiasm.

41

And then last month, I find a diary of my grandmother's, and she writes of the special love her cousin Gabriella has for music, her special gift, and I think — ah-ha, if this music lies anywhere, it is with this Gabriella."

He picked up my right hand and started playing with my fingers. "Besides, confess to me, Vic: in your mind's eye you are at your home feverishly searching through your mother's music, whether I am present or not."

I laughed, a little shakily: the intensity in his face made him look so like Gabriella when she was swept up in music that my heart turned over with yearning.

"So I am right? We can pay the bill and leave?"

The wait staff, hoping to close the restaurant, had left the bill on our table some time earlier. I tried to pay it, but Vico snatched it from me. He took a thick stack of bills from his billfold. Counting under his breath he peeled off two hundreds and a fifty and laid them on the check. Like many Europeans he'd assumed the tip was included in the total: I added four tens and went to retrieve the Trans Am.

IV

As we got out of the car I warned Vico not to talk in the stairwell. "We don't want the dogs to hear me and wake Mr. Contreras."

"He is a malevolent neighbor? You need me perhaps to guard you?"

"He's the best-natured neighbor in the world. Unfortunately, he sees his role in my life as Cerberus, with a whiff of Othello thrown in. It's late enough without spending an hour on why I'm bringing you home with me."

We managed to tiptoe up the stairs without rousing anyone. Inside my apartment we collapsed with the giggles of teenagers who've walked past a cop after curfew. Somehow it seemed natural to fall from laughter into each other's arms. I was the first to break away. Vico gave me a look I couldn't interpret — mockery seemed to dominate.

My cheeks stinging, I went to the hall closet and pulled out Gabriella's trunk once more. I lifted out her evening gown again, fingering the lace panels in the bodice. They were silver, carefully edged in black. Shortly before her final illness Gabriella managed to organize a series of concerts that she hoped would launch her career again, at least in a small way, and it was for these that she had the dress made. Tony and I sat in the front row of Mandel Hall, almost swooning with our passion for her. The gown cost her two years of free lessons for the couturier's daughter, the last few given when she had gone bald from chemotherapy.

As I stared at the dress, wrapped in melancholy, I realized Vico was pulling books and scores from the trunk and going through them with quick careful fingers. I'd saved dozens of Gabriella's books of operas and lieder, but nothing like her whole collection. I wasn't going to tell Vico that, though: he'd probably demand that we break into old Mr. Fortieri's shop to see if any of the scores were still lying about.

At one point Vico thought he had found something, a handwritten score tucked into the pages of *Idomeneo*. I came to look. Someone, not my mother, had meticulously copied out a concerto. As I bent to look more closely, Vico pulled a small magnifying glass from his wallet and began to scrutinize the paper.

I eyed him thoughtfully. "Does the music or the notation look anything like our great-grandmother's?"

He didn't answer me, but held the score up to the light to inspect the margins. I finally took the pages from him and scanned the clarinet line.

"I'm no musicologist, but this sounds baroque to me." I flipped to the end, where the initials "CF" were inscribed with a flourish: Carlo Fortieri might have copied this for my mother — a true labor of love: copying music is a slow, painful business.

"Baroque?" Vico grabbed the score back from me and looked at it more intensely. "But this paper is not that old, I think."

"I think not, also. I have a feeling it's something one of my mother's friends copied out for a chamber group they played in: she sometimes took the piano part."

He put the score to one side and continued burrowing in the trunk. Near the bottom he came on a polished wooden box, big enough to fit snugly against the short side of the trunk. He grunted as he prised it free, then gave a little crow of delight as he saw it was filled with old papers.

"Take it easy, cowboy," I said as he started tossing them to the floor. "This isn't the city dump."

He gave me a look of startling rage at my reproof, then covered it so quickly with a laugh that I couldn't be sure I'd seen it. "This old wood is beautiful. You should keep this out where you can look at it."

"It was Gabriella's, from Pitigliano." In it, carefully wrapped in her winter underwear, she'd laid the eight Venetian glasses that were her sole legacy of home. Fleeing in haste in the night, she had chosen to transport a fragile load, as if that gained her control of her own fragile destiny.

Vico ran his long fingers over the velvet lining the case. The green had turned yellow and black along the creases. I took the box away from him, and began replacing my school essays and report cards — my mother used to put my best school reports in the case.

At two Vico had to admit defeat. "You have no idea where it is? You didn't sell it, perhaps to meet some emergency bill or pay for that beautiful sports car?"

"Vico! What on earth are you talking about? Putting aside the insult, what do you think a score by an unknown nineteenth-century woman is worth?"

"Ah, *mi scusi,* Vic — I forget that everyone doesn't value these Verazi pieces as I do."

"Yes, my dear cousin, and I didn't just fall off a turnip truck, either." I switched to English in my annoyance. "Not even the most enthusiastic grandson would fly around the world with this much mystery. What's the story — are the Verazis making you their heir if you produce her music? Or are you looking for something else altogether?"

"Turnip truck? What is this turnip truck?"

"Forget the linguistic excursion and come clean, Vico. Meaning, confession is good for the soul, so speak up. What are you really looking for?"

He studied his fingers, grimy from paging through the music, then looked up at me with a quick frank smile. "The truth is, Fortunato Magi may have seen some of her music. He was Puccini's uncle, you know, and very influential among the Italian composers of the end of the century. My great-grandmother used to talk about Magi reading Claudia Fortezza's music. She was only a daughter-in-law, and anyway, Claudia Fortezza was dead years before she married into the family, so I never paid any attention to it. But then when I found my grandmother's diaries, it seemed possible that there was some truth to it. It's even possible that Puccini used some of Claudia Fortezza's music, so if we can find it, it might be valuable."

I thought the whole idea was ludicrous — it

wasn't even as though the Puccini estate were collecting royalties that one might try to sue for. And even if they were — you could believe almost any highly melodic vocal music sounded like Puccini. I didn't want to get into a fight with Vico about it, though: I had to be at work early in the morning.

"There wasn't any time you can remember Gabriella talking about something very valuable in the house?" he persisted.

I was about to shut him off completely when I suddenly remembered my parents' argument that I'd interrupted. Reluctantly, because he saw I'd thought of something, I told Vico about it.

"She was saying it wasn't hers to dispose of. I suppose that might include her grandmother's music. But there wasn't anything like that in the house when my father died. And believe me, I went through all the papers." Hoping for some kind of living memento of my mother, something more than her Venetian wineglasses.

Vico seized my arms in his excitement. "You see! She did have it, she must have sold it anyway. Or your father did, after she died. Who would they have gone to?"

I refused to give him Mr. Fortieri as a gift. If Gabriella had been worried about the ethics of disposing of someone else's belongings she probably would have consulted him. Maybe even asked him to sell it, if she came to that in the end, but Vico didn't need to know that.

"You know someone, I can tell," he cried.

"No. I was a child. She didn't confide in me. If my father sold it he would have been embarrassed to let me know. It's going on for three in the morning, Vico, and I have to work in a few hours. I'm going to call you a cab and get you back to the Garibaldi."

"You work? Your long lost cousin Vico comes to Chicago for the first time and you cannot kiss off your boss?" He blew across his fingers expressively.

"I work for myself." I could hear the brusqueness creep into my voice — his exigency was taking away some of his charm. "And I have one job that won't wait past tomorrow morning."

"What kind of work is it you do that cannot be deferred?"

"Detective. Private investigator. And I have to be on a — a —" — I couldn't think of the Italian, so I used English — "shipping dock in four hours."

"Ah, a detective." He pursed his lips. "I see now why this Murray was warning me about you. You and he are lovers? Or is that a shocking question to ask an American woman?"

"Murray's a reporter. His path crosses mine from time to time." I went to the phone and summoned a cab.

"And, Cousin, I may take this handwritten score with me? To study more leisurely?"

"If you return it."

"I will be here with it tomorrow afternoon — when you return from your detecting."

I went to the kitchen for some newspaper to wrap it in, wondering about Vico. He didn't seem to have much musical knowledge. Perhaps he was ashamed to tell me he couldn't read music and was going to take it to some third party who could give him a stylistic comparison between this score and something of our grandmother's.

The cab honked under the window a few minutes later. I sent him off on his own with a chaste cousinly kiss. He took my retreat from passion with the same mockery that had made me squirm earlier.

V

All during the next day, as I huddled behind a truck taking pictures of a handoff between the vice president of an electronics firm and a driver, as I tailed the driver south to Kankakee and photographed another handoff to a man in a sports car, traced the car to its owner in Libertyville and reported back to the electronics firm in Naperville, I wondered about Vico and the score. What was he really looking for?

Last night I hadn't questioned his story too closely — the late night and pleasure in my new cousin had both muted my suspicions. Today the bleak air chilled my euphoria. A quest for a great-grandmother's music might bring one pleasure, but surely not inspire such avidity as Vico displayed. He'd grown up in poverty in Milan without knowing who his father, or even his grandfather were. Maybe it was a quest for roots that was driving my cousin so passionately.

I wondered, too, what item of value my mother had refused to sell thirty summers ago. What wasn't *hers* to sell, that she would stubbornly sacrifice better medical care for it? I realized I felt hurt: I thought I was so dear to her she told me everything. The idea that she'd kept a secret from me made it hard for me to think clearly.

When my dad died, I'd gone through everything in the little house on Houston before selling it. I'd never found anything that seemed worth that much agony, so either she did sell it in the end — or my dad had done so — or she had given it to someone else. Of course, she might have buried it deep in the house. The only place I could imagine her hiding something was in her piano, and if that was the case I was out of luck: the piano had been lost in the fire that destroyed my apartment ten years ago.

But if it — whatever it was — was the same thing Vico was looking for, some old piece of music — Gabriella would have consulted Mr. Fortieri. If she hadn't gone to him, he might know who else she would have turned to. While I waited in a Naperville mall for my prints to be developed I tried phoning him. He was eighty now, but still actively working, so I wasn't surprised when he didn't answer the phone.

I snoozed in the president's antechamber until

he could finally snatch ten minutes for my report. When I finished, a little after five, I stopped in his secretary's office to try Mr. Fortieri again. Still no answer.

With only three hours sleep, my skin was twitching as though I'd put it on inside out. Since seven this morning I'd logged a hundred and ninety miles. I wanted nothing now more than my bed. Instead I rode the packed expressway all the way northwest to the O'Hare cutoff.

Mr. Fortieri lived in the Italian enclave along north Harlem Avenue. It used to be a day's excursion to go there with Gabriella: we would ride the Number Six bus to the Loop, transfer to the Douglas line of the el, and at its end take yet another bus west to Harlem. After lunch in one of the storefront restaurants, my mother stopped at Mr. Fortieri's to sing or talk while I was given an old clarinet to take apart to keep me amused. On our way back to the bus we bought polenta and olive oil in Frescobaldi's Deli. Old Mrs. Frescobaldi would let me run my hands through the bags of cardamom, the voluptuous scent making me stomp around the store in an exaggerated imitation of the drunks along Commercial Avenue. Gabriella would hiss embarrassed invectives at me, and threaten to withhold my gelato if I didn't behave.

The street today has lost much of its charm. Some of the old stores remain, but the chains have set out tendrils here as elsewhere. Mrs.

Frescobaldi couldn't stand up to Jewel, and Vespucci's, where Gabriella bought all her shoes, was swallowed by the nearby mall.

Mr. Fortieri's shop, on the ground floor of his dark-shuttered house, looked forlorn now, as though it missed the lively commerce of the street. I rang the bell without much hope: no lights shone from either story.

"I don't think he's home," a woman called from the neighboring walk.

She was just setting out with a laundry-laden shopping cart. I asked her if she'd seen Mr. Fortieri at all today. She'd noticed his bedroom light when she was getting ready for work — he was an early riser, just like her, and this time of year she always noticed his bedroom light. In fact, she'd just been thinking it was strange she didn't see his kitchen light on — he was usually preparing his supper about now, but maybe he'd gone off to see his married daughter in Wilmette.

I remembered Barbara Fortieri's wedding. Gabriella had been too sick to attend, and had sent me by myself. The music had been sensational, but I had been angry and uncomfortable and hadn't paid much attention to anything — including the groom. I asked the woman if she knew Barbara's married name — I might try to call her father there.

"Oh, you know her?"

"My mother was a friend of Mr. Fortieri's — Gabriella Sestieri — Warshawski, I mean." Talking to my cousin had sunk me too deep in my mother's past.

"Sorry, honey, never met her. She married a boy she met at college, I can't think of his name, just about the time my husband and I moved in here, and they went off to those lakefront suburbs together."

She made it sound like as daring a trip as any her ancestors had undertaken braving the Atlantic. Fatigue made it sound funny to me and I found myself doubling over to keep the woman from seeing me shake with wild laughter. The thought of Gabriella telling me "No gelato if you do not behave this minute" only made it seem funnier and I had to bend over, clutching my side.

"You okay there, honey?" The woman hesitated, not wanting to be involved with a stranger.

"Long day," I gasped. "Sudden — cramp — in my side."

I waved her on, unable to speak further. Losing my balance, I reeled against the door. It swung open behind me and I fell hard into the open shop, banging my elbow against a chair.

The fall sobered me. I rubbed my elbow, crooning slightly from pain. Bracing against the chair I hoisted myself to my feet. It was only then that it dawned on me that the chair was overturned — alarming in any shop, but especially that of someone as fastidious as Mr. Fortieri.

Without stopping to reason I backed out the door, closing it by wrapping my hand in my jacket before touching the knob. The woman with the laundry cart had gone on down the street. I hunted in my glove compartment for my flashlight, then ran back up the walk and into the shop.

I found the old man in the back, in the middle of his workshop. He lay amid his tools, the stem of an oboe still in his left hand. I fumbled for his pulse. Maybe it was the nervous beating of my own heart, but I thought I felt a faint trace of life. I found the phone on the far side of the room, buried under a heap of books that had been taken from the shelves and left where they landed.

VI

"Damn it, Warshawski, what were you doing here anyway?" Sergeant John McGonnigal and I were talking in the back room of Mr. Fortieri's shop while evidence technicians ravaged the front.

I was as surprised to see him as he was me: I'd worked with him, or around him, anyway, for years downtown at the Central District. No one down there had told me he'd transferred — kind of surprising, because he'd been the right-hand man of my dad's oldest friend on the force, Bobby Mallory. Bobby was nearing retirement now; I was guessing McGonnigal had moved out to Montclare to establish a power base independent of his protector. Bobby doesn't like me messing with murder, and McGonnigal sometimes apes his boss, or used to.

Even at his most irritable, when he's inhaling Bobby's frustration, McGonnigal realizes he can trust me, if not to tell the whole truth, at least not to lead him astray or blow a police operation. Tonight he was exasperated simply by the coincidence of mine being the voice that summoned him to a crime scene — the nature of their work makes most cops a little superstitious. He wasn't willing to believe I'd come out to the Montclare neighborhood just to ask about music. As a sop, I threw in my long-lost cousin who was trying to track down a really obscure score.

"And what is that?"

"Sonatas by Claudia Fortezza Verazi." Okay, maybe I sometimes led him a little bit astray.

"Someone tore this place up pretty good for a while before the old guy showed up. It looks as though he surprised the intruder and thought he could defend himself with — what did you say he was holding? an oboe? You think your cousin did that? Because the old guy didn't have any Claudia whoever whoever sonatas?"

I tried not to jump at the question. "I don't think so." My voice came from far away, in a small thread, but at least it didn't quaver.

I was worrying about Vico myself. I hadn't told him about Mr. Fortieri, I was sure of that. But maybe he'd found the letter Fortieri wrote Gabriella, the one I'd tucked into the score of *Don Giovanni*. And then came out here, looking for — whatever he was really hunting -- and found it, so he stabbed Mr. Fortieri to hide his

55

— Had he come to Chicago to make a fool of me in his search for something valuable? And how had McGonnigal leaped on that so neatly? I must be tired beyond measure to have revealed my fears.

"Let's get this cousin's name . . . Damn it, Vic, you can't sit on that. I move to this district three months ago. The first serious assault I bag who should be here but little Miss Muppet right under my tuffet. You'd have to be on drugs to put a knife into the guy, but you know something or you wouldn't be here minutes after it happened."

"Is that the timing? Minutes before my arrival?"

McGonnigal hunched his shoulders impatiently. "The medics didn't stop to figure out that kind of stuff — his blood pressure was too low. Take it as read that the old man'd be dead if you hadn't shown so pat — you'll get your citizen's citation the next time the mayor's handing out medals. Maybe Fortieri'd been bleeding half an hour, but no more. So, I want to talk to your cousin. And then I'll talk to someone else, and someone else and someone after that. You know how a police investigation runs."

"Yes, I know how they run." I felt unbearably tired as I gave him Vico's name, letter by slow letter, to relay to a patrolman. "Did your guys track down Mr. Fortieri's daughter?"

"She's with him at the hospital. And what does *she* know that you're not sharing with me?"

"She knew my mother. I should go see her.

56

It's hard to wait in a hospital while people you don't know cut on your folks."

He studied me narrowly, then said roughly that he'd seen a lot of that himself, lately, his sister had just lost a kidney to lupus, and I should get some sleep instead of hanging around a hospital waiting room all night.

I longed to follow his advice, but beneath the rolling waves of fatigue that crashed against my brain was a sense of urgency. If Vico had been here, had found what he was looking for, he might be on his way to Italy right now.

The phone rang. McGonnigal stuck an arm around the corner and took it from the patrolman who answered it. After a few grunts he hung up.

"Your cousin hasn't checked out of the Garibaldi, but he's not in his room. As far as the hall staff know he hasn't been there since breakfast this morning, but of course guests don't sign in and out as they go. You got a picture of him?"

"I met him yesterday for the first time. We didn't exchange high school yearbooks. He's in his mid-thirties, maybe an inch or two taller than me, slim, reddish-brown hair that's a little long on the sides and combed forward in front, and eyes almost the same color."

I swayed and almost fell as I walked to the door. In the outer room the chaos was greater than when I'd arrived. On top of the tumbled books and instruments lay gray print powder and yellow crime-scene tape. I skirted the mess as best I could, but when I climbed into the Trans Am I left a streak of gray powder on the floor mats.

VII

Although her thick hair now held more gray than black, I knew Barbara Fortieri as soon as I stepped into the surgical waiting room (now Barbara Carmichael, now fifty-two, summoned away from flute lessons to her father's bedside). She didn't recognize me at first: I'd been a teenager when she last saw me, and twenty-seven years had passed.

After the usual exclamations of surprise, of worry, she told me her father had briefly opened his eyes at the hospital, just before they began running the anesthetic, and had uttered Gabriella's name.

"Why was he thinking about your mother? Had you been to see him recently? He talks about you sometimes. And about her."

I shook my head. "I wanted to see him, to find out if Gabriella had consulted him about selling something valuable the summer she got sick, the summer of 1965."

Of course Barbara didn't know a thing about the matter. She'd been in her twenties then, engaged to be married, doing her masters in performance at Northwestern in flute and piano, with no attention to spare for the women who were in and out of her father's shop.

I recoiled from her tone as much as her words, the sense of Gabriella as one of an adoring harem. I uttered a stiff sentence of regret over her father's attack and turned to leave.

She put a hand on my arm. "Forgive me, Victoria: I liked your mother. All the same, it used to bug me, all the time he spent with her. I thought he was being disloyal to the memory of my own mother . . . anyway, my husband is out of town. The thought of staying here alone, waiting on news. . . ."

So I stayed with her. We talked emptily, to fill the time, of her classes, the recitals she and her husband gave together, the fact that I wasn't married, and, no, I didn't keep up with my music. Around nine one of the surgeons came in to say that Mr. Fortieri had made it through surgery. The knife had pierced his lung and he had lost a lot of blood. To make sure he didn't suffer heart damage they were putting him on a ventilator, in a drug-induced coma, for a few days. If we were his daughters we could go see him, but it would be a shock and he wanted us to be prepared.

We both grimaced at the assumption that we were sisters. I left Barbara at the door of the intensive care waiting room and dragged myself to the Trans Am. A fine mist was falling, outlining street lamps with a gauzy halo. I tilted the rearview mirror so that I could see my face in the silver light. Those angular cheekbones were surely Slavic, and my eyes Tony's clear deep gray. Surely. I was surely Tony Warshawski's daughter.

The streets were slippery. I drove with extreme care, frightened of my own fatigue. Safe at home the desire for sleep consumed me like a ravening appetite. My fingers trembled on the keys with my longing for my bed.

Mr. Contreras surged into the hall when he heard me open the stairwell door. "Oh, there you are, doll. I found your cousin hanging around the entrance waiting for you, least, I didn't know he was your cousin, but he explained it all, and I thought you wouldn't want him standing out there, not knowing how long it was gonna be before you came home."

"Ah, *cara cugina!*" Vico appeared behind my neighbor, but before he could launch into his recitative the chorus of dogs drowned him, barking and squeaking as they barreled past him to greet me.

I stared at him, speechless.

"How are you? Your working it was good?"

"My working was difficult. I'm tired."

"So, maybe I take you to dinner, to the dancing, you are lively." He was speaking English in deference to Mr. Contreras, whose only word of Italian is "grappa."

"Dinner and dancing and I'll feel like a corpse. Why don't you go back to your hotel and let me get some sleep."

"Naturally, naturally. You are working hard

60

all the day and I am playing. I have your —
your *partitura* —"

"Score."

"*Buono*. Score. I have her. I will take her upstairs and put her away very neat for you and
leave you to your resting."

"I'll take it with me." I held out my hand.

"No, no. We are leaving one big mess last night,
I know that, and I am greedy last night, making
you stay up when today you work. So I come
with you, clean — *il disordine* — disorderliness?,
then you rest without worry. You smell flowers
while *I* work."

Before I could protest further he ducked back
into Mr. Contreras's living room and popped out
with a large portmanteau. With a flourish he extracted a bouquet of spring flowers, and the score,
wrapped this time in a cream envelope, and put
his arm around me to shepherd me up the stairs.
The dogs and the old man followed him, all four
making so much racket that the medical resident
who'd moved in across the hall from Mr. Contreras came out.

"Please! I just got off a thirty-six-hour shift
and I'm trying to sleep. If you can't control those
damned dogs I'm going to issue a complaint to
the city."

Vico butted in just as Mr. Contreras, drawing
a deep breath, prepared to unleash a major aria
in defense of his beloved animals. *Mi scusa, Signora, mi scusa*. It is all my doing. I am here
from Italy to meet my cousin for the first time.

I am so excited I am not thinking, I am making noise, I am disturbing the rest your beautiful eyes require. . . ."

I stomped up the stairs without waiting for the rest of the flow. Vico caught up with me as I was closing the door. "This building attracts hardworking ladies who need to sleep. Your poor neighbor. She is at a hospital where they work her night and day. What is it about America, that ladies must work so hard? I gave her some of your flowers; I knew you wouldn't mind, and they made her so happy, she will give you no more complaints about the ferocious beasts."

He had switched to Italian, much easier to understand on his lips than English. Flinging himself on the couch he launched happily into a discussion of his day with the "partitura." He had found, through our mutual acquaintance Mr. Ranier, someone who could interpret the music for him. I was right: it was from the Baroque, and not only that, most likely by Pergolesi.

"So not at all possibly by our great-grandmother. Why would your mother have a handwritten score by a composer she could find in any music store?"

I was too tired for finesse. "Vico, where were you at five this afternoon?"

He flung up his hands. "Why are you like a policeman all of a sudden, eh, *cugina*?"

"It's a question the police may ask you. I'd like to know, myself."

A wary look came into his eyes — not anger,

which would have been natural, or even bewilderment — although he used the language of a puzzled man: I couldn't be jealous of him, although it was a compliment when we had only just met, so what on earth was I talking about? And why the police? But if I really wanted to know, he was downstairs, with my neighbor.

"And for that matter, Vic, where were you at five o'clock?"

"On the Kennedy Expressway. Heading toward north Harlem Avenue."

He paused a second too long before opening his hands wide again. "I don't know your city, cousin, so that tells me nothing."

"*Bene*. Thank you for going to so much trouble over the score. Now you must let me rest."

I put a hand out for it, but he ignored me and rushed over to the mound of papers we'd left in the hall last night with a cry that I was to rest, he was to work now.

He took the Pergolesi from its envelope. "The music is signed at the end, with the initials 'CF.' Who would that be?"

"Probably whoever copied it for her. I don't know."

He laid it on the bottom of the trunk and placed a stack of operas on top of it. My lips tight with anger I lifted the libretti out in order to get at the Pergolesi. Vico rushed to assist me but only succeeded in dropping everything, so that music and old papers both fluttered to the floor. I was too tired to feel anything except a tightening of the screws in my forehead. Without speaking I took the score from him and retreated to the couch.

Was this the same concerto Vico had taken with him the night before? I'd been naive to let him walk off with a document without some kind of proper safeguard. I held it up to the light, but saw nothing remarkable in the six pages, no signs that a secret code had been erased, or brought to light, nothing beyond a few carefully corrected notes in measure 168. I turned to the end where the initials "CF" were written in the same careful black ink as the notes.

Vico must have found Fortieri's letter to my mother stuffed inside *Don Giovanni* and tracked him down. No, he'd been here at five. So the lawyer, Ranier, was involved. Vico had spent the day with him: together they'd traced Mr. Fortieri. Vico came here for an alibi while the lawyer searched the shop. I remembered Ranier's eyes, granite chips in his soft face. He could stab an old man without a second's compunction.

Vico, a satisfied smile on his face, came to the couch for Gabriella's evening gown. "This goes on top, right, this beautiful concert dress. And now, *cugina,* all is tidy. I will leave you to your dreams. May they be happy ones."

He scooped up his portmanteau and danced into the night, blowing me a kiss as he went.

VIII

I fell heavily into sleep, and then into dreams about my mother. At first I was watching her with Mr. Fortieri as they laughed over their coffee in the little room behind the shop where McGonnigal and I had spoken. Impatient with my mother for her absorption in someone else's company I started smearing strawberry gelato over the oboe Mr. Fortieri was repairing. Bobby Mallory and John McGonnigal appeared, wearing their uniforms, and carried me away. I was screaming with rage or fear as Bobby told me my naughtiness was killing my mother.

And then suddenly I was with her in the hospital as she was dying, her dark eyes huge behind a network of tubes and bottles. She was whispering my name through her parched lips, mine and Francesca Salvini's. *"Maestra Salvini . . . nella cassa . . . Vittora, mia carissima, dale . . ."* she croaked. My father, holding her hands, demanded of me what she was saying.

I woke as I always did at this point in the dream, my hair matted with sweat. "Maestra Salvini is in the box," I had told Tony helplessly at the time. "She wants me to give her something."

I always thought my mother was struggling with

65

the idea that her voice teacher might be dead, that that was why her letters were returned unopened. Francesca Salvini on the Voice had filled my ears from my earliest childhood. As Gabriella staged her aborted comeback, she longed to hear some affirmation from her teacher. She wrote her at her old address in Pitigliano, and in care of the Siena Opera, as well as through her cousin Frederica — not knowing that Frederica herself had died two years earlier.

"Cassa" — "box" — isn't the usual Italian word for coffin, but it could be used as a crude figure just as it is in English. It had always jarred on me to hear it from my mother — her speech was precise, refined, and she tolerated no obscenities. And as part of her last words — she lapsed into a coma later that afternoon from which she never awoke — it always made me shudder to think that was on her mind, Salvini in a box, buried, as Gabriella was about to be.

But my mother's urgency was for the pulse of life. As though she had given me explicit instructions in my sleep I rose from the bed, walked to the hall without stopping to dress, and pulled open the trunk once more. I took out everything and sifted through it over and over, but nowhere could I see the olivewood box that had held Gabriella's glasses on the voyage to America. I hunted all through the living room, and then, in desperation, went through every surface in the apartment.

I remembered the smug smile Vico had given

me on his way out the door last night. He'd stuffed the box into his portmanteau and disappeared with it.

IX

Vico hadn't left Chicago, or at least he hadn't settled his hotel bill. I got into his room at the Garibaldi by calling room service from the hall phone and ordering champagne. When the service trolley appeared from the bar I followed the waiter into the elevator, saw which room he knocked on as I sauntered past him down the hall, then let myself in with my picklocks when he'd taken off again in frustration. I knew my cousin wasn't in, or at least wasn't answering his phone — I'd already called from across the street.

I didn't try to be subtle in my search. I tossed everything from the drawers onto the floor, pulled the mattress from the bed, and pried the furniture away from the wall. Fury was making me wanton: by the time I'd made sure the box wasn't in the room the place looked like the remains of a shipwreck.

If Vico didn't have the box he must have handed it off to Ranier. The import-export lawyer, who specialized in remarkable *objets,* doubtless knew the value of an old musical score and how to dispose of it.

The bedside clock was buried somewhere under

the linens. I looked at my watch — it was past four now. I let myself out of the room, trying to decide whether Ranier would store the box at his office or his home. There wasn't any way of telling, but it would be easier to break into his office, especially at this time of day.

I took a cab to the west Loop rather than trying to drive and park in the rush-hour maelstrom. The November daylight was almost gone. Last night's mist had turned into a biting sleet. People fled for their home-bound transportation, heads bent into the wind. I paid off the cab and ran out of the ice into the Caleb Building's coffee shop to use the phone. When Ranier answered I gave myself a high nasal voice and asked for Cindy.

"She's left for the day. Who is this?"

"Amanda Parton. I'm in her book group and I wanted to know if she remembered —"

"You'll have to call her at home. I don't want this kind of personal drivel discussed in my office." He hung up.

Good, good. No personal drivel on company time. Only theft. I mixed with the swarm of people in the Caleb's lobby and rode up to the thirty-seventh floor. A metal door without any letters or numbers on it might lead to a supply closet. Working quickly, while the hall was briefly empty, I unpicked the lock. Behind lay a mass of wires, the phone and signal lines for the floor, and a space just wide enough for me to stand in. I pulled the door almost shut and stared through the crack.

A laughing group of men floated past on their way to a Blackhawks game. A solitary woman, hunched over a briefcase, scowled at me. I thought for a nervous moment that she was going to test the door, but she was apparently lost in unpleasant thoughts all her own. Finally, around six, Ranier emerged, talking in Italian with Vico. My cousin looked as debonair as ever, with a marigold tucked in his lapel. Where he'd found one in mid-November I don't know but it looked quite jaunty against his brown worsted. The fragment of conversation I caught seemed to be about a favorite restaurant in Florence, not about my mother and music.

I waited another ten minutes, to make sure they weren't standing at the elevator, or returning for a forgotten umbrella, then slipped out of the closet and down to Ranier's import-export law office. Someone leaving an adjacent firm looked at me curiously as I slid the catch back. I flashed a smile, said I hated working nights. He grunted in commiseration and went on to the elevator.

Cindy's chair was tucked against her desk, a white cardigan draped primly about the arms. I didn't bother with her area but went to work on the inner door. Here Ranier had been more careful. It took me ten minutes to undo it. I was angry and impatient and my fingers kept slipping on the hafts.

Lights in these modern buildings are set on

master timers for quadrants of a story, so that they all turn on or off at the same time. Outside full night had arrived; the high harsh lamps reflected my wavering outline in the black windows. I might have another hour of fluorescence flooding my search before the building masters decided most of the denizens had gone home for the day.

When I reached the inner office my anger mounted to murderous levels: my mother's olivewood box lay in pieces in the garbage. I pulled it out. They had pried it apart, and torn out the velvet lining. One shred of pale green lay on the floor. I scrabbled through the garbage for the rest of the velvet and saw a crumpled page in my mother's writing.

Gasping for air I stuck my hand in to get it. The whole wastebasket rose to greet me. I clutched at the edge of the desk but it seemed to whirl past me and the roar of a giant wind deafened me.

I managed to get my head between my knees and hold it there until the dizziness subsided. Weak from my emotional storm, I moved slowly to Ranier's couch to read Gabriella's words. The page was dated the 30th of October 1967, her last birthday, and the writing wasn't in her usual bold, upright script. Pain medication had made all her movements shaky at that point.

The letter began *"Carissima,"* without any other address, but it was clearly meant for me. My cheeks burned with embarrassment that her farewell note would be to her daughter, not her husband. "At least not to a lover, either," I muttered, thinking with more embarrassment of Mr. Fortieri, and my explicit dream.

My dearest,

I have tried to put this where you may someday find it. As you travel through life you will discard that which has no meaning for you, but I believe — hope — this box and my glasses will always stay with you on your journey. You must return this valuable score to Francesca Salvini if she is still alive. If she is dead, you must do with it as the circumstances of the time dictate to you. You must under no circumstances sell it for your own gain. If it has the value that Maestra Salvini attached to it it should perhaps be in a museum.

It hung always in a frame next to the piano in Maestra Salvini's music room, on the ground floor of her house. I went to her in the middle of the night, just before I left Italy, to bid her farewell. She feared she, too, might be arrested — she had been an uncompromising opponent of the Fascists. She gave it to me to safeguard in America, lest it fall into lesser hands, and I cannot agree to sell it only to buy medicine. So I am hiding this from your papa, who would violate my trust to feed more money to the doctors. And there is no need. Already, after all, these drugs they give me make me ill

71

and destroy my voice. Should I use her treasure to add six months to my life, with only the addition of much more pain? You, my beloved child, will understand that that is not living, that mere survival of the organism.

Oh, my darling one, my greatest pain is that I must leave you alone in a world full of dangers and temptations. Always strive for justice, never accept the second-rate in yourself, my darling, even though you must accept it from the world around you. I grieve that I shall not live to see you grown, in your own life, but remember: *Il mio amore per te è l'amor che muove il sole e l'altre stelle.*

My love for you is the love that moves the sun and all the other stars. She used to croon that to me as a child. It was only in college I learned that Dante said it first.

I could see her cloudy with pain, obsessed with her commitment to save Salvini's music, scoring open the velvet of the box and sealing it in the belief I would find it. Only the pain and the drugs could have led her to something so improbable. For I would never have searched unless Vico had come looking for it. No matter how many times I recalled the pain of those last words, *"nella cassa,"* I wouldn't have made the connection to this box. This lining. This letter.

I smoothed the letter and put it in a flat side compartment of my case. With the sense that my mother was with me in the room some of my anger calmed. I was able to begin the search for Francesca Salvini's treasure with a degree of rationality.

Fortunately Ranier relied for security on the building's limited access: I'd been afraid he might have a safe. Instead he housed his papers in the antique credenza. Inside the original decorative lock he'd installed a small modern one, but it didn't take long to undo it. My anger at the destruction of Gabriella's box made me pleased when the picklocks ran a deep scratch across the marquetry front of the cabinet.

I found the score in a file labeled "Sestieri-Verazi." The paper was old, parchment that had frayed and discolored at the edges, and the writing on it — clearly done by hand — had faded in places to a pale brown. Scored for oboe, two horns, a violin, and a viola, the piece was eight pages long. The notes were drawn with exquisite care. On the second, third, and sixth pages someone had scribbled another set of bar lines above the horn part and written in notes in a fast careless hand, much different from the painstaking care of the rest of the score. In two places he'd scrawled "da capo" in such haste that the letters were barely distinguishable. The same impatient writer had scrawled some notes in the margin, and at the end. I couldn't read the script, although I thought it might be German. Nowhere could I find a signature on the document to tell me who the author was.

I placed the manuscript on the top of the credenza and continued to inspect the file. A letter from a Signor Arnoldo Piave in Florence introduced Vico to Ranier as someone on the trail of a valuable musical document in Chicago. Signor Ranier's help in locating the parties involved would be greatly appreciated. Ranier had written in turn to a man in Germany "well-known to be interested in 18th-century musical manuscripts," to let him know Ranier might soon have something "unusual" to show him.

I had read that far when I heard a key in the outer door. The cleaning crew I could face down, but if Ranier had returned . . . I swept the score from the credenza and tucked it in the first place that met my eye — behind the Modigliani that hung above it. A second later Ranier and Vico stormed into the room. Ranier was holding a pistol, which he trained on me.

"I knew it!" Vico cried in Italian. "As soon as I saw the state of my hotel room I knew you had come to steal the score."

"Steal the score? My dear Vico!" I was pleased to hear a tone of light contempt in my voice.

Vico started toward me but backed off at a sharp word from Ranier. The lawyer told me to put my hands on top of my head and sit on the couch. The impersonal chill in his eyes was more frightening than anger. I obeyed.

"Now what?" Vico demanded of Ranier.

"Now we had better take her out to — well, the place name won't mean anything to you. A forest west of town. One of the sheriff's deputies will take care of her."

There are sheriff's deputies who will do murder for hire in unincorporated parts of Cook County. My body would be found by dogs or children under a heap of rotted leaves in the spring.

"So you have Mob connections," I said in English. "Do you pay them, or they you?"

"I don't think it matters." Ranier was still indifferent. "Let's get going. . . . Oh, Verazi," he added in Italian, "before we leave, just check for the score, will you?"

"What is this precious score?" I asked.

"It's not important for you to know."

"You steal it from my apartment, but I don't need to know about it? I think the state will take a different view."

Before Ranier finished another cold response Vico cried out that the manuscript was missing.

"Then search her bag," Ranier ordered.

Vico crossed behind him to snatch my case from the couch. He dumped the contents on the floor. A Shawn Colwin tape, a tampon that had come partially free of its container, loose receipts, and a handful of dog biscuits joined my work notebook, miniature camera, and binoculars in an unprofessional heap. Vico opened the case wide and shook it. The letter from my mother remained in the inner compartment.

"Where is it?" Ranier demanded.

"Don't ask, don't tell," I said, using English again.

"Verazi, get behind her and tie her hands. You'll find some rope in the bottom of my desk."

Ranier wasn't going to shoot me in his office: too much to explain to the building management. I fought hard. When Ranier kicked me in the stomach I lost my breath, though, and Vico caught my arms roughly behind me. His marigold was crushed, and he would have a black eye before tomorrow morning. He was panting with fury, and smacked me again across the face when he finished tying me. Blood dripped from my nose onto my shirt. I wanted to blot it and momentarily gave way to rage at my helplessness. I thought of Gabriella, of the love that moves the sun and all the other stars, and tried to avoid the emptiness of Ranier's eyes.

"Now tell me where the manuscript is," Ranier said in the same impersonal voice.

I leaned back in the couch and shut my eyes. Vico hit me again.

"Okay, okay," I muttered. "I'll tell you where the damned thing is. But I have one question first."

"You're in no position to bargain," Ranier intoned.

I ignored him. "Are you really my cousin?"

Vico bared his teeth in a canine grin. "Oh, yes, *cara cugina,* be assured, we are relatives. That naughty Frederica whom everyone in the family despised was truly my grandmother. Yes, she slunk off to Milan to have a baby in the slums without a father. And my mother was so impressed by her example that she did the same. Then when those two worthy women died, the one of tuberculosis, the other of excess heroin, the noble Verazis rescued the poor gutter child and brought him up in splendor in Florence. They packed all my grandmother's letters into a box and swept them up with me and my one toy, a horse that someone else had thrown in the garbage, and that my mother brought home from one of her nights out. My aunt discarded the horse and replaced it with some very hygienic toys, but the papers she stored in her attic.

"Then when my so-worthy uncle, who could never thank himself enough for rescuing this worthless brat, died, I found all my grandmother's papers. Including letters from your mother, and her plea for help in finding Francesca Salvini so that she could return this most precious musical score. And I thought, what have these Verazis ever done for me, but rubbed my nose in dirt? And you, that same beautiful blood flows in you as in them. And as in me!"

"And Claudia Fortezza, our great-grandmother? Did she write music, or was that all a fiction?"

"Oh, no doubt she dabbled in music as all the ladies in our family like to, even you, looking at that score the other night and asking me about the notation! Oh, yes, like all those stuck-up Verazi cousins, laughing at me because I'd never seen a piano before! I thought you would fall for such a tale, and it amused me to have you

77

hunting for her music when it never existed."

His eyes glittered amber and flecks of spit covered his mouth by the time he finished. The idea that he looked like Gabriella seemed obscene. Ranier slapped him hard and ordered him to calm down.

"She wants us excited. It's her only hope for disarming me." He tapped the handle of the gun lightly on my left kneecap. "Now tell me where the score is, or I'll smash your kneecap and make you walk on it."

My hands turned clammy. "I hid it down the hall. There's a wiring closet. . . . The metal door near the elevators. . . ."

"Go see," Ranier ordered Verazi.

My cousin returned a few minutes later with the news that the door was locked.

"Are you lying?" Ranier growled at me. "How did you get into it?"

"Same as into here," I muttered. "Picklocks. In my hip pocket."

Ranier had Vico take them from me, then seemed disgusted that my cousin didn't know how to use them. He decided to take me down to unlock the closet myself.

"No one's working late on this side of the floor tonight, and the cleaning staff don't arrive until nine. We should be clear."

They frog-marched me down the hall to the closet before untying my hands. I knelt to work the lock. As it clicked free Vico grabbed the door and yanked it open. I fell forward into the wires.

Grabbing a large armful I pulled with all my strength. The hall turned black and an alarm began to blare.

Vico grabbed my left leg. I kicked him in the head with my right. He let go. I turned and grabbed him by the throat and pounded his head against the floor. He got hold of my left arm and pulled it free. Before he could hit me I rolled clear and kicked again at his head. I hit only air. My eyes adjusted to the dark: I could make out his shape as a darker shape against the floor, squirming out of reach.

"Roll clear and call out!" Ranier shouted at him. "On the count of five I'm going to shoot."

I dove for Ranier's legs and knocked him flat. The gun went off as he hit the floor. I slammed my fist into the bridge of his nose and he lost consciousness. Vico reached for the gun. Suddenly the hall lights came on. I blinked in the brightness and rolled toward Vico, hoping to kick the gun free before he could focus and fire.

"Enough! Hands behind your heads, all of you." It was a city cop. Behind him stood one of the Caleb's security force.

X

It didn't take me as long to sort out my legal problems as I'd feared. Ranier's claim, that I'd broken into his office and he was protecting himself, didn't impress the cops: if Ranier was defending his office why was he shooting at me out in the hall? Besides, the city cops had long had an eye on him: they had a pretty good idea he was connected to the Mob, but no real evidence. I had to do some fancy tap dancing on why I'd been in his office to begin with, but I was helped by Bobby Mallory's arrival on the scene. Assaults in the Loop went across his desk, and one with his oldest friend's daughter on the rap sheet brought him into the holding cells on the double.

For once I told him everything I knew. And for once he was not only empathetic, but helpful: he retrieved the score for me — himself — from behind the Modigliani, along with the fragments of the olivewood box. Without talking to the state's attorney, or even suggesting that it should be impounded to make part of the state's case. It was when he started blowing his nose as someone translated Gabriella's letter for him — he didn't trust me to do it myself — that I figured he'd come through for me.

"But what is it?" he asked, when he'd handed me the score.

I hunched a shoulder. "I don't know. It's old music that belonged to my mother's voice teacher. I figure Max Loewenthal can sort it out."

Max is the executive director of Beth Israel, the hospital where Lotty Herschel is chief of perinatology, but he collects antiques and knows a lot about music. I told him the story later that day and gave the score to him. Max is usually imperturbably urbane, but when he inspected the music his face flushed and his eyes glittered unnaturally.

"What is it?" I cried.

"If it's what I think — no, I'd better not say. I have a friend who can tell us. Let me give it to her."

Vico's blows to my stomach made it hard for me to move, otherwise I might have started pounding on Max. The glitter in his eye made me demand a receipt for the document before I parted with it.

At that his native humor returned. "You're right, Victoria: I'm not immune from cupidity. I won't abscond with this, I promise, but maybe I'd better give you a receipt just the same."

XI

It was two weeks later that Max's music expert was ready to give us a verdict. I figured Bobby Mallory and Barbara Carmichael deserved to hear the news firsthand, so I invited them all to dinner, along with Lotty. Of course, that meant I had to include Mr. Contreras and the dogs. My neighbor decided the occasion was important enough to justify digging his one suit out of mothballs.

Bobby arrived early, with his wife Eileen, just as Barbara showed up. She told me her father had recovered sufficiently from his attack to be revived from his drug-induced coma, but he was still too weak to answer questions. Bobby added that they'd found a witness to the forced entry of Fortieri's house. A boy hiding in the alley had seen two men going in through the back. Since he was smoking a reefer behind a garage he hadn't come forward earlier, but when John McGonnigal assured him they didn't care about his dope — this one time — he picked Ranier's face out of a collection of photos.

"And the big guy promptly donated his muscle to us — a part-time deputy, who's singing like a bird, on account of he's p-o'd about being fingered." He hesitated, then added, "If you won't press charges they're going to send Verazi home, you know."

I smiled unhappily. "I know."

Eileen patted his arm. "That's enough shop for now. Victoria, who is it who's coming tonight?"

Max rang the bell just then, arriving with both Lotty and his music expert. A short skinny brunette, she looked like a street urchin in her jeans and outsize sweater. Max introduced her as Isabel Thompson, an authority on rare music from the Newberry Library.

"I hope we haven't kept dinner waiting — Lotty was late getting out of surgery," Max added.

"Let's eat later," I said. "Enough suspense. What have I been lugging unknowing around Chicago all this time?"

"She wouldn't tell us anything until you were here to listen," Max said. "So we are as impatient as you."

Ms. Thompson grinned. "Of course, this is only a preliminary opinion, but it looks like a concerto by Marianne Martines."

"But the insertions, the writing at the end," Max began, when Bobby demanded to known who Marianne Martines was.

"She was an eighteenth-century Viennese composer. She was known to have written over four hundred compositions, but only about sixty have survived, so it's exciting to find a new one." She folded her hands in her lap, a look of mischief in her eyes.

"And the writing, Isabel?" Max demanded.

She grinned. "You were right, Max: it is Mozart's. A suggestion for changes in the horn line. He started to describe them, then decided just to write them in above her original notation. He added a reminder that the two were going to play together the following Monday — they often played piano duets, sometimes privately, sometimes for an audience."

"Hah! I knew it! I was sure!" Max was almost dancing in ecstasy. "So I put some Krugs down to chill. Liquid gold to toast the moment I held in my hand a manuscript that Mozart held."

He pulled a couple of bottles of champagne from his briefcase. I fetched my mother's Venetian glasses from the dining room. Only five remained whole of the eight she had transported so carefully. One had shattered in the fire that destroyed my old apartment, and another when some thugs broke into it one night. A third had been repaired and could still be used. How could I have been so careless with my little legacy.

"But whose is it now?" Lotty asked, when we'd all drunk and exclaimed enough to calm down.

"That's a good question," I said. "I've been making some inquiries through the Italian government. Francesca Salvini died in 1943 and she didn't leave any heirs. She wanted Gabriella to dispose of it in the event of her death. In the absence of a formal will the Italian government might make a claim, but her intention as expressed in Gabriella's letter might give me the right to it, as long as I didn't keep it or sell it just for my own gain."

"We'd be glad to house it," Ms. Thompson offered.

"Seems to me your ma would have wanted someone in trouble to benefit." Bobby was speaking gruffly to hide his embarrassment. "What's something like this worth?"

Ms. Thompson pursed her lips. "A private collector might pay a quarter of a million. We couldn't match that, but we'd probably go to a hundred or hundred and fifty thousand."

"So what mattered most to your ma, Vicki, besides you? Music. Music and victims of injustice. You probably can't do much about the second, but you ought to be able to help some kids learn some music."

Barbara Carmichael nodded in approval. "A scholarship fund to provide Chicago kids with music lessons. It's a great idea, Vic."

We launched the Gabriella-Salvini program some months later with a concert at the Newberry. Mr. Fortieri attended, fully recovered from his wounds. He told me that Gabriella had come to consult him the summer before she died, but she hadn't brought the score with her. Since she'd never mentioned it to him before he thought her illness and medications had made her delusional.

"I'm sorry, Victoria: it was the last time she was well enough to travel to the northwest side, and I'm sorry that I disappointed her. It's been troubling me ever since Barbara told me the news."

I longed to ask him whether he'd been my mother's lover. But did I want to know? What if he, too, had moved the sun and all the other stars for her — I'd hate to know that. I sent him to a front-row chair and went to sit next to Lotty.

In Gabriella's honor the Cellini Wind Ensemble had come from London to play the benefit. They played the Martines score first as the composer had written it, and then as Mozart revised it. I have to confess I liked the original better, but as Gabriella often told me, I'm no musician.

The Pietro Andromache

I

"YOU ONLY AGREED to hire him because of his art collection. Of that I'm sure." Lotty Herschel bent down to adjust her stockings. "And don't waggle your eyebrows like that — it makes you look like an adolescent Groucho Marx."

Max Loewenthal obediently smoothed his eyebrows, but said, "It's your legs, Lotty; they remind me of my youth. You know, going into the Underground to wait out the air raids, looking at the ladies as they came down the escalators. The updraft always made their skirts billow."

"You're making this up, Max. I was in those Underground stations, too, and as I remember the ladies were always bundled in coats and children."

Max moved from the doorway to put an arm around Lotty. "That's what keeps us together, *Lottchen:* I am a romantic and you are severely logical. And you know we didn't hire Caudwell because of his collection. Although I admit I am eager to see it. The board wants Beth Israel to develop a transplant program. It's the only way we're going to become competitive —"

"Don't deliver your publicity lecture to me," Lotty snapped. Her thick brows contracted to a solid black line across her forehead. "As far as I am concerned he is a cretin with the hands of a Caliban and the personality of Attila."

Lotty's intense commitment to medicine left no room for the mundane consideration of money. But as the hospital's executive director, Max was on the spot with the trustees to see that Beth Israel ran at a profit. Or at least at a smaller loss than they'd achieved in recent years. They'd brought Caudwell in in part to attract more paying patients — and to help screen out some of the indigent who made up 12 percent of Beth Israel's patient load. Max wondered how long the hospital could afford to support personalities as divergent as Lotty and Caudwell with their radically differing approaches to medicine.

He dropped his arm and smiled quizzically at her. "Why do you hate him so much, Lotty?"

"*I* am the person who has to justify the patients I admit to this — this troglodyte. Do you realize he tried to keep Mrs. Mendes from the operating room when he learned she had AIDS? He wasn't even being asked to sully his hands with her blood and he didn't want me performing surgery on her."

Lotty drew back from Max and pointed an accusing finger at him. "You may tell the board that if he keeps questioning my judgment they

87

will find themselves looking for a new perinatologist. I am serious about this. You listen this afternoon, Max, you hear whether or not he calls me 'our little baby doctor.' I am fifty-eight years old, I am a Fellow of the Royal College of Surgeons besides having enough credentials in this country to support a whole hospital, and to him I am a 'little baby doctor.' "

Max sat on the daybed and pulled Lotty down next to him. "No, no, *Lottchen:* don't fight. Listen to me. Why haven't you told me any of this before?"

"Don't be an idiot, Max: you are the director of the hospital. I cannot use our special relationship to deal with problems I have with the staff. I said my piece when Caudwell came for his final interview. A number of the other physicians were not happy with his attitude. If you remember, we asked the board to bring him in as a cardiac surgeon first and promote him to chief of staff after a year if everyone was satisfied with his performance."

"We talked about doing it that way," Max admitted. "But he wouldn't take the appointment except as chief of staff. That was the only way we could offer him the kind of money he could get at one of the university hospitals or Humana. And, Lotty, even if you don't like his personality you must agree that he is a first-class surgeon."

"I agree to nothing." Red lights danced in her black eyes. "If he patronizes me, a fellow physician, how do you imagine he treats his patients?

88

You cannot practice medicine if —"

"Now it's my turn to ask to be spared a lecture," Max interrupted gently. "But if you feel so strongly about him, maybe you shouldn't go to his party this afternoon."

"And admit that he can beat me? Never."

"Very well then." Max got up and placed a heavily brocaded wool shawl over Lotty's shoulders. "But you must promise me to behave. This is a social function we are going to, remember, not a gladiator contest. Caudwell is trying to repay some hospitality this afternoon, not to belittle you."

"I don't need lessons in conduct from you: Herschels were attending the emperors of Austria while the Loewenthals were operating vegetable stalls on the Ring," Lotty said haughtily.

Max laughed and kissed her hand. "Then remember these regal Herschels and act like them, *Eure Hoheit.*"

II

Caudwell had bought an apartment sight unseen when he moved to Chicago. A divorced man whose children are in college only has to consult with his own taste in these matters. He asked the Beth Israel board to recommend a realtor, sent his requirements to them — twenties construction, near Lake Michigan, good security,

89

modern plumbing — and dropped seven hundred and fifty thousand for an eight-room condo facing the lake at Scott Street.

Since Beth Israel paid handsomely for the privilege of retaining Dr. Charlotte Herschel as their perinatologist, nothing required her to live in a five-room walk-up on the fringes of Uptown, so it was a bit unfair of her to mutter "Parvenu" to Max when they walked into the lobby.

Max relinquished Lotty gratefully when they got off the elevator. Being her lover was like trying to be companion to a Bengal tiger: you never knew when she'd take a lethal swipe at you. Still, if Caudwell was insulting her — and her judgment — maybe he needed to talk to the surgeon, explain how important Lotty was for the reputation of Beth Israel.

Caudwell's two children were making the obligatory Christmas visit. They were a boy and a girl, Deborah and Steve, within a year of the same age, both tall, both blond and poised, with a hearty sophistication born of a childhood spent on expensive ski slopes. Max wasn't very big, and as one took his coat and the other performed brisk introductions, he felt himself shrinking, losing in self-assurance. He accepted a glass of special *cuvée* from one of them — was it the boy or the girl, he wondered in confusion — and fled into the melee.

He landed next to one of Beth Israel's trustees, a woman in her sixties wearing a gray textured minidress whose black stripes were constructed

90

of feathers. She commented brightly on Caudwell's art collection, but Max sensed an undercurrent of hostility: wealthy trustees don't like the idea that they can't out buy the staff.

While he was frowning and nodding at appropriate intervals, it dawned on Max that Caudwell did know how much the hospital needed Lotty. Heart surgeons do not have the world's smallest egos: when you ask them to name the world's three leading practitioners, they never can remember the names of the other two. Lotty was at the top of her field, and she, too, was used to having things her way. Since her confrontational style was reminiscent more of the Battle of the Bulge than the Imperial Court of Vienna, he didn't blame Caudwell for trying to force her out of the hospital.

Max moved away from Martha Gildersleeve to admire some of the paintings and figurines she'd been discussing. A collector himself of Chinese porcelains, Max raised his eyebrows and mouthed a soundless whistle at the pieces on display. A small Watteau and a Charles Demuth watercolor were worth as much as Beth Israel paid Caudwell in a year. No wonder Mrs. Gildersleeve had been so annoyed.

"Impressive, isn't it."

Max turned to see Arthur Gioia looming over him. Max was shorter than most of the Beth Israel staff, shorter than everyone but Lotty. But Gioia, a tall muscular immunologist, loomed over everyone. He had gone to the University of Arkansas on a football scholarship and had even spent a season playing tackle for Houston before starting medical school. It had been twenty years since he last lifted weights, but his neck still looked like a redwood stump.

Gioia had led the opposition to Caudwell's appointment. Max had suspected at the time that it was due more to a medicine man's not wanting a surgeon as his nominal boss than from any other cause, but after Lotty's outburst he wasn't so sure. He was debating whether to ask the doctor how he felt about Caudwell now that he'd worked with him for six months when their host surged over to him and shook his hand.

"Sorry I didn't see you when you came in, Loewenthal. You like the Watteau? It's one of my favorite pieces. Although a collector shouldn't play favorites any more than a father should, eh, sweetheart?" The last remark was addressed to the daughter, Deborah, who had come up behind Caudwell and slipped an arm around him.

Caudwell looked more like a Victorian sea dog than a surgeon. He had a round red face under a shock of yellow-white hair, a hearty Santa Claus laugh, and a bluff, direct manner. Despite Lotty's vituperations, he was immensely popular with his patients. In the short time he'd been at the hospital, referrals to cardiac surgery had increased 15 percent.

His daughter squeezed his shoulder playfully.

"I know you don't play favorites with us, Dad, but you're lying to Mr. Loewenthal about your collection; come on, you know you are."

She turned to Max. "He has a piece he's so proud of he doesn't like to show it to people — he doesn't want them to see he's got vulnerable spots. But it's Christmas, Dad, relax, let people see how you feel for a change."

Max looked curiously at the surgeon, but Caudwell seemed pleased with his daughter's familiarity. The son came up and added his own jocular cajoling.

"This really is Dad's pride and joy. He stole it from Uncle Griffen when Grandfather died and kept Mother from getting her mitts on it when they split up."

Caudwell did bark out a mild reproof at that. "You'll be giving my colleagues the wrong impression of me, Steve. I didn't steal it from Grif. Told him he could have the rest of the estate if he'd leave me the Watteau and the Pietro."

"Of course he could've bought ten estates with what those two would fetch," Steve muttered to his sister over Max's head.

Deborah relinquished her father's arm to lean over Max and whisper back, "Mom could've used them, too."

Max moved away from the alarming pair to say to Caudwell, "A Pietro? You mean Pietro d'Alessandro? You have a model, or an actual sculpture?"

Caudwell gave his staccato admiral's laugh. "The real McCoy, Loewenthal. The real McCoy. An alabaster."

"An alabaster?" Max raised his eyebrows. "Surely not. I thought Pietro worked only in bronze and marble."

"Yes, yes," chuckled Caudwell, rubbing his hands together. "Everyone thinks so, but there were a few alabasters in private collections. I've had this one authenticated by experts. Come take a look at it — it'll knock your breath away. You come, too, Gioia," he barked at the immunologist. "You're Italian, you'll like to see what your ancestors were up to."

"A Pietro alabaster?" Lotty's clipped tones made Max start — he hadn't noticed her joining the little group. "I would very much like to see this piece."

"Then come along, Dr. Herschel, come along." Caudwell led them to a small hallway, exchanging genial greetings with his guests as he passed, pointing out a John William Hill miniature they might not have seen, picking up a few other people who for various reasons wanted to see his prize.

"By the way, Gioia, I was in New York last week, you know. Met an old friend of yours from Arkansas. Paul Nierman."

"Nierman?" Gioia seemed to be at a loss. "I'm afraid I don't remember him."

"Well, he remembered you pretty well. Sent you all kinds of messages — you'll have to stop by my office on Monday and get the full strength."

Caudwell opened a door on the right side of the hall and let them into his study. It was an octagonal room carved out of the corner of the building. Windows on two sides looked out on Lake Michigan. Caudwell drew salmon drapes as he talked about the room, why he'd chosen it for his study even though the view kept his mind from his work.

Lotty ignored him and walked over to a small pedestal which stood alone against the paneling on one of the far walls. Max followed her and gazed respectfully at the statue. He had seldom seen so fine a piece outside a museum. About a foot high, it depicted a woman in classical draperies hovering in anguish over the dead body of a soldier lying at her feet. The grief in her beautiful face was so poignant that it reminded you of every sorrow you had ever faced.

"Who is it meant to be?" Max asked curiously.

"Andromache," Lotty said in a strangled voice. "Andromache mourning Hector."

Max stared at Lotty, astonished equally by her emotion and her knowledge of the figure — Lotty was totally uninterested in sculpture.

Caudwell couldn't restrain the smug smile of a collector with a true coup. "Beautiful, isn't it? How do you know the subject?"

"I should know it." Lotty's voice was husky with emotion. "My grandmother had such a Pietro. An alabaster given her great-grandfather

95

by the Emperor Joseph the Second himself for his help in consolidating imperial ties with Poland."

She swept the statue from its stand, ignoring a gasp from Max, and turned it over. "You can see the traces of the imperial stamp here still. And the chip on Hector's foot which made the Hapsburg wish to give the statue away to begin with. How came you to have this piece? Where did you find it?"

The small group that had joined Caudwell stood silent by the entrance, shocked at Lotty's outburst. Gioia looked more horrified than any of them, but he found Lotty overwhelming at the best of times — an elephant confronted by a hostile mouse.

"I think you're allowing your emotions to carry you away, Doctor." Caudwell kept his tone light, making Lotty seem more gauche by contrast. "I inherited this piece from my father, who bought it — legitimately — in Europe. Perhaps from your — grandmother, was it? But I suspect you are confused about something you may have seen in a museum as a child."

Deborah gave a high-pitched laugh and called loudly to her brother, "Dad may have stolen it from Uncle Grif, but it looks like Grandfather snatched it to begin with anyway."

"Be quiet, Deborah," Caudwell barked sternly.

His daughter paid no attention to him. She laughed again and joined her brother to look at the imperial seal on the bottom of the statue.

96

Lotty brushed them aside. "*I* am confused about the seal of Joseph the Second?" she hissed at Caudwell. "Or about this chip on Hector's foot? You can see the line where some philistine filled in the missing piece. Some person who thought his touch would add value to Pietro's work. Was that you, *Doctor*? Or your father?"

"Lotty." Max was at her side, gently prising the statue from her shaking hands to restore it to its pedestal. "Lotty, this is not the place or the manner to discuss such things."

Angry tears sparkled in her black eyes. "Are you doubting my word?"

Max shook his head. "I'm not doubting you. But I'm also not supporting you. I'm asking you not to talk about this matter in this way at this gathering."

"But, Max: either this man or his father is a thief!"

Caudwell strolled up to Lotty and pinched her chin. "You're working too hard, Dr. Herschel. You have too many things on your mind these days. I think the board would like to see you take a leave of absence for a few weeks, go someplace warm, get yourself relaxed. When you're this tense, you're no good to your patients. What do you say, Loewenthal?"

Max didn't say any of the things he wanted to — that Lotty was insufferable and Caudwell intolerable. He believed Lotty, believed that the piece had been her grandmother's. She knew too much about it, for one thing. And for another, a lot of artworks belonging to European Jews were now in museums or private collections around the world. It was only the most god-awful coincidence that the Pietro had ended up with Caudwell's father.

But how dare she raise the matter in the way most likely to alienate everyone present? He couldn't possibly support her in such a situation. And at the same time, Caudwell's pinching her chin in that condescending way made him wish he were not chained to a courtesy that would have kept him from knocking the surgeon out even if he'd been ten years younger and ten inches taller.

"I don't think this is the place or the time to discuss such matters," he reiterated as calmly as he could. "Why don't we all cool down and get back together on Monday, eh?"

Lotty gasped involuntarily, then swept from the room without a backward glance.

Max refused to follow her. He was too angry with her to want to see her again that afternoon. When he got ready to leave the party an hour or so later, after a long conversation with Caudwell that taxed his sophisticated urbanity to the utmost, he heard with relief that Lotty was long gone. The tale of her outburst had of course spread through the gathering at something faster than the speed of sound; he wasn't up to defending her to Martha Gildersleeve, who demanded an explanation of him in the elevator going down.

He went home for a solitary evening in his

house in Evanston. Normally such time brought him pleasure, listening to music in his study, lying on the couch with his shoes off, reading history, letting the sounds of the lake wash over him.

Tonight, though, he could get no relief. Fury with Lotty merged into images of horror, the memories of his own disintegrated family, his search through Europe for his mother. He had never found anyone who was quite certain what became of her, although several people told him definitely of his father's suicide. And stamped over these wisps in his brain was the disturbing picture of Caudwell's children, their blond heads leaning backward at identical angles as they gleefully chanted, "Grandpa was a thief, Grandpa was a thief," while Caudwell edged his visitors out of the study.

By morning he would somehow have to reconstruct himself enough to face Lotty, to respond to the inevitable flood of calls from outraged trustees. He'd have to figure out a way of soothing Caudwell's vanity, bruised more by his children's behavior than anything Lotty had said. And find a way to keep both important doctors at Beth Israel.

Max rubbed his gray hair. Every week this job brought him less joy and more pain. Maybe it was time to step down, to let the board bring in a young MBA who would turn Beth Israel's finances around. Lotty would resign then, and it would be an end to the tension between her and Caudwell.

Max fell asleep on the couch. He awoke around five muttering, "By morning, by morning." His joints were stiff from cold, his eyes sticky with tears he'd shed unknowingly in his sleep.

But in the morning things changed. When Max got to his office he found the place buzzing, not with news of Lotty's outburst but word that Caudwell had missed his early morning surgery. Work came almost completely to a halt at noon when his children phoned to say they'd found the surgeon strangled in his own study and the Pietro Andromache missing. And on Tuesday, the police arrested Dr. Charlotte Herschel for Lewis Caudwell's murder.

III

Lotty would not speak to anyone. She was out on two hundred fifty thousand dollars' bail, the money raised by Max, but she had gone directly to her apartment on Sheffield after two nights in County Jail without stopping to thank him. She would not talk to reporters, she remained silent during all conversations with the police, and she emphatically refused to speak to the private investigator who had been her close friend for many years.

Max, too, stayed behind an impregnable shield of silence. While Lotty went on indefinite leave, turning her practice over to a series of colleagues, Max continued to go to the hospital every day. But he, too, would not speak to reporters: he wouldn't even say "No comment." He talked to the police only after they threatened to lock him up as a material witness, and then every word had to be pried from him as if his mouth were stone and speech Excalibur. For three days V. I. Warshawski left messages which he refused to return.

On Friday, when no word came from the detective, when no reporter popped up from a nearby urinal in the men's room to try to trick him into speaking, when no more calls came from the state's attorney, Max felt a measure of relaxation as he drove home. As soon as the trial was over he would resign, retire to London. If he could only keep going until then, everything would be — not all right, but bearable.

He used the remote release for the garage door and eased his car into the small space. As he got out he realized bitterly he'd been too optimistic in thinking he'd be left in peace. He hadn't seen the woman sitting on the stoop leading from the garage to the kitchen when he drove in, only as she uncoiled herself at his approach.

"I'm glad you're home — I was beginning to freeze out here."

"How did you get into the garage, Victoria?"

The detective grinned in a way he usually found engaging. Now it seemed merely predatory. "Trade secret, Max. I know you don't want to see me, but I need to talk to you."

He unlocked the door into the kitchen. "Why not just let yourself into the house if you were cold? If your scruples permit you into the garage, why not into the house?"

She bit her lip in momentary discomfort but said lightly, "I couldn't manage my picklocks with my fingers this cold."

The detective followed him into the house. Another tall monster; five foot eight, athletic, light on her feet behind him. Maybe American mothers put growth hormones or steroids in their children's cornflakes. He'd have to ask Lotty. His mind winced at the thought.

"I've talked to the police, of course," the light alto continued behind him steadily, oblivious to his studied rudeness as he poured himself a cognac, took his shoes off, found his waiting slippers, and padded down the hall to the front door for his mail.

"I understand why they arrested Lotty — Caudwell had been doped with a whole bunch of Xanax and then strangled while he was sleeping it off. And, of course, she was back at the building Sunday night. She won't say why, but one of the tenants I.D.'d her as the woman who showed up around ten at the service entrance when he was walking his dog. She won't say if she talked to Caudwell, if he let her in, if he was still alive."

Max tried to ignore her clear voice. When that proved impossible he tried to read a journal which had come in the mail.

"And those kids, they're marvelous, aren't

they? Like something out of the *Fabulous Furry Freak Brothers*. They won't talk to me but they gave a long interview to Murray Ryerson over at the *Star*.

"After Caudwell's guests left, they went to a flick at the Chestnut Street Station, had a pizza afterwards, then took themselves dancing on Division Street. So they strolled in around two in the morning — confirmed by the doorman — saw the light on in the old man's study. But they were feeling no pain and he kind of over-reacted — their term — if they were buzzed, so they didn't stop in to say goodnight. It was only when they got up around noon and went in that they found him."

V. I. had followed Max from the front hallway to the door of his study as she spoke. He stood there irresolutely, not wanting his private place desecrated with her insistent, air-hammer speech, and finally went on down the hall to a little-used living room. He sat stiffly on one of the brocade armchairs and looked at her remotely when she perched on the edge of its companion.

"The weak piece in the police story is the statue," V. I. continued.

She eyed the Persian rug doubtfully and unzipped her boots, sticking them on the bricks in front of the fireplace.

"Everyone who was at the party agrees that Lotty was beside herself. By now the story has spread so far that people who weren't even in the apartment when she looked at the statue swear they heard her threaten to kill him. But if that's the case, what happened to the statue?"

Max gave a slight shrug to indicate total lack of interest in the topic.

V. I. plowed on doggedly. "Now some people think she might have given it to a friend or a relation to keep for her until her name is cleared at the trial. And these people think it would be either her Uncle Stefan here in Chicago, her brother Hugo in Montreal, or you. So the Mounties searched Hugo's place and are keeping an eye on his mail. And the Chicago cops are doing the same for Stefan. And I presume someone got a warrant and went through here, right?"

Max said nothing, but he felt his heart beating faster. Police in his house, searching his things? But wouldn't they have to get his permission to enter? Or would they? Victoria would know, but he couldn't bring himself to ask. She waited for a few minutes, but when he still wouldn't speak, she plunged on. He could see it was becoming an effort for her to talk, but he wouldn't help her.

"But I don't agree with those people. Because I know that Lotty is innocent. And that's why I'm here. Not like a bird of prey, as you think, using your misery for carrion. But to get you to help me. Lotty won't speak to me, and if she's that miserable I won't force her to. But surely, Max, you won't sit idly by and let her be railroaded for something she never did."

Max looked away from her. He was surprised

to find himself holding the brandy snifter and set it carefully on a table beside him.

"Max!" Her voice was shot with astonishment. "I don't believe this. You actually think she killed Caudwell."

Max flushed a little, but she'd finally stung him into a response. "And you are God who sees all and knows she didn't?"

"I see more than you do," V. I. snapped. "I haven't known Lotty as long as you have, but I know when she's telling the truth."

"So you are God." Max bowed in heavy irony. "You see beyond the facts to the innermost souls of men and women."

He expected another outburst from the young woman, but she gazed at him steadily without speaking. It was a look sympathetic enough that Max felt embarrassed by his sarcasm and burst out with what was on his mind.

"What else am I to think? She hasn't said anything, but there's no doubt that she returned to his apartment Sunday night."

It was V. I.'s turn for sarcasm. "With a little vial of Xanax that she somehow induced him to swallow? And then strangled him for good measure? Come on, Max, you know Lotty: honesty follows her around like a cloud. If she'd killed Caudwell, she'd say something like, "Yes, I bashed the little vermin's brains in.' Instead she's not speaking at all."

Suddenly the detective's eyes widened with incredulity. "Of course. She thinks you killed

Caudwell. You're doing the only thing you can to protect her — standing mute. And she's doing the same thing. What an admirable pair of archaic knights."

"No!" Max said sharply. "It's not possible. How could she think such a thing? She carried on so wildly that it was embarrassing to be near her. I didn't want to see her or talk to her. That's why I've felt so terrible. If only I hadn't been so obstinate, if only I'd called her Sunday night. How could she think I would kill someone on her behalf when I was so angry with her?"

"Why else isn't she saying anything to anyone?" Warshawski demanded.

"Shame, maybe," Max offered. "You didn't see her on Sunday. I did. That is why I think she killed him, not because some man let her into the building."

His brown eyes screwed shut at the memory. "I have seen Lotty in the grip of anger many times, more than is pleasant to remember, really. But never, never have I seen her in this kind of — uncontrolled rage. You could not talk to her. It was impossible."

The detective didn't respond to that. Instead she said, "Tell me about the statue. I heard a couple of garbled versions from people who were at the party, but I haven't found anyone yet who was in the study when Caudwell showed it to you. Was it really her grandmother's, do you think? And how did Caudwell come to have it if it was?"

Max nodded mournfully. "Oh, yes. It was really her family's, I'm convinced of that. She could not have known in advance about the details, the flaw in the foot, the imperial seal on the bottom. As to how Caudwell got it, I did a little looking into that myself yesterday. His father was with the Army of Occupation in Germany after the war. A surgeon attached to Patton's staff. Men in such positions had endless opportunities to acquire artworks after the war."

V. I. shook her head questioningly.

"You must know something of this, Victoria. Well, maybe not. You know the Nazis helped themselves liberally to artwork belonging to Jews everywhere they occupied Europe. And not just to Jews — they plundered Eastern Europe on a grand scale. The best guess is that they stole sixteen million pieces — statues, paintings, altarpieces, tapestries, rare books. The list is beyond reckoning, really."

The detective gave a little gasp. "Sixteen million! You're joking."

"Not a joke, Victoria. I wish it were so, but it is not. The U.S. Army of Occupation took charge of as many works of art as they found in the occupied territories. In theory, they were to find the rightful owners and try to restore them. But in practice few pieces were ever traced, and many of them ended up on the black market.

"You only had to say that such-and-such a piece was worth less than five thousand dollars and you were allowed to buy it. For an officer on

Patton's staff, the opportunities for fabulous acquisitions would have been endless. Caudwell said he had the statue authenticated, but of course he never bothered to establish its provenance. Anyway, how could he?" Max finished bitterly. "Lotty's family had a deed of gift from the emperor, but that would have disappeared long since with the dispersal of their possessions."

"And you really think Lotty would have killed a man just to get this statue back? She couldn't have expected to keep it. Not if she'd killed someone to get it, I mean."

"You are so practical, Victoria. You are too analytical, sometimes, to understand why people do what they do. That was not just a statue. True, it is a priceless artwork, but you know Lotty, you know she places no value on such possessions. No, it meant her family to her, her past, her history, everything that the war destroyed forever for her. You must not imagine that because she never discusses such matters that they do not weigh on her."

V. I. flushed at Max's accusation. "You should be glad I'm analytical. It convinces me that Lotty is innocent. And whether you believe it or not I'm going to prove it."

Max lifted his shoulders slightly in a manner wholly European. "We each support Lotty according to our lights. I saw that she met her bail, and I will see that she gets expert counsel. I am not convinced that she needs you making innermost secrets public."

108

V. I.'s gray eyes turned dark with a sudden flash of temper. "You're dead wrong about Lotty. I'm sure the memory of the war is a pain that can never be cured, but Lotty lives in the present, she works in hope for the future. The past does not obsess and consume her as, perhaps, it does you."

Max said nothing. His wide mouth turned in on itself in a narrow line. The detective laid a contrite hand on his arm.

"I'm sorry, Max. That was below the belt."

He forced the ghost of a smile to his mouth.

"Perhaps it's true. Perhaps it's why I love these ancient things so much. I wish I could believe you about Lotty. Ask me what you want to know. If you promise to leave as soon as I've answered and not to bother me again, I'll answer your questions."

IV

Max put in a dutiful appearance at the Michigan Avenue Presbyterian Church Monday afternoon for Lewis Caudwell's funeral. The surgeon's former wife came, flanked by her children and her husband's brother Griffen. Even after three decades in America Max found himself puzzled sometimes by the natives' behavior: since she and Caudwell were divorced, why had his ex-wife draped herself in black? She was even wearing a veiled hat reminiscent of Queen Victoria.

The children behaved in a moderately subdued fashion, but the girl was wearing a white dress shot with black lightning forks which looked as though it belonged at a disco or a resort. Maybe it was her only dress or her only dress with black in it, Max thought, trying hard to look charitably at the blond Amazon — after all, she had been suddenly and horribly orphaned.

Even though she was a stranger both in the city and the church, Deborah had hired one of the church parlors and managed to find someone to cater coffee and light snacks. Max joined the rest of the congregation there after the service.

He felt absurd as he offered condolences to the divorced widow: did she really miss the dead man so much? She accepted his conventional words with graceful melancholy and leaned slightly against her son and daughter. They hovered near her with what struck Max as a stagey solicitude. Seen next to her daughter, Mrs. Caudwell looked so frail and undernourished that she seemed like a ghost. Or maybe it was just that her children had a hearty vitality that even a funeral couldn't quench.

Caudwell's brother Griffen stayed as close to the widow as the children would permit. The man was totally unlike the hearty sea dog surgeon. Max thought if he'd met the brothers standing side by side he would never have guessed their relationship. He was tall, like his niece and nephew, but without their robustness. Caudwell

110

had had a thick mop of yellow-white hair; Griffen's domed head was covered by thin wisps of gray. He seemed weak and nervous, and lacked Caudwell's outgoing bonhomie; no wonder the surgeon had found it easy to decide the disposition of their father's estate in his favor. Max wondered what Griffen had gotten in return.

Mrs. Caudwell's vague, disoriented conversation indicated that she was heavily sedated. That, too, seemed strange. A man she hadn't lived with for four years and she was so upset at his death that she could only manage the funeral on drugs? Or maybe it was the shame of coming as the divorced woman, not a true widow? But then why come at all?

To his annoyance, Max found himself wishing he could ask Victoria about it. She would have some cynical explanation — Caudwell's death meant the end of the widow's alimony and she knew she wasn't remembered in the will. Or she was having an affair with Griffen and was afraid she would betray herself without tranquilizers. Although it was hard to imagine the uncertain Griffen as the object of a strong passion.

Since he had told Victoria he didn't want to see her again when she left on Friday, it was ridiculous of him to wonder what she was doing, whether she was really uncovering evidence that would clear Lotty. Ever since she had gone he had felt a little flicker of hope in the bottom of his stomach. He kept trying to drown it, but it wouldn't quite go away.

Lotty, of course, had not come to the funeral, but most of the rest of the Beth Israel staff was there, along with the trustees. Arthur Gioia, his giant body filling the small parlor to the bursting point, tried finding a tactful balance between honesty and courtesy with the bereaved family; he made heavy going of it.

A sable-clad Martha Gildersleeve appeared under Gioia's elbow, rather like a furry football he might have tucked away. She made bright, unseemly remarks to the bereaved family about the disposal of Caudwell's artworks.

"Of course, the famous statue is gone now. What a pity. You could have endowed a chair in his honor with the proceeds from that piece alone." She gave a high, meaningless laugh.

Max sneaked a glance at his watch, wondering how long he had to stay before leaving would be rude. His sixth sense, the perfect courtesy that governed his movements, had deserted him, leaving him subject to the gaucheries of ordinary mortals. He never peeked at his watch at functions, and at any prior funeral he would have deftly pried Martha Gildersleeve from her victim. Instead he stood helplessly by while she tortured Mrs. Caudwell and other bystanders alike.

He glanced at his watch again. Only two minutes had passed since his last look. No wonder people kept their eyes on their watches at dull meetings: they couldn't believe the clock could move so slowly.

He inched stealthily toward the door, exchanging empty remarks with the staff members and trustees he passed. Nothing negative was said about Lotty to his face, but the comments cut off at his approach added to his misery.

He was almost at the exit when two newcomers appeared. Most of the group looked at them with indifferent curiosity, but Max suddenly felt an absurd stir of happiness. Victoria, looking sane and modern in a navy suit, stood in the doorway, eyebrows raised, scanning the room. At her elbow was a police sergeant Max had met with her a few times. The man was in charge of Caudwell's death, too: it was that unpleasant association that kept the name momentarily from his mind.

V. I. finally spotted Max near the door and gave him a discreet sign. He went to her at once.

"I think we may have the goods," she murmured. "Can you get everyone to go? We just want the family, Mrs. Gildersleeve, and Gioia."

"*You* may have the goods," the police sergeant growled. "I'm here unofficially and reluctantly."

"But you're here." Warshawski grinned, and Max wondered how he ever could have found the look predatory. His own spirits rose enormously at her smile. "You know in your heart of hearts that arresting Lotty was just plain dumb. And now I'm going to make you look real smart. In public, too."

Max felt his suave sophistication return with the rush of elation that an ailing diva must have when she finds her voice again. A touch here, a word there, and the guests disappeared like

113

the hosts of Sennacherib. Meanwhile he solicitously escorted first Martha Gildersleeve, then Mrs. Caudwell to adjacent armchairs, got the brother to fetch coffee for Mrs. Gildersleeve, the daughter and son to look after the widow.

With Gioia he could be a bit more ruthless, telling him to wait because the police had something important to ask him. When the last guest had melted away, the immunologist stood nervously at the window rattling his change over and over in his pockets. The jingling suddenly was the only sound in the room. Gioia reddened and clasped his hands behind his back.

Victoria came into the room beaming like a governess with a delightful treat in store for her charges. She introduced herself to the Caudwells.

"You know Sergeant McGonnigal, I'm sure, after this last week. I'm a private investigator. Since I don't have any legal standing, you're not required to answer any questions I have. So I'm not going to ask you any questions. I'm just going to treat you to a travelogue. I wish I had slides, but you'll have to imagine the visuals while the audio track moves along."

"A private investigator!" Steve's mouth formed an exaggerated "O"; his eyes widened in amazement. "Just like Bogie."

He was speaking, as usual, to his sister. She gave her high-pitched laugh and said, "We'll win first prize in the 'How I Spent My Winter Vacation' contests. Our daddy was murdered. Zowie. Then his most valuable possession was

114

snatched. Powie. But he'd already stolen it from the Jewish doctor who killed him. Yowie! And then a P.I. to wrap it all up. Yowie! Zowie! Powie!"

"Deborah, please," Mrs. Caudwell sighed. "I know you're excited, sweetie, but not right now, okay?"

"Your children keep you young, don't they, ma'am?" Victoria said. "How can you ever feel old when your kids stay seven all their lives?"

"Oo, ow, she bites, Debbie, watch out, she bites!" Steve cried.

McGonnigal made an involuntary movement, as though restraining himself from smacking the younger man. "Ms. Warshawski is right: you are under no obligation to answer any of her questions. But you're bright people, all of you: you know I wouldn't be here if the police didn't take her ideas very seriously. So let's have a little quiet and listen to what she's got on her mind."

Victoria seated herself in an armchair near Mrs. Caudwell's. McGonnigal moved to the door and leaned against the jamb. Deborah and Steve whispered and poked each other until one or both of them shrieked. They then made their faces prim and sat with their hands folded on their laps, looking like bright-eyed choirboys.

Griffen hovered near Mrs. Caudwell. "You know you don't have to say anything, Vivian. In fact, I think you should return to your hotel and lie down. The stress of the funeral — then these strangers —"

Mrs. Caudwell's lips curled bravely below the bottom of her veil. "It's all right, Grif; if I managed to survive everything else, one more thing isn't going to do me in."

"Great." Victoria accepted a cup of coffee from Max. "Let me just sketch events for you as I saw them last week. Like everyone else in Chicago, I read about Dr. Caudwell's murder and saw it on television. Since I know a number of people attached to Beth Israel, I may have paid more attention to it than the average viewer, but I didn't get personally involved until Dr. Herschel's arrest on Tuesday."

She swallowed some coffee and set the cup on the table next to her with a small snap. "I have known Dr. Herschel for close to twenty years. It is inconceivable that she would commit such a murder, as those who know her well should have realized at once. I don't fault the police, but others should have known better: she is hot tempered. I'm not saying killing is beyond her — I don't think it's beyond any of us. She might have taken the statue and smashed Dr. Caudwell's head in in the heat of rage. But it beggars belief to think she went home, brooded over her injustices, packed a dose of prescription tranquilizer, and headed back to the Gold Coast with murder in mind."

Max felt his cheeks turn hot at her words. He started to interject a protest but bit it back.

"Dr. Herschel refused to make a statement all week, but this afternoon, when I got back from my travels, she finally agreed to talk to me. Sergeant McGonnigal was with me. She doesn't deny that she returned to Dr. Caudwell's apartment at ten that night — she went back to apologize for her outburst and to try to plead with him to return the statue. He didn't answer when the doorman called up, and on impulse she went around to the back of the building, got in through the service entrance, and waited for some time outside the apartment door. When he neither answered the doorbell nor returned home himself, she finally went away around eleven o'clock. The children, of course, were having a night on the town."

"*She* says," Gioia interjected.

"Agreed." V. I. smiled. "I make no bones about being a partisan: I accept her version. The more so because the only reason she didn't give it a week ago was that she herself was protecting an old friend. She thought perhaps this friend had bestirred himself on her behalf and killed Caudwell to avenge deadly insults against her. It was only when I persuaded her that these suspicions were as unmerited as — well, as accusations against herself — that she agreed to talk."

Max bit his lip and busied himself with getting more coffee for the three women. Victoria waited for him to finish before continuing.

"When I finally got a detailed account of what took place at Caudwell's party, I heard about three people with an ax to grind. One always has to ask, what ax and how big a grindstone? That's what I've spent the weekend finding out. You might as well know that I've been to Little Rock and to Havelock, North Carolina."

Gioia began jingling the coins in his pockets again. Mrs. Caudwell said softly, "Grif, I am feeling a little faint. Perhaps —"

"Home you go, Mom," Steve cried out with alacrity.

"In a few minutes, Mrs. Caudwell," the sergeant said from the doorway. "Get her feet up, Warshawski."

For a moment Max was afraid that Steve or Deborah was going to attack Victoria, but McGonnigal moved over to the widow's chair and the children sat down again. Little drops of sweat dotted Griffen's balding head; Gioia's face had a greenish sheen, foliage on top of his redwood neck.

"The thing that leapt out at me," Victoria continued calmly, as though there had been no interruption, "was Caudwell's remark to Dr. Gioia. The doctor was clearly upset, but people were so focused on Lotty and the statue that they didn't pay any attention to that.

"So I went to Little Rock, Arkansas, on Saturday and found the Paul Nierman whose name Caudwell had mentioned to Gioia. Nierman lived in the same fraternity with Gioia when they were undergraduates together twenty-five years ago. And he took Dr. Gioia's anatomy and physiology exams his junior year when Gioia was in danger of academic probation, so he could stay

118

on the football team.

"Well, that seemed unpleasant, perhaps disgraceful. But there's no question that Gioia did all his own work in medical school, passed his boards, and so on. So I didn't think the board would demand a resignation for this youthful indiscretion. The question was whether Gioia thought they would, and if he would have killed to prevent Caudwell making it public."

She paused, and the immunologist blurted out, "No. No. But Caudwell — Caudwell knew I'd opposed his appointment. He and I — our approaches to medicine were very opposite. And as soon as he said Nierman's name to me, I knew he'd found out and that he'd torment me with it forever. I — I went back to his place Sunday night to have it out with him. I was more determined than Dr. Herschel and got into his unit through the kitchen entrance; he hadn't locked that.

"I went to his study, but he was already dead. I couldn't believe it. It absolutely terrified me. I could see he'd been strangled and — well, it's no secret that I'm strong enough to have done it. I wasn't thinking straight. I just got clean away from there — I think I've been running ever since."

"You!" McGonnigal shouted. "How come we haven't heard about this before?"

"Because you insisted on focusing on Dr. Herschel," V. I. said nastily. "I knew he'd been there

119

because the doorman told me. He would have told you if you'd asked."

"This is terrible," Mrs. Gildersleeve interjected. "I am going to talk to the board tomorrow and demand the resignations of Dr. Gioia and Dr. Herschel."

"Do," Victoria agreed cordially. "You could also tell them the reason you got to stay for this discussion was because Murray Ryerson at the *Herald-Star* was doing a little checking for me here in Chicago. He found out that part of the reason you were so jealous of Caudwell's collection is that you're living terribly in debt. I won't humiliate you in public by telling people what your money has gone to, but you've had to sell your husband's art collection and you have a third mortgage on your house. A valuable statue with no documented history would have taken care of everything."

Martha Gildersleeve shrank inside her sable. "You don't know anything about this."

"Well, Murray talked to Pablo and Eduardo. . . . Yes, I won't say anything else. So anyway, Murray checked whether either Gioia or Mrs. Gildersleeve had the statue. They didn't, so —"

"You've been in my house?" Mrs. Gildersleeve shrieked.

V. I. shook her head. "Not me. Murray Ryerson." She looked apologetically at the sergeant. "I knew you'd never get a warrant for me, since you'd made an arrest. And you'd never have got it in time, anyway."

She looked at her coffee cup, saw it was empty and put it down again. Max took it from the table and filled it for her a third time. His fingertips were itching with nervous irritation; some of the coffee landed on his trouser leg.

"I talked to Murray Saturday night from Little Rock. When he came up empty here, I headed for North Carolina. To Havelock, where Griffen and Lewis Caudwell grew up and where Mrs. Caudwell still lives. And I saw the house where Griffen lives, and talked to the doctor who treats Mrs. Caudwell, and —"

"You really are a pooper snooper, aren't you," Steve said.

"Pooper snooper, pooper snooper," Deborah chanted. "Don't get enough thrills of your own so you have to live on other people's shit."

"Yeah, the neighbors talked to me about you two." Victoria looked at them with contemptuous indulgence. "You've been a two-person wolf pack terrifying most of the people around you since you were three. But the folks in Havelock admired how you always stuck up for your mother. You thought your father got her addicted to tranquilizers and then left her high and dry. So you brought her newest version with you and were all set — you just needed to decide when to give it to him. Dr. Herschel's outburst over the statue played right into your hands. You figured your father had stolen it from your uncle to begin with — why not send it back to him and let Dr. Herschel take the rap?"

"It wasn't like that," Steve said, red spots burning in his cheeks.

"What was it like, son?" McGonnigal had moved next to him.

"Don't talk to them — they're tricking you," Deborah shrieked. "The pooper snooper and her gopher gooper."

"She — Mommy used to love us before Daddy made her take all this shit. Then she went away. We just wanted him to see what it was like. We started putting Xanax in his coffee and stuff; we wanted to see if he'd fuck up during surgery, let his life get ruined. But then he was sleeping there in the study after his stupid-ass party, and we thought we'd just let him sleep through his morning surgery. Sleep forever, you know, it was so easy, we used his own Harvard necktie. I was so fucking sick of hearing 'Early to bed, early to rise' from him. And we sent the statue to Uncle Grif. I suppose the pooper snooper found it there. He can sell it and Mother can be all right again."

"Grandpa stole it from Jews and Daddy stole it from Grif, so we thought it worked out perfectly if we stole it from Daddy," Deborah cried. She leaned her blond head next to her brother's and shrieked with laughter.

V

Max watched the line of Lotty's legs change as she stood on tiptoe to reach a brandy snifter. Short, muscular from years of racing at top speed from one point to the next, maybe they weren't as svelte as the long legs of modern American girls, but he preferred them. He waited until her feet were securely planted before making his announcement.

"The board is bringing in Justin Hardwick for a final interview for chief of staff."

"Max!" She whirled, the Bengal fire sparkling in her eyes. "I know this Hardwick and he is another like Caudwell, looking for cost-cutting and no poverty patients. I won't have it."

"We've got you and Gioia and a dozen others bringing in so many nonpaying patients that we're not going to survive another five years at the present rate. I figure it's a balancing act. We need someone who can see that the hospital survives so that you and Art can practice medicine the way you want to. And when he knows what happened to his predecessor, he'll be very careful not to stir up our resident tigress."

"Max!" She was hurt and astonished at the same time. "Oh. You're joking, I see. It's not very funny to me, you know."

"My dear, we've got to learn to laugh about

123

it: it's the only way we'll ever be able to forgive ourselves for our terrible misjudgments." He stepped over to put an arm around her. "Now where is this remarkable surprise you promised to show me."

She shot him a look of pure mischief, Lotty on a dare as he first remembered meeting her at eighteen. His hold on her tightened and he followed her to her bedroom. In a glass case in the corner, complete with a humidity-control system, stood the Pietro Andromache.

Max looked at the beautiful, anguished face. I understand your sorrows, she seemed to say to him. I understand your grief for your mother, your family, your history, but it's all right to let go of them, to live in the present and hope for the future. It's not a betrayal.

Tears pricked his eyelids, but he demanded, "How did you get this? I was told the police had it under lock and key until lawyers decided on the disposition of Caudwell's estate."

"Victoria," Lotty said shortly. "I told her the problem and she got it for me. On the condition that I not ask how she did it. And Max, you know — *damned* well — that it was not Caudwell's to dispose of."

It was Lotty's. Of course it was. Max wondered briefly how Joseph the Second had come by it to begin with. For that matter, what had Lotty's great-great-grandfather done to earn it from the emperor? Max looked into Lotty's tiger eyes and kept such reflections to himself. Instead he inspected Hector's foot where the filler had been carefully scraped away to reveal the old chip.

Strung Out

I

PEOPLE BORN NEAR the corner of 90th and Commercial used to have fairly predictable futures. The boys grew up to work in the mills; the girls took jobs in the bakeries or coffee shops. They married each other and scrimped to make a down payment on a neighborhood bungalow and somehow fit their large families into its small rooms.

Now that the mills are history, the script has changed. Kids are still marrying, still having families, but without the certainty of the steel industry to buoy their futures. The one thing that seems to stay the same, though, is the number who stubbornly cling to the neighborhood even now that the jobs are gone. It's a clannish place, South Chicago, and people don't leave it easily.

When Monica Larush got pregnant our senior year in high school and married football hero Gary Oberst, we all just assumed they were on their way to becoming another large family in a small bungalow. She wasn't a friend of mine, so I didn't worry about the possible ruin of her life. Anyway,

126

having recently lost my own mother to cancer, I wasn't too concerned about other girls' problems.

Monica's and my lives only intersected on the basketball court. Like me, she was an aggressive athlete, but she clearly had a high level of talent as well. In those days, though, a pregnant girl couldn't stay in school, so she missed our championship winter. The team brought her a game ball. We found her, fat and pasty, eating Fritos in angry frustration in front of the TV in her mother's kitchen. When we left, we made grotesque jokes about her swollen face and belly, our only way of expressing our embarrassment and worry.

Gary and Monica rewrote their script, though. Gary got a job on the night shift at Inland Steel and went to school during the day. After the baby — Gary Junior — was born, Monica picked up her GED. The two of them scrimped, not for a down payment, but to make it through the University of Illinois's Chicago campus. Gary took a job as an accountant with a big Loop firm, Monica taught high school French, and they left the neighborhood. Moved north was what I heard.

And that was pretty much all I knew — or cared — about them before Lily Oberst's name and face started popping up in the papers. She was apparently mopping up junior tennis competition. Tennis boosters and athletic-apparel makers were counting the minutes until she turned pro.

127

I actually first heard about her from my old basketball coach, Mary Ann McFarlane. Mary Ann's first love had always been tennis. When she retired from teaching at sixty, she continued to act as a tennis umpire at local high school and college tournaments. I saw her once a year when the Virginia Slims came to Chicago. She worked as a linesperson there for the pittance the tour paid — not for the bucks, but for the excitement. I always came during the last few days and had dinner with her in Greek Town at the end of the finals.

"I've been watching Lily Oberst play up at the Skokie Valley club," Mary Ann announced one year. "Kid's got terrific stuff. If they don't ruin her too young she could be — well, I won't say another Martina. Martinas come once a century. But a great one."

"Lily Oberst?" I shook my head, fishing for why the name sounded familiar.

"You don't remember Monica? Didn't you girls keep in touch after your big year? Lily is her and Gary's daughter. I used to coach Monica in tennis besides basketball, but I guess that wasn't one of your sports."

After that I read the stories in detail and got caught up on twenty years of missing history. Lily grew up in suburban Glenview, the second of two children. The *Herald-Star* explained that both her parents were athletic and encouraged her and her brother to go out for sports. When a camp coach brought back the word that Lily

128

might have some tennis aptitude, her daddy began working with her every day. She had just turned six then.

Gary put up a net for her in the basement and would give her an ice cream bar every time she could hit the ball back twenty-five times without missing.

"He got mad when it got too easy for me," Lily said, giggling, to the reporter. "Then he'd raise the net whenever I got to twenty-four."

When it became clear that they had a major tennis talent on their hands, Monica and Gary put all their energy into developing it. Monica quit her job as a teacher so that she could travel to camps and tournaments with Lily. Gary, by then regional director for a pharmaceutical firm, persuaded his company to put in the seed money for Lily's career. He himself took a leave of absence to work as her personal trainer. Even now that she was a pro Monica and Gary went with her everywhere. Of course Lily had a professional coach, but her day always started with a workout with Daddy.

Gary Junior didn't get much print attention. He apparently didn't share the family's sports mania. Five years older than Lily, he was in college studying for a degree in chemical engineering, and hoping to go off to Procter & Gamble in Cincinnati.

Lily turned pro the same year Jennifer Capriati did. Since Capriati was making history, joining the pros at thirteen, Lily, two years older, didn't get the national hoopla. But Chicago went wild. Her arrival in the Wimbledon quarterfinals that year was front-page news all over town. Her 6–2, 6–0 loss there to Monica Seles was shown live in every bar in the city. Fresh-faced and smiling under a spiky blond hairdo, she grinned through her braces and said it was just a thrill to be on the same court with players like Seles and Graf. The city fell in love.

So when it was announced that she was coming to Chicago to play in the Slims in February the tournament generated more publicity than it had ever known. After a year and a half on the pro circuit Lily was ranked eighth in the world, but the pictures of her arrival at the family home still showed an ingenuous grin. Her Great Dane, standing on his hind legs with his paws on her shoulders, was licking her face.

Mary Ann McFarlane called me a few days after the Obersts arrived back in town. "Want to come up to Glenview and watch the kid work out? You could catch up with Monica at the same time."

That sounded like a treat that would appeal to Monica about as much as it did to me. But I had never seen a tennis prodigy in the making. I agreed to drive out to Glenview on Friday morning. Mary Ann and I would have lunch with Monica after Lily's workout.

The Skokie Valley Tennis Club was just off the Edens Expressway at Dempster. Lily's workout started at eight but I hadn't felt the need to watch a sixteen-year-old, however prodigious, run laps. I arrived at the courts a little after ten.

When I asked a woman at the reception desk to direct me to Lily, she told me the star's workout was off-limits to the press today. I explained who I was. She consulted higher authority over the phone. Mary Ann had apparently greased the necessary skids: I was allowed past a bored guard lounging against a hall door. After showing him my driver's license, I was directed down the hall to the private court where Lily was practicing. A second guard there looked at my license again and then opened the door for me.

Lily had the use of three nets if she needed them. A small grandstand held only three people: Mary Ann and Monica and a young man in a workout suit with "Artemis" blazoned across the back. I recognized Monica from the newspaper photos, but they didn't do justice to her perfectly styled gold hair, the makeup enhancing her oval face, or the casual elegance of her clothes. I had a fleeting memory of her fat, pasty face as she sat eating Fritos twenty years ago. I would never have put those two images together. As the old bromide has it, living well is the best revenge.

Mary Ann squeezed my hand as I sat on her other side. "Good to see you, Vic," she whispered. "Monica — here's Vic."

We exchanged confused greetings across our old coach, me congratulating her on her daughter's success, she exclaiming at how I hadn't changed a bit. I didn't know if that was a compliment or not.

The man was introduced as Monte Allison, from Artemis Products' marketing department. Artemis supplied all of Lily's tennis clothes and shoes, as well as a seven-figure endorsement contract. Allison was just along to protect the investment, Mary Ann explained. The equipment maker heard her and ostentatiously turned his left shoulder to us.

On the court in front of us Lily was hitting tennis balls. A kid in white shorts was serving to her backhand. A dark man in shabby gray sweats stood behind her encouraging her and critiquing her stroke. And a third man in bright white clothes offered more forceful criticisms from the sidelines.

"Get into the shot, Lily. Come'n, honey, you're not concentrating."

"Gary," Mary Ann muttered at me. "That's Paco Callabrio behind her."

I don't know much about tennis, but even I'd heard of Callabrio. After dominating men's tennis in the sixties he had retired to his family home in Majorca. But five years ago he'd come out of seclusion to coach a few selected players. Lily had piqued his interest when he saw her at the French Open last year; Monica had leaped at the opportunity to have her daughter work with him. Apparently Gary was less impressed. As the morning wore on Gary's advice began clashing with Paco's more and more often.

In the midst of a heated exchange over Lily's upswing I sensed someone moving onto the bench behind me. I turned to see a young woman leaning at her ease against the bleacher behind her. She was dressed in loose-fitting trousers that accentuated the long, lean lines of her body.

Lily saw the newcomer at the same time I did. She turned very red, then very white. While Paco and Gary continued arguing, she signaled to the young man to start hitting balls to her again. She'd been too tired to move well a minute ago, but the woman's arrival infused her with new energy.

Mary Ann had also turned to stare. "Nicole Rubova," she muttered to me.

I raised my eyebrows. Another of the dazzling Czech players who'd come to the States in Martina's wake. She was part of the generation between Martina and Capriati, a year or so older than Graf but with time ahead of her still to fight for the top spots. Her dark, vivid beauty made her a mediagenic foil to Graf's and Lily's blondness, but her sardonic humor kept her from being really popular with the press.

"Gary's afraid she's going to rape his baby. He won't let Lily go out alone with any of the women on the circuit." Mary Ann continued to mutter at me.

I raised my brows again, this time amazed at Mary Ann's pithy remarks. She'd never talked so bluntly to me when she was my basketball coach.

By now Gary had also seen Rubova in the stands. Like Lily he changed color, then grew even more maniacal in his demands on his daughter. When Paco advised a rest around eleven-thirty, Gary shook his head emphatically.

"You can't spoil her, Paco. Believe me, I know this little girl. She's got great talent and a heart of gold, but she's lazy. You've got to drive her."

Lily was gray with exhaustion. While they argued over her she leaned over, her hands on her knees, and gasped for air.

"Mr. Oberst," Paco said, his chilly formality emphasizing his dislike, "you want Lily to be a great star. But a girl who plays when she is this fatigued will only injure herself, if she doesn't burn out completely first. I say the workout is over for the day."

"And I say she got to Wimbledon last year thanks to my methods," Gary yelled.

"And she almost had to forfeit her round of sixteen match because you were coaching her so blatantly from the seats," Paco shouted back. "Your methods stink, Oberst."

Gary stepped toward the Catalan, then abruptly turned his back on him and yelled at his daughter, "Lily, pick up your racket. Come on, girl. You know the rules."

"Really, Oberst," Monte Allison called tentatively down to the floor from the stands. "We can't injure Lily — that won't help any of us."

Monica nodded in emphatic agreement, but Gary paid no attention to either of them. Lily looked imploringly from Paco to Gary. When the coach said nothing else, she bent to pick up her racket and continued returning balls. She was missing more than she was hitting now and was moving leadenly around the court. Paco watched for about a minute, then turned on his heel and marched toward a door in the far wall. As he disappeared through it, Monica got up from Mary Ann's left and hurried after him.

I noticed a bright pink anorak with rabbit fur around the hood next to where she'd been sitting, and two furry leather mittens with rabbits embroidered on them.

"That's Lily's," Mary Ann said. "Monica must have forgotten she was holding them for her. I'll give them to the kid if she makes it through this session."

My old coach's face was set in angry lines. I felt angry, too, and kept half rising from my seat, wondering if I ought to intervene. Paco's departure had whipped Gary into a triumphant frenzy. He shooed the kid serving balls away and started hitting ground strokes to his daughter at a furious pace. She took it for about five minutes before collapsing on the floor in tears.

"I just can't do it anymore, Daddy. I just can't."

Gary put his own racket down and smiled in triumph.

A sharp clap came from behind me, making me jump. "Bravo, Gary!" Nicole cried. "What a man you are! Yes, indeed, you've proved you can frighten your little girl. Now the question is: Which matters more to you? That Lily become the great player her talent destines her to be? Or that you prove that you own her?"

She jumped up lightly from the bench and ran down to the court. She put an arm around Lily and said something inaudible to the girl. Lily looked from her to her father and shook her head, flushing with misery. Nicole shrugged. Before leaving the court she and Gary exchanged a long look. Only an optimist would have found the seeds of friendship in it.

II

The Slims started the next Monday. The events at the Skokie Valley Tennis Club made me follow the newspaper reports eagerly, but the tournament seemed to be progressing without any open fireworks. One or two of the higher seeds were knocked out early, but Martina, Rubova, Lily, and one of the Maleeva sisters were all winning on schedule, along with Zina Garrison. Indeed, Martina, coming off knee surgery, seemed to be playing with the energy of a woman half her age.

I called Mary Ann McFarlane Thursday night to make sure she had my pass to the quarterfinal matches on Friday. Lily was proving such a hit that tickets were hard to get.

"Oh, yes," she assured me. "We linespersons don't have much leverage, but I got Monica to leave a pass for you at the will-call window. Dinner Sunday night?"

I agreed readily. Driving down to the Pavilion on Friday, I was in good time for the noon match, which pitted Martina against Frederica Lujan.

Lujan was seeded twelfth to Martina's third in world rankings, but the gap between their games seemed much wider than those numbers. In fact, halfway through the first set Martina suddenly turned her game up a notch and turned an even match into a rout. She was all over the court, going down for shots that should have been unhittable.

An hour later we got the quarterfinal meeting the crowd had come to see: Lily against Nicole Rubova. When Lily danced onto the court, a vision in pink and white with a sweatband pulling her blond spikes back from her face, the stands roared with pleasure. Nicole got a polite round of applause, but she was only there to give their darling a chance to play.

A couple of minutes after they'd started their warm-up, Monica came in. She sat close to the court, about ten rows in front of me. The man she joined was Paco Callabrio. He had stood next to Lily on the court as she came out for her warm-ups, patted her encouragingly on the ass, and climbed into the stands. Monica must have persuaded him not to quit in fury last week.

At first I assumed Gary was boycotting the match, either out of dislike of Paco or for fear his overt coaching would cause Lily to forfeit.

As play progressed, though, I noticed him on the far side of the court, behind the chair umpire, making wild gestures if Lily missed a close shot, or if he thought the linespersons were making bad calls.

When play began Rubova's catlike languor vanished. She obviously took her conditioning seriously, moving well around the court and playing the net with a brilliant ferocity. Mary Ann might be right — she might have designs on Lily's body — but it didn't make her play the youngster with any gentleness.

Lily, too, had a range of motion that was exciting to watch. She was big, already five ten, with long arms and a phenomenal reach. Whether due to Gary's drills or not, her backhand proved formidable; unlike most women on the circuit she could use it one handed.

Lily pushed her hard but Rubova won in three sets, earning the privilege of meeting Navratilova the next afternoon. It seemed to me that Lily suddenly began hitting the ball rather tentatively in the last few games of the final set. I wasn't knowledgeable enough to know if she had suddenly reached her physical limit, or if she was buckling under Rubova's attack.

The crowd, disappointed in their favorite's loss, gave the Czech only a lukewarm hand as she collected her rackets and exited. Paco, Monica, and Gary all disappeared from the stands as Lily left the court to a standing ovation.

Mary Ann had been a linesperson on the far

sideline during the Rubova match. Neither of the players had given the umpire a hard time. Rubova at one point drew a line on the floor with her racket, a sarcastic indicator of where she thought Mary Ann was spotting Lily. Another time Lily cried out in frustration to the chair umpire; I saw Monica's shoulders tense and wondered if the prodigy was prone to tantrums. More likely she was worried by what Gary — turning puce on the far side — might do to embarrass her. Other than that the match had gone smoothly.

Doubles quarterfinals were on the agenda for late afternoon. I wasn't planning on watching those, so I wandered down to the court to have a word with Mary Ann before I left.

She tried to talk me into staying. "Garrison has teamed up with Rubova. They should be fun to watch — both are real active girls."

"Enough for me for one day. What'd you think of the kid in tournament play?"

Mary Ann spread her hands. "She's going to go a long way. Nicole outplayed her today, but she won't forever. Although — I don't know — it looked to me in the last couple of games as though she might have been favoring her right shoulder. I couldn't be sure. I just hope Gary hasn't got her to injure herself with his hit-till-you-drop coaching methods. I'm surprised Paco's hanging on through it."

I grinned suggestively at her. "Maybe Monica has wonderful powers of persuasion."

Mary Ann looked at me calmly. "You're trying

139

to shock me, Vic, but believe me, I was never a maiden aunt. And anyway, nothing on this circuit would shock me. . . . They have free refreshments downstairs for players and crew. And press and hangers-on. Want to come have some coffee before you go? Some of the girls might even be there."

"And be a hanger-on? Sure, why not?" Who knows, maybe Martina would meet me and remember an urgent need for some detective work.

A freight elevator protected by guards carried the insiders to the lower depths. Mary Ann, in her linesperson's outfit, didn't need to show any identification. I came in for more scrutiny, but my player's-guest badge got me through.

The elevator decanted us onto a grubby corridor. Young people of both sexes hurried up and down its length, carrying clipboards at which they frowned importantly.

"PR staff," Mary Ann explained. "They feed all the statistics from the match to different wire services and try to drum up local interest in the tournament. Tie-ins with the auto show, that kind of thing."

Older, fatter people stood outside makeshift marquees with coffee and globular brownies. At the end of the hall I could see Paco and Monica huddled together. Gary wasn't in sight.

"Lily may have gone back in for a massage; I think she already did her press interview. Gary must be inside with her. He won't let her get a workover alone."

"Inside the locker room?" I echoed. "I know she's Daddy's darling, but don't the other women object to him being there while they're changing? And can she really stand having him watch her get massaged?"

"There's a lounge." Mary Ann shepherded me into the refreshment tent — really a niche roped off from the cement corridor with a rather pathetic plastic canopy overhead. "Friends and lovers of the stars can sit there while the girls dress inside. I don't expect he actually hangs around the massage table. Don't go picturing some fabulous hideaway, though. This is a gym at a relatively poor university. It's purely functional. But they do have a cement cubbyhole for the masseuse — that sets it apart from the normal school gym."

I suddenly realized I was hungry — it was long past lunchtime. The Slims catering was heavy on volume and carbohydrates. I rejected fried chicken wings and rice and filled a plastic bowl with some doubtful-looking chili. Mary Ann picked up a handful of cookies to eat with her coffee.

We settled at an empty table in the far corner and ate while Mary Ann pointed out the notables to me. Zina Garrison's husband was at the buffet next to Katarina Maleeva. The two were laughing together, trying to avoid a fat reporter who was unabashedly eavesdropping on them.

A well-groomed woman near the entrance to the marquee was Clare Rutland, the doyenne of the tour, Mary Ann explained. She had no formal title with the Slims, but seemed to be able to keep its temperamental stars happy, or at least functioning.

As I ate my chili, six or seven people stopped to talk to Rutland. They'd nod at her remarks and race off again. I imagined tennis stars' wishes, from lotus blossoms to Lotus racers, being satisfied at the wave of her hand.

Mary Ann, talking to acquaintances, began picking up some of the gossip buzzing the room: Lily might have strained her shoulder. Maybe torn her rotator cuff. In this kind of environment the worst scenarios are generated rapidly from the whiff of an idea. And Gary apparently had been thrown out of Lily's press conference and was now sulking in the women's lounge.

A collective cry from the group across the room made me jerk my head around. Nicole Rubova was sprinting down the hall, wet, a towel haphazardly draping her midriff.

"Clare," she gasped.

Clare Rutland was on her feet as soon as she heard the outcry, almost before Rubova came into view. She took off her cardigan and draped it across the player's shoulders. Rubova was too far from us for me to be able to hear her, but the reporters in the room crowded around her, tournament etiquette forgotten.

It only took a minute for Mary Ann to get the main point of the story from one of them: Gary Oberst was on the couch in the players' lounge. Someone had wrapped a string from a tennis racket around his neck a few times.

It was only later that everyone realized Lily herself had disappeared.

III

Clare Rutland curled one foot toward her chin and massaged her stockinged toes. Her face, rubbed free of makeup, showed the strain of the day in its sharply dug lines.

"This could kill the Slims," she remarked to no one in particular.

It was past midnight. I was in the windowless press room with her, Mary Ann, and a bunch of men, including Jared Brookings, who owned the PR firm handling the Slims in Chicago. Brookings had come in in person around nine, to see what could be done to salvage the tournament. He'd sent his fresh-faced minions packing long ago. They'd phoned him in terror when the police arrested Nicole Rubova, and clearly were not up to functioning in the crisis.

Arnold Krieger was there, too, with a handful of other reporters whose names I never learned. Krieger was the fat man who'd been listening in on Zina Garrison's husband earlier in the dining area. He covered tennis for one of the wire services and had made himself at home in the press room when the cops commandeered it for their headquarters.

"She'll be out on bond in the morning, right?" Krieger palmed a handful of nuts into his mouth as he started to talk, so his words came out clogged. "So she can play Martina at one, per the schedule."

Clare looked at him in dismay but didn't speak.

Brookings put his fingertips together. "It all depends, doesn't it? We can't be too careful. We've spent two decades building these girls up, but the whole fabric could collapse at any minute."

I could see Mary Ann's teacher instincts debating whether to correct his mixed metaphors and deciding against it. "The problem isn't just having one of the stars arrested for murder," she said bluntly. "Lily Oberst is a local heroine and now everyone is going to read that an evil lesbian who had designs on her killed her father because he stood between them. Chicago might rip Nicole apart. They certainly won't support the tournament."

"Besides," Clare Rutland added in a dull voice, "two of the top seeds withdrew when they heard about Rubova's arrest. They've gone off to locate a lawyer to handle the defense. The other Czechs may not play any more Slims this year if a cloud hangs over Rubova. Neither will Freddie Lujan. If they drop out, others may follow suit."

"If a cloud hangs over Rubova, it's over the whole tour," Monte Allison, the Artemis Products representative, spoke for the first time. "We may withdraw *our* sponsorship for the rest of the year

— I can't speak for Philip Morris, of course. That's a corporate decision, naturally, not mine, but we'll be making it tomorrow or — no, tomorrow's Saturday. We'll make it Monday. Early."

I'd never yet known a corporation that could make an important decision early Monday just because one of its vice presidents said so in a forceful voice. But Allison was fretful because none of the tennis people was paying attention to him. Since Artemis also helped Philip Morris promote the tour, Allison was likely to urge that they withdraw their sponsorship just because he didn't like the way Clare Rutland kept snubbing him.

I muttered as much to Mary Ann.

"If they have to make a decision Monday, it gives you two days to solve the crime, Vic," she said loudly.

"You don't believe Rubova killed Oberst?" I asked her, still sotto voce.

"I believe the police wanted to arrest her because they didn't like her attitude," Mary Ann snapped.

The investigation had been handled by John McGonnigal, a violent crimes sergeant I know. He's a good cop, but a soignée, sardonic woman does not bring out the best in him. And by the time he'd arrived Nicole had dressed, in a crimson silk jumpsuit that emphasized the pliable length of her body, and withdrawn from shock into mockery.

145

When McGonnigal saw me slide into the interrogation room behind Rubova, he gave an exaggerated groan but didn't actively try to exclude me from his questioning sessions. Those gave me a sense of where everyone claimed to have been when Gary was killed, but no idea at all if McGonnigal was making a mistake in arresting Nicole Rubova.

Police repugnance at female-female sexuality might have helped him interpret evidence so that it pointed at her. I hadn't been able to get the forensic data, but the case against Rubova seemed to depend on two facts: she was the only person known to be alone with Gary in the locker room. And one of her rackets had a big section of string missing from it. This last seemed to be a rather slender thread to hang her on. It would have taken a good while to unthread enough string from a racket to have enough for a garrote. I didn't see where she'd had the time to do it.

McGonnigal insisted she'd spent Lily's press conference at it, dismissing claims from Frederica Lujan that she'd been talking to Nicole while it was going on. Some helpful person had told him that Frederica and Nicole had had an affair last year, so McGonnigal decided the Spanish player would say anything to help a friend.

None of the Slims people questioned my sitting in on the inquiry — they were far too absorbed in their woes over the tournament. The men didn't pay any attention to Mary Ann's comment to me now, but Clare Rutland moved slightly on the couch so that she was facing my old coach directly. "Who is this, Mary Ann?"

"V. I. Warshawski. About the best private investigator in the city." Mary Ann continued to speak at top volume.

"Is that why you came to the matches today?" The large hazel eyes looked at me with intense interest. I felt the power she exerted over tennis divas directed at me.

"I came because I wanted to watch Lily Oberst. I grew up playing basketball with her mother. Mary Ann here was our coach. After watching Gary train Lily last week I would have thought the kid might have killed him herself — he seemed extraordinarily brutal."

Clare smiled, for the first time since Nicole Rubova had come running down the hall in her towel ten hours ago. "If every tennis kid killed her father because of his brutal coaching, we wouldn't have any parents left on the circuit. Which might only improve the game. But Oberst was one of the worst. Only — why did she have to do it *here*? She must have known — only I suppose when you're jealous you don't think of such things."

"So you think Rubova killed the guy?"

Clare spread her hands, appealing for support. "You don't?"

"You know her and I don't, so I assume you're a better judge of her character. But she seems too cool, too poised, to kill a guy for the reason everyone's imputing to her. Maybe she was interested in Lily. But I find it impossible to believe she'd kill the girl's father because he tried to short-circuit her. She's very sophisticated, very smart, and very cool. If she *really* wanted to have an affair with Lily, she'd have figured out a way. I'm not sure she wanted to — I think it amused her to see Lily blush and get flustered, and to watch Gary go berserk. But if she did want to kill Gary she'd have done so a lot more subtly, not in a fit of rage in the locker room. One other thing: If — *if* — she killed him like that, on the spot, it must have been for some other reason than Lily."

"Like what?" Arnold Krieger had lost interest in Monte Allison and was eavesdropping on me, still chewing cashews.

I hunched a shoulder. "You guys tell me. You're the ones who see these prima donnas week in and week out."

Clare nodded. "I see what you mean. But then, who did kill Oberst?"

"I don't know the players and I don't have access to the forensic evidence. But — well, Lily herself would be my first choice."

A furious uproar started from Allison and Brookings, with Clare chiming in briefly. Mary Ann silenced them all with a coach's whistle — she still could put her fingers in her mouth and produce a sound like a steam engine.

"She must have been awfully tired of Gary sitting in her head," I continued when Mary Ann had shut them up. "She could hardly go to the bathroom without his permission. I learned today that he chose her clothes, her friends, ran her practice sessions, drove away her favorite coaches. You name it."

The police had found Lily quickly enough — she'd apparently had a rare fight with Gary and stormed away to Northwestern Hospital without telling Monica. Without her entourage it had taken her a while to persuade the emergency room that her sore shoulder should leap ahead of other emergencies. Once they realized who she was, though, they summoned their sports medicine maven at once. He swept her off in a cloud of solicitude for X rays, then summoned a limo to take her home to Glenview. There still would have been plenty of time for her to kill Gary before she left the Pavilion.

"Then there's Monica," I went on. "She and Paco Callabrio have been pretty friendly — several people hinted at it during their interviews this afternoon. She and Gary started dating when they were fifteen. That's twenty-four years with a bully. Maybe she figured she'd had enough.

"I don't like Paco for the spot very well. He's like Nicole — he's got a life, and an international reputation; he didn't need to ruin it by killing the father of one of his pupils. Although, apparently he came out of retirement because of financial desperation. So maybe he was worried about losing Lily as a client, and his affair with Monica deranged him enough that he killed Oberst."

"So you think it's one of those three?" Clare asked.

I shrugged. "Could be. Could be Allison here, worried about his endorsement contract. He watched Gary driving Lily to the breaking point. Artemis could lose seven, eight million dollars if Lily injured herself so badly she couldn't play anymore."

Allison broke off his conversation with Brookings when he heard his name. "What the hell are you saying? That's outrageous. We're behind Lily all the way. I could sue you —"

"Control yourself, Monte," Clare said coldly. "No one's accusing you of anything except high-level capitalism. The detective is just suggesting why someone besides Nicole might have killed Gary Oberst. Anything else?"

"The hottest outsider is Arnold Krieger here."

Two of the anonymous reporters snickered. Krieger muttered darkly but didn't say anything. The tale of Lily's interview with him had come out very early in McGonnigal's questioning.

Tennis etiquette dictates that the loser meet journalists first. The winner can then shower and dress at her leisure. After her match Lily had bounced out, surrounded by Paco, Gary, and Monica. She'd giggled with the press about her game, said she didn't mind losing to Nicole because Nicole was a great player, but she, Lily, had given the game her best, and anyway, she was glad to have a few extra days at home with Ninja, her Great Dane, before flying off to Palm

Springs for an exhibition match. People asked about her shoulder. She'd said it was sore but nothing serious. She was going over to Northwestern for X rays just to be on the safe side.

Arnold Krieger then asked whether she felt she ever played her best against Rubova. "After all, most people know she's just waiting for the chance to get you alone. Doesn't that unnerve you?"

Lily started to giggle again, but Gary lost his temper and jumped Krieger on the spot. Security guards pried his hands from the journalist's throat; Gary was warned out of the press room. In fact, he was told that one more episode would get him barred from the tour altogether.

The cops loved that, but they couldn't find anyone who'd seen Krieger go into the locker room afterwards. In fact, most of us could remember his staying near the food, playing tag team with Garrison's husband.

"Don't forget, it was Rubova's racket the string was missing from," Krieger reminded me belligerently.

Clare eyed Krieger as though measuring him for an electric chair, then turned back to me. "What do you charge?"

"Fifty dollars an hour. Plus any unusual expenses — things above the cost of gas or local phone bills."

"I'm hiring you," Clare said briskly.

"To do what? Clear Nicole's name, or guarantee the tour can go on? I can only do the first — if she's not guilty. If it turns out to be Lily, or

151

any of the other players, the Slims are going to be under just as much of a cloud as they are now."

Clare Rutland scowled, but she was used to being decisive. "Clear Nicole for me. I'll worry about the Slims after that. What do you need me to do to make it official?"

"I'll bring a contract by for you tomorrow, but right now what I really want is to take a look at the women's locker room."

"You can't do that," one of the anonymous reporters objected. "The police have sealed it."

"The police are through with it," I said. "They've made their arrest. I just need someone with a key to let me in."

Clare pinched the bridge of her nose while she thought about it. Maybe it was the objections the men kept hurling at her that made her decide. She stood up briskly, slipped her feet into their expensive suede pumps, and told me to follow her. Mary Ann and I left the press room in her wake. Behind us I could hear Allison shouting, "You can't do this."

IV

I tore the police seal without compunction. If they'd been in the middle of an investigation I would have honored it, but they'd had their chance, made their arrest.

152

The locker room was a utilitarian set of cement cubes. The attempt to turn the outermost cube into a lounge merely made it look forlorn. It held a few pieces of secondhand furniture, a large bottle of spring water, and a telephone.

Gary had been sitting on a couch plunked into the middle of the floor. Whoever killed him had stood right behind him, wrapping the racket string around his throat before he had time to react — the police found no evidence that he had been able even to lift a hand to try to pull it loose. A smear of dried blood on the back cushion came from where the string had cut through the skin of his neck.

Whoever had pulled the garrote must have cut her — or his — hands as well. I bummed a pad of paper from Clare and made a note to ask McGonnigal whether Nicole had any cuts. And whether he'd noticed them on anyone else. It was quite possible he hadn't bothered to look.

The lounge led to the shower room. As Mary Ann had warned, the place was strictly functional — no curtains, no gleaming fittings. Just standard brown tile that made my toes curl inside my shoes as I felt mold growing beneath them, and a row of small, white-crusted shower heads.

Beyond the showers was a bare room with hooks for coats or equipment bags and a table for the masseuse. A door led to the outer hall.

"It's locked at all times, though," Clare said.

"*All* the time? I expect someone has a key."

She took the notepad from me and scribbled

on it. "I'll track that down for you in the morning."

A barrel of used towels stood between the showers and the massage room. For want of anything better to do I poked through them, but nothing unusual came to light.

"Normally all the laundry is cleared out at the end of the day, along with the garbage, but the maintenance crews couldn't come in tonight, of course," Clare explained.

The garbage bins were built into the walls. It was easy to lift the swinging doors off and pull the big plastic liners out. I took them over to the masseuse's corner and started emptying them onto the table piece by piece. I did them in order of room, starting with the lounge. Police detritus — coffee cups, ashes, crumpled forms — made up the top layer. In the middle of the styrofoam and ash, I found two leather mittens with bunnies embroidered on them. The palms were cut to ribbons.

I went through the rest of the garbage quickly, so quickly I almost missed the length of nylon wrapped in paper towels. One end poked out as I perfunctorily shook the papers; I saw it just as I was about to sweep everything off the massage table back into the bag.

"It's racket string," Mary Ann said tersely.

"Yes," I agreed quietly.

It was a piece about five inches long. I unrolled all the paper toweling and newsprint a sheet at a time. By the time I finished I had three more little pieces. Since the garrote that killed Gary had been deeply embedded in his throat, these might have been cut from Nicole's racket to point suspicion at her.

"But the mittens . . ." My old coach couldn't bring herself to say more.

Clare Rutland was watching me, her face frozen. "The mittens are Lily's, aren't they? Her brother got them for her for Christmas. She showed them off to everyone on the tour when we had our first post-Christmas matches. Why don't you give them to me, Vic? The string should be enough to save Nicole."

I shook my head unhappily. "Could be. We'd have to have the lab make sure these pieces came from her racket. Anyway, I can't do that, Clare. I'm not Gary Oberst's judge and jury. I can't ignore evidence that I've found myself."

"But, Vic," Mary Ann said hoarsely, "how can you do that to Lily? Turn on her? I always thought you tried to help other women. And you saw yourself what her life was like with Gary. How can you blame her?"

I felt the muscles of my face distort into a grimace. "I don't blame her. But how can you let her go through her life without confronting herself? It's a good road to madness, seeing yourself as above and beyond the law. The special treatment she gets as a star is bound to make her think that way to some degree already. If we let her kill her father and get away with it, we're doing her the worst possible damage."

Mary Ann's mouth twisted in misery. She stared at me a long minute. "Oh, *damn* you, Vic!" she cried, and pushed her way past me out of the locker room.

The last vestiges of Clare Rutland's energy had fallen from her face, making her cheeks look as though they had collapsed into it. "I agree with Mary Ann, Vic. We ought to be able to work something out. Something that would be good for Lily as well as Nicole."

"No," I cried.

She lunged toward me and grabbed the mittens. But I was not only younger and stronger, my Nikes gave me an advantage over her high heels. I caught up with her before she'd made it to the shower-room door and gently took the mittens from her.

"Will you let me do one thing? Will you let me see Lily before you talk to the police?"

"What about Nicole?" I demanded. "Doesn't she deserve to be released as soon as possible?"

"If the lawyer the other women have dug up for her doesn't get her out, you can call Sergeant McGonnigal first thing in the morning. Anyway, go ahead and give him the string now. Won't that get her released?"

"I can't do that. I can't come with two separate pieces of evidence found in the identical place but delivered to the law eight hours apart. And no, I damned well will not lie about it for you. I'll do this much for you: I'll let you talk to Lily. But I'll be with you."

Anyway, once the cops have made an arrest they don't like to go back on it. They were just as likely to say that Nicole had cut the string out herself as part of an elaborate bluff.

Clare smiled affably. "Okay. We'll go first thing in the morning."

"No, Ms. Rutland. You're a hell of a woman, but you're not going to run me around the way you do the rest of the tour. If I wait until morning, you'll have been on the phone with Lily and Monica and they'll be in Majorca. We go tonight. Or I stick to you like your underwear until morning."

Her mouth set in a stubborn line, but she didn't waste her time fighting lost battles. "We'll have to phone first. They're bound to be in bed, and they have an elaborate security system. I'll have to let them know we're coming."

I breathed down her neck while she made the call, but she simply told Monica it was important that they discuss matters tonight, before the story made national headlines.

"I'm sorry, honey, I know it's a hell of an hour. And you're under a hell of a lot of strain. But this is the first moment I've had since Nicole found Gary. And we just can't afford to let it go till morning."

Monica apparently found nothing strange in the idea of a two A.M. discussion of Lily's tennis future. Clare told her I was with her and would be driving, so she turned the phone over to me for instructions. Monica also didn't question what

I was doing with Clare, for which I was grateful. My powers of invention weren't very great by this point.

V

A single spotlight lit the gate at Nine Nightingale Lane. When I leaned out the window and pressed the buzzer, Monica didn't bother to check that it was really us: she released the lock at once. The gate swung in on well-oiled hinges.

Inside the gate the house and drive were dark. I switched my headlights on high and drove forward cautiously, trying to make sure I stayed on the tarmac. My lights finally picked out the house. The drive made a loop past the front door. I pulled over to the edge and turned off the engine.

"Any idea why the place is totally dark?" I asked Clare.

"Maybe Lily's in bed and Monica doesn't want to wake her up."

"Lily can't sleep just knowing there's a light on somewhere in the house? Try a different theory."

"I don't have any theories," Clare said sharply. "I'm as baffled as you are, and probably twice as worried. Could someone have come out here and jumped her, be lying in ambush for us?"

My mouth felt dry. The thought had occurred to me as well. Anyone could have lifted Lily's mittens from the locker room while she was playing. Maybe Arnold Krieger had done so. Gotten someone to let him in through the permanently locked end of the women's locker room, lifted the mittens, garroted Gary, and slipped out the back way again while Rubova was still in the shower. When he realized we were searching the locker room, he came to Glenview ahead of us. He'd fought hard to keep me from going into the locker room, now that I thought about it.

My gun, of course, was locked away in the safe in my bedroom. No normal person carries a Smith & Wesson to a Virginia Slims match.

"Can you drive a stick shift?" I asked Clare. "I'm going inside, but I want to find a back entrance, avoid a trap if I can. If I'm not out in twenty minutes, drive off and get a neighbor to call the cops. And lock the car doors. Whoever's in the house knows we're here: they released the gate for us."

The mittens were zipped into the inside pocket of my parka. I decided to leave them there. Clare might still destroy them in a moment of chivalry if I put them in the trunk for safekeeping.

I took a pencil flash from the glove compartment. Using it sparingly, I picked my way around the side of the house. A dog bayed nearby. Ninja, the Great Dane. But he was in the house. If Arnold Krieger or someone else had come out to get a jump on us, they would have killed the dog, or the dog would have disabled them. I felt the hair

159

stand up on the back of my neck.

A cinder-block cube had been attached to the back of the house. I shone the flash on it cautiously. It had no windows. It dawned on me that they had built a small indoor court for Lily, for those days when she couldn't get to the club. It had an outside door that led to the garden. When I turned the knob, the door moved inward.

"I'm in here, Vic." Monica's voice came to me in the darkness. "I figured you'd avoid the house and come around the back."

"Are you all right?" I whispered loudly. "Who's inside with Lily?"

Monica laughed. "Just her dog. You worried about Paco interrupting us? He's staying downtown in a hotel. Mary Ann called me. She told me you'd found Lily's mittens. She wanted me to take Lily and run, but I thought I'd better stay to meet you. I've got a shotgun, Vic. Gary was obsessive about Lily's safety, except, of course, on the court. Where he hoped she'd run herself into early retirement."

"You going to kill me to protect your daughter? That won't help much. I mean, I'll be dead, but then the police will come looking, and the whole ugly story will still come out."

"You always were kind of a smart mouth. I remember that from our high school days. And how much I hated you the day you came to see me with the rest of the team when I was pregnant with little Gary." Her voice had a conversational quality. "No. I can persuade the cops that I thought my home was being invaded. Someone coming to hurt Lily on top of all she's already been through today. Mary Ann may figure it out, but she loves Lily too much to do anything to hurt her."

"Clare Rutland's out front with the car. She's going for help before too long. Her story would be pretty hard to discount."

"She's going to find the gate locked when she gets there. And even Clare, endlessly clever, will find it hard to scale a ten-foot electrified fence. No, it will be seen as a terrible tragedy. People will give us their sympathy. Lily's golden up here, after all."

I felt a jolt under my rib cage. "*You* killed Gary."

She burst out laughing. "Oh, my goodness, yes, Vic. Did you just figure that out, smart-ass that you are? I was sure you were coming up here to gun for me. Did you really think little Lily, who could hardly pee without her daddy, had some sudden awakening and strangled him?"

"Why, Monica? Because she may have hurt her shoulder? You couldn't just get him to lay off? I noticed you didn't even try at her practice session last week."

"I always hated that about you," she said, her tone still flat. "Your goddamned high-and-mightiness. You don't — didn't — ever stop Gary from doing some damned thing he was doing. How do you think I got pregnant with little Gary?

161

Because his daddy said lie down and spread your legs for me, pretty please? Get out of your dream world. I got pregnant the old-fashioned way: he raped me. We married. We fought — each other and everything around us. But we made it out of that hellhole down there just like you did. Only not as easily."

"It wasn't easy for me," I started to say, but I sensed a sudden movement from her and flung myself onto the floor. A tennis ball bounced off the wall behind me and ricocheted from my leg.

Monica laughed again. "I have the shotgun. But I kind of like working with a racket. I was pretty good once. Never as good as Lily, though. And when Lily was born — when we realized what her potential was — I saw I could move myself so far from South Chicago it would never be able to grab me again."

Another *thwock* came in the dark and another ball crashed past me.

"Then Gary started pushing her so hard, I was afraid she'd be like Andrea Jaeger. Injured and burned out before she ever reached her potential. I begged him, pleaded with him. We'd lose that Artemis contract and everything else. But Gary's the kind of guy who's always right."

This time I was ready for the swish of her racket in the dark. Under cover of the ball's noise, I rolled across the floor in her direction. I didn't speak, hoping the momentum of her anger would keep her going without prompting.

"When Lily came off the court today favoring

her shoulder, I told him I'd had it, that I wanted him out of her career. That Paco knew a thousand times more how to coach a girl with Lily's talent than he did. But Mr. Ever-right just laughed and ranted. He finally said Lily could choose. Just like she'd chosen him over Nicole, she'd choose him over Paco."

I kept inching my way forward until I felt the net. One of the balls had stopped there; I picked it up.

Monica hadn't noticed my approach. "Lily came up just then and heard what he said. On top of the scene he'd made at her little press doohickey it was too much for her. She had a fit and left the room. I went down the hall to an alcove where Johnny Lombardy — the stringer — kept his spool. I just cut a length of racket string from his roll, went back to the lounge, and — God, it was easy."

"And Nicole's racket?" I asked hoarsely, hoping my voice would sound as though it was farther away.

"Just snipped a few pieces out while she was in the shower. She's another one like you — snotty know-it-all. It won't hurt her to spend some time in jail."

She fired another ball at the wall and then, unexpectedly, flooded the room with light. Neither of us could see, but she at least was prepared for the shock. It gave her time to locate me as I scrambled to my feet. I found myself tangled in the net and struggled furiously while she steadied the gun on her shoulder.

I wasn't going to get my leg free in time. Just before she fired, I hurled the ball I'd picked up at her. It hit her in the face. The bullet tore a hole in the floor inches from my left foot. I finally yanked my leg from the net and launched myself at her.

VI

"I'm sorry, Vic. That you almost got killed, I mean. Not that I called Monica — she needed me. Not just then, but in general. She never had your, oh, centeredness. She needed a mother."

Mary Ann and I were eating in Greek Town. The Slims had limped out of Chicago a month ago, but I hadn't felt like talking to my old coach since my night with Monica. But Clare Rutland had come to town to meet with one of the tour sponsors, and to hand me a check in person. And she insisted that the three of us get together. After explaining how she'd talked the sponsors and players into continuing, Clare wanted to know why Mary Ann had called Monica that night.

"Everyone needs a mother, Mary Ann. That's the weakest damned excuse I ever heard for trying to help someone get away with murdering her husband."

Mary Ann looked at me strangely. "Maybe Monica is right about you, Victoria: too high-

and-mighty. But it was Lily I was trying to help. I wouldn't have done it if I'd known Monica was going to try to kill you. But you can take care of yourself. You survived the encounter. She didn't."

"What do you mean?" I demanded. "All I did was bruise her face getting her not to shoot me. And no one's going to give her the death penalty. I'd be surprised if she served more than four years."

"You don't understand, Vic. She didn't have anything besides the . . . the scrappiness that got her and Gary out of South Chicago. Oh, she learned how to dress, and put on makeup, and what kinds of things North Shore people eat for dinner. Now that the fight's gone out of her she doesn't have anything inside her to get her through the bad times. You do."

Clare Rutland interrupted hastily. "The good news is that Lily will recover. We have her working with a splendid woman, psychotherapist, I mean. She's playing tennis as much as she wants, which turns out to be a lot. And the other women on the circuit are rallying around in a wonderful way. Nicole is taking her to Maine to spend the summer at her place near Bar Harbor with her."

"Artemis dropped their endorsement contract," I said. "It was in the papers here."

"Yes, but she's already made herself enough to get through the next few years without winning another tournament. Let's be honest. She could live the rest of her life on what she's made in

165

endorsements so far. Anyway, I hear Nike and Reebok are both sniffing around. No one's going to do anything until after Monica's trial — it wouldn't look right. But Lily will be fine."

We dropped it there. Except for the testimony I had to give at Monica's trial I didn't think about her or Lily too much as time went by. Sobered by my old coach's comments, I kept my time on the stand brief. Mary Ann, who came to the trial every day, seemed to be fighting tears when I left the courtroom, but I didn't stop to talk to her.

The following February, though, Mary Ann surprised me by phoning me.

"I'm not working on the lines this year," she said abruptly. "I've seen too much tennis close up. But Lily's making her first public appearance at the Slims, and she sent me tickets for all the matches. Would you like to go?"

I thought briefly of telling her to go to hell, of saying I'd had enough tennis — enough of the Obersts — to last me forever. But I found myself agreeing to meet her outside the box office on Harrison the next morning.

At the Old Swimming Hole

I

THE GYM WAS dank — chlorine and sweat combined in a hot, sticky mass. Shouts from the trainers, from the swimmers, from the spectators, bounced from the high metal ceilings and back and forth from the benches lining the pool on two sides. The cacophony set up an unpleasant buzzing in my head.

I was not enjoying myself. My shirt was soaked through with sweat. Anyway, I was too old to sit cheering on a bleacher for two hours. But Alicia had been insistent — I had to be there in person for her to get points on her sponsor card.

Alicia Alonso Dauphine and I went to high school together. Her parents had bestowed a prima ballerina's name on her, but Alicia showed no aptitude for fine arts. From her earliest years, all she wanted was to muck around with engines. At eighteen, off she went to the University of Illinois to study aeronautics.

Despite her lack of interest in dance, Alicia

was very athletic. Next to airplanes, the only thing she really cared about was competitive swimming. I used to cheer her when she was NCAA swimming champ, always with a bit of irritation about being locked in a dank, noisy gym for hours at a time — swimming is not a great spectator sport. But after all, what are friends for?

When Alicia joined Berman Aircraft as an associate engineer, we drifted our separate ways. We met occasionally at weddings, confirmations, bar mitzvahs (my, how our friends were aging! Childlessness seemed to suspend us in time, but each new ceremony in their lives marked a new milestone toward old age for the women we had played with in school).

Then last week I'd gotten a call from Alicia. Berman was mounting a team for a citywide corporate competition — money would be raised through sponsors for the American Cancer Society. Both Alicia's mother and mine had died of cancer — would I sponsor her for so many meters? Doubling my contribution if she won? It was only after I'd made the pledge that I realized she expected me there in person. One of her sponsors had to show up to testify that she'd done it, and all the others were busy with their homes and children, and come on, V.I., what do you do all day long? I need you.

How can you know you're being manipulated and still let it happen? I hunched an impatient shoulder and turned back to the starting blocks.

From where I sat, Alicia was just another

bathing-suited body with a cap. Her distinctive cheekbones were softened and flattened by the dim fluorescence. Not a wisp of her thick black hair trailed around her face. She was wearing a bright red tank suit — no extra straps or flounces to slow her down in the water.

The swimmers had been wandering around the side of the pool, swinging their arms to stretch out the muscles, not talking much while the timers argued some inaudible point with the referee. Now a police whistle shrilled faintly in the din and the competitors snapped to attention, moving toward the starting blocks at the far end of the pool.

We were about to watch the fifty-meter freestyle. I looked at the hand-scribbled card Alicia had given me before the meet. After the fifty-meter, she was in a 4 × 50 relay. Then I could leave.

The swimmers were mounting the blocks when someone began complaining again. The woman from the Ajax insurance team seemed to be having a problem with the lane marker on the inside of her lane. The referee reshuffled the swimmers, leaving the offending lane empty. The swimmers finally mounted the blocks again. Timers got into position.

Standing to see the start of the race, I was no longer certain which of the women was Alicia. Two of the other six contenders also wore red tank suits; with their features smoothed by caps and dimmed lighting, they all became anonymous.

One red suit was in lane two, one in lane three, one in lane six.

The referee raised the starting gun. Swimmers got set. Arms swung back for the dive. Then the gun, and seven bodies flung themselves into the water. Perfect dive in lane six — had to be Alicia, surfacing, pulling away from all but one other swimmer, a fast little woman from the brokerage house of Feldstein, Holtz and Woods.

Problems for the red-suited woman in lane two. I hadn't seen her dive, but she was having trouble righting herself, couldn't seem to make headway in the lane. Now everyone was noticing her. Whistles were blowing; the man on the loudspeaker tried ineffectually to call for silence.

I pushed my way through the crowds on the benches and vaulted over the barrier dividing the spectators from the water. Useless over the din to order someone into the pool for her. Useless to point out the growing circle of red. I kicked off running shoes and dove from the side. Swimming underwater to the second lane. Not Alicia. Surely not. Seeing the water turn red around me. Find the woman. Surface. Drag her to the edge where, finally, a few galvanized hands pulled her out.

I scrambled from the pool and picked out someone in a striped referee's shirt. "Get a fire department ambulance as fast as you can." He stared at me with a stupid gape to his jaw. "Dial 911, damn it. Do it now!" I pushed him toward the door, hard, and he suddenly broke into a trot.

I knelt beside the woman. She was breathing, but shallowly. I felt her gently. Hard to find the source of bleeding with the wet suit, but I thought it came from the upper back. Demanding help from one of the bystanders, I carefully turned her to her side. Blood was oozing now, not pouring, from a wound below her left shoulder. Pack it with towels, elevate her feet, keep the crowd back. Wait. Wait. Watch the shallow breathing turn to choking. Mouth-to-mouth does no good. Who knows cardiopulmonary resuscitation? A muscular young man in skimpy bikini shorts comes forward and works at her chest. By the time the paramedics hustle in with stretcher and equipment, the shallow, choking breath has stopped. They take her to the hospital, but we all know it's no good.

As the stretcher-bearers trotted away, the rest of the room came back into focus. Alicia was standing at my side, black hair hanging damply to her shoulders, watching me with fierce concentration. Everyone else seemed to be shrieking in unison; the sound reechoing from the rafters was more unbearable than ever.

I stood up, put my mouth close to Alicia's ear, and asked her to take me to whoever was in charge. She pointed to a man in an Izod T-shirt standing on the other side of the hole left by the dead swimmer's body.

I went to him immediately. "I'm V. I. War-shawski. I'm a private detective. That woman was murdered — shot through the back. Whoever

171

shot her probably left during the confusion. But you'd better get the cops here now. And tell everyone over your megaphone that no one leaves until the police have seen them."

He looked contemptuously at my dripping jeans and shirt. "Do you have anything to back up this preposterous statement?"

I held out my hands. "Blood," I said briefly, then grabbed the microphone from him. "May I have your attention, please." My voice bounced around the hollow room. "My name is V. I. Warshawski; I am a detective. There has been a serious accident in the pool. Until the police have been here and talked to us, none of us must leave this area. I am asking the six timers who were at the far end of the pool to come here now."

There was silence for a minute, then renewed clamor. A handful of people picked their way along the edge of the pool toward me. The man in the Izod shirt was fulminating but lacked the guts to try to grab the mike.

When the timers came up to me, I said, "You six are the only ones who definitely could not have killed the woman. I want you to stand at the exits." I tapped each in turn and sent them to a post — two to the doors on the second floor at the top of the bleachers, two to the ground-floor exits, and one each to the doors leading to the men's and women's dressing rooms.

"Don't let anyone, regardless of *anything* he or she says, leave. If they have to use the bathroom, tough — hold it until the cops get here. Anyone tries to leave, keep them here. If they want to fight, let them go but get as complete a description as you can."

They trotted off to their stations. I gave Izod back his mike, made my way to a pay phone in the corner, and dialed the Eleventh Street homicide number.

II

Sergeant McGonnigal was not fighting sarcasm as hard as he might have. "You sent the guy to guard the upstairs exit and he waltzed away, probably taking the gun with him. He must be on his knees in some church right now thanking God for sending a pushy private investigator to this race."

I bit my lips. He couldn't be angrier with me than I was with myself. I sneezed and shivered in my damp, clammy clothes. "You're right, Sergeant. I wish you'd been at the meet instead of me. You'd probably have had ten uniformed officers with you who could've taken charge as soon as the starting gun was fired and avoided this mess. Do any of the timers know who the man was?"

We were in an office that the school athletic department had given the police for their investigation-scene headquarters. McGonnigal had

173

been questioning all the timers, figuring their closeness to the pool gave them the best angle on what had happened. One was missing, the man I'd sent to the upper balcony exit.

The sergeant grudgingly told me he'd been over that ground with the other timers. None of them knew who the missing man was. Each of the companies in the meet had supplied volunteers to do the timing and other odd jobs. Everyone just assumed this man was from someone else's firm. No one had noticed him that closely; their attention was focused on the action in the pool. My brief glance at him gave the police their best description: medium height, short brown hair, wearing a pale green T-shirt and faded white denim shorts. Yes, baggy enough for a gun to fit in a pocket unnoticed.

"You know, Sergeant, I asked for the six timers at the far end of the pool because they were facing the swimmers, so none of them could have shot the dead woman in the back. This guy came forward. That means there's a timer missing — either the person actually down at the far end was in collusion, or you're missing a body."

McGonnigal made an angry gesture — not at me. Himself for not having thought of it before. He detailed two uniformed cops to round up all the volunteers and find out who the errant timer was.

"Any more information on the dead woman?"

McGonnigal picked up a pad from the paper-littered desk in front of him. "Her name was

Louise Carmody. You know that. She was twenty-four. She worked for the Ft. Dearborn Bank and Trust as a junior lending officer. You know that. Her boss is very shocked — you probably could guess that. And she has no enemies. No dead person ever does."

"Was she working on anything sensitive?"

He gave me a withering glance. "What twenty-four-year-old junior loan officer works on anything sensitive?"

"Lots," I said firmly. "No senior person ever does the grubby work. A junior officer crunches numbers or gathers basic data for crunching. Was she working on any project that someone might not want her to get data for?"

McGonnigal shrugged wearily but made a note on a second pad — the closest he would come to recognizing that I might have a good suggestion.

I sneezed again. "Do you need me for anything else? I'd like to get home and dry off."

"No, go. I'd just as soon you weren't around when Lieutenant Mallory arrives, anyway."

Bobby Mallory was McGonnigal's boss. He was also an old friend of my father, who had been a beat sergeant until his death fifteen years earlier. Bobby did not like women on the crime scene in any capacity — victim, perpetrator, or investigator — and he especially did not like his old friend Tony's daughter on the scene. I appreciated McGonnigal's unwillingness to witness any acrimony between his boss and me, and was getting up to leave when the uniformed cops came back.

175

The sixth timer had been found in a supply closet behind the men's lockers. He was concussed and groggy from a head wound and couldn't remember how he got to where he was. Couldn't remember anything past lunchtime. I waited long enough to hear that and slid from the room.

Alicia was waiting for me at the far end of the hall. She had changed from her suit into jeans and a pullover and was squatting on her heels, staring fiercely at nothing. When she saw me coming, she stood up and pushed her black hair out of her eyes.

"You look a mess, V.I."

"Thanks. I'm glad to get help and support from my friends after they've dragged me into a murder investigation."

"Oh, don't get angry — I didn't mean it that way. I'm sorry I dragged you into a murder investigation. No, I'm not, actually. I'm glad you were on hand. Can we talk?"

"After I put some dry clothes on and stop looking a mess."

She offered me her jacket. Since I'm five eight to her five four, it wasn't much of a cover, but I draped it gratefully over my shoulders to protect myself from the chilly October evening.

At my apartment Alicia followed me into the bathroom while I turned on the hot water. "Do you know who the dead woman was? The police wouldn't tell us."

"Yes," I responded irritably. "And if you'll give me time to warm up, I'll tell you. Bathing is not a group sport in this apartment."

She trailed back out of the bathroom, her face set in tense lines. When I joined her in the living room some twenty minutes later, a towel around my damp hair, she was sitting in front of the television set changing channels.

"No news yet," she said briefly. "Who was the dead girl?"

"Louise Carmody. Junior loan officer at the Ft. Dearborn. You know her?"

Alicia shook her head. "Do the police know why she was shot?"

"They're just starting to investigate. What do you know about it?"

"Nothing. Are they going to put her name on the news?"

"Probably, if the family's been notified. Why is this important?"

"No reason. It just seems so ghoulish, reporters hovering around her dead body and everything."

"Could I have the truth, please?"

She sprang to her feet and glared at me. "It is the truth."

"Screw that. You don't know her name, you spin the TV dials to see the reports, and now you think it's ghoulish for the reporters to hover around? . . . Tell you what I think, Alicia. I think you know who did the shooting. They shuffled the swimmers, nobody knew who was in which lane. You started out in lane two, and you'd be dead if the woman from Ajax hadn't complained. Who wants to kill you?"

Her black eyes glittered in her white face. "No one. Why don't you have a little empathy, Vic? I might have been killed. There was a madman out there who shot a woman. Why don't you give me some sympathy?"

"I jumped into a pool to pull that woman out. I sat around in wet clothes for two hours talking to the cops. I'm beat. You want sympathy, go someplace else. The little I have is reserved for myself tonight.

"I'd really like to know why I had to be at the pool, if it wasn't to ward off a potential attacker. And if you'd told me the real reason, Louise Carmody might still be alive."

"Damn you, Vic, stop doubting every word I say. I told you why I needed you there — someone had to sign the card. Millie works during the day. So does Fredda. Katie has a new baby. Elene is becoming a grandmother for the first time. Get off my goddamn back."

"If you're not going to tell me the truth, and if you're going to scream at me about it, I'd just as soon you left."

She stood silent for a minute. "Sorry, Vic. I'll get a better grip on myself."

"Great. You do that. I'm fixing some supper — want any?"

She shook her head. When I returned with a plate of pasta and olives, Joan Druggen was just announcing the top local story. Alicia sat with her hands clenched as they stated the dead woman's name. After that, she didn't say much.

Just asked if she could crash for the night — she lived in Warrenville, a good hour's drive from town, near Berman's aeronautic engineering labs.

I gave her pillows and a blanket for the couch and went to bed. I was pretty angry: I figured she wanted to sleep over because she was scared, and it infuriated me that she wouldn't talk about it.

When the phone woke me at 2:30, my throat was raw, the start of a cold brought on by sitting around in wet clothes for so long. A heavy voice asked for Alicia.

"I don't know who you're talking about," I said hoarsely.

"Be your age, Warshawski. She brought you to the gym. She isn't at her own place. She's gotta be with you. You don't want to wake her up, give her a message. She was lucky tonight. We want the money by noon, or she won't be so lucky a second time."

He hung up. I held the receiver a second longer and heard another click. The living room extension. I pulled on a dressing gown and padded down the hallway. The apartment door shut just as I got to the living room. I ran to the top of the stairs; Alicia's footsteps were echoing up and down the stairwell.

"Alicia! Alicia — you can't go out there alone. Come back here!"

The slamming of the entryway door was my only answer.

III

I didn't sleep well, my cold mixing with worry and anger over Alicia. At eight I hoisted my aching body out of bed and sat sneezing over some steaming fruit juice while I tried to focus my brain on possible action. Alicia owed somebody money. That somebody was pissed off enough to kill because he didn't have it. Bankers do not kill wayward loan customers. Loan sharks do, but what could Alicia have done to rack up so much indebtedness? Berman probably paid her seventy or eighty thousand a year for the special kinds of designs she did on aircraft wings. And she was the kind of client a bank usually values. So what did she need money for that only a shark would provide?

The clock was ticking. I called her office. She'd phoned in sick; the secretary didn't know where she was calling from but had assumed home. On a dim chance I tried her home phone. No answer. Alicia had one brother, Tom, an insurance agent on the far south side. After a few tries I located his office in Flossmoor. He hadn't heard from Alicia for weeks. And no, he didn't know who she might owe money to.

Reluctantly Tom gave me their father's phone number in Florida. Mr. Dauphine hadn't heard from his daughter, either.

"If she calls you, or if she shows up, *please* let me know. She's in trouble up here, and the only way I can help her is by knowing where she is." I gave him the number without much expectation of hearing from him again.

I did know someone who might be able to give me a line on her debts. A year or so earlier, I'd done a major favor for Don Pasquale, a local mob leader. If she owed him money, he might listen to my intercession. If not, he might be able to tell me whom she had borrowed from.

Torfino's, an Elmwood Park restaurant where the don had a part-time office, put me through to his chief assistant, Ernesto. A well-remembered gravel voice told me I sounded awful.

"Thank you, Ernesto," I snuffled. "Did you hear about the death of Louise Carmody at the University of Illinois gym last night? She was probably shot by mistake, poor thing. The intended victim was a woman named Alicia Dauphine. We grew up together, so I feel a little solicitous on her behalf. She owes a lot of money to someone: I wondered if you know who."

"Name isn't familiar, Warshawski. I'll check around and call you back."

My cold made me feel as though I was at the bottom of a fish tank. I couldn't think fast enough or hard enough to imagine where Alicia might have gone to ground. Perhaps at her house, believing if she didn't answer the phone no one would think she was home? It wasn't a very clever idea, but it was the best I could do in my muffled, snuffled state.

The old farmhouse in Warrenville that Alicia had modernized lay behind the local high school. The boys were out practicing football. They were wearing light jerseys. I had on my winter coat — even though the day was warm, my cold made me shiver and want to be bundled up. Although we were close enough that I could see their mouthpieces, they didn't notice me as I walked around the house looking for signs of life.

Alicia's car was in the garage, but the house looked cold and unoccupied. As I made my way to the back, a black-and-white cat darted out from the bushes and began weaving itself around my ankles, mewing piteously. Alicia had three cats. This one wanted something to eat.

Alicia had installed a sophisticated burglar alarm system — she had an office in her home and often worked on preliminary designs there. An expert had gotten through the system into the pantry — some kind of epoxy had been sprayed on the wires to freeze them. Then, somehow disabling the phone link, the intruder had cut through the wires.

My stomach muscles tightened, and I wished futilely for the Smith & Wesson locked in my safe at home. My cold really had addled my brains for me not to take it on such an errand. Still, where burglars lead shall P.I.s hesitate? I opened the window, slid a leg over, and landed on the pantry floor. My feline friend followed more gracefully. She promptly abandoned me to start sniffing at the pantry walls.

Cautiously opening the door I slid into the kitchen. It was deserted, the refrigerator and clock motors humming gently, a dry dishcloth draped over the sink. In the living room another cat joined me and followed me into the electronic wonderland of Alicia's study. She had used built-in bookcases to house her computers and other gadgets. The printers were tucked along a side wall, and wires ran everywhere. Whoever had broken in was not interested in merchandise — the street value of her study contents would have brought in a nice return, but they stood unharmed.

By now I was dreading the trek upstairs. The second cat, a tabby, trotted briskly ahead of me, tail waving like a flag. Alicia's bedroom door was shut. I kicked it open with my right leg and pressed myself against the wall. Nothing. Dropping to my knees I looked in. The bed, tidily covered with an old-fashioned white spread, was empty. So was the bathroom. So was the guest room and an old sun porch glassed in and converted to a solarium.

The person who broke in had not come to steal — everything was preternaturally tidy. So he (she?) had come to attack Alicia. The hair stood up on the nape of my neck. Where was he? Not in the house. Hiding outside?

I started down the stairs again when I heard a noise, a heavy scraping. I froze, trying to locate the source. A movement caught my eye at the line of vision. The hatch to the crawl space had been shoved open; an arm swung down. For a split second only I stared at the arm and the gun in its grip, then leaped down the stairs two at a time.

A heavy thud — the man jumping onto the upper landing. The crack as the gun fired. A jolt in my left shoulder, and I gasped with shock and fell the last few steps to the bottom. Righted myself. Reached for the deadlock on the front door. Heard an outraged squawk, loud swearing, and a crash that sounded like a man falling downstairs. Then I had the door open and was staggering outside while an angry bundle of fur poured past me. One of the cats, a heroine, tripping my assailant and saving my life.

IV

I never really lost consciousness. The football players saw me stagger down the sidewalk and came trooping over. In their concern for me they failed to tackle the gunman, but they got me to a hospital, where a young intern eagerly set about removing the slug from my shoulder; the winter coat had protected me from major damage. Between my cold and the gunshot, I was just as happy to let him incarcerate me for a few days.

They tucked me into bed, and I fell into a

heavy, uneasy sleep. I had jumped into the black waters of Lake Michigan in search of Alicia, trying to reach her ahead of a shark. She was lurking just out of reach. She didn't know that her oxygen tank ran out at noon.

When I finally woke, soaked with sweat, it was dark outside. The room was lit faintly by a fluorescent light over the sink. A lean man in a brown wool business suit was sitting next to the bed. When he saw me looking at him, he reached into his coat.

If he was going to shoot me, there wasn't a thing I could do about it — I was too limp from my heavy sleep to move. Instead of a gun, though, he pulled out an I.D. case.

"Miss Warshawski? Peter Carlton, Federal Bureau of Investigation. I know you're not feeling well, but I need to talk to you about Alicia Dauphine."

"So the shark ate her," I said.

"What?" he demanded sharply. "What does that mean?"

"Nothing. Where is she?"

"We don't know. That's what we want to talk to you about. She went home with you after the swimming meet yesterday. Correct?"

"Gosh, Mr. Carlton. I love watching my tax dollars at work. If you've been following her, you must have a better fix on her whereabouts than I do. I last saw her around two-thirty this morning. If it's still today, that is."

"What did she talk to you about?"

My mind was starting to unfog. "Why is the bureau interested in Ms. Dauphine?"

He didn't want to tell me. All he wanted was every word Alicia had said to me. When I wouldn't budge, he started in on why I was in her house and what I had noticed there.

Finally I said, "Mr. Carlton, if you can't tell me why you're interested in Ms. Dauphine, there's no way I can respond to your questions. I don't believe the bureau — or the police — or anyone, come to that — has any right to pry into the affairs of citizens in the hopes of turning up some scandal. You tell me why you're interested, and I'll tell you if I know anything relevant to that interest."

With an ill grace he said, "We believe she has been selling Defense Department secrets to the Chinese."

"No," I said flatly. "She wouldn't."

"Some wing designs she was working on have disappeared. She's disappeared. And a Chinese functionary in St. Charles has disappeared."

"Sounds pretty circumstantial to me. The wing designs might be in her home. They could easily be on a disk someplace — she did all her drafting on computer."

They'd been through her computer files at home and at work and found nothing. Her boss did not have copies of the latest design, only of the early stuff. I thought about the heavy voice on the phone demanding money, but loyalty to Alicia made me keep it to myself — give her

186

a chance to tell her story first.

I did give him everything Alicia had said, her nervousness and her sudden departure. That I was worried about her and went to see if she was in her house. And was shot by an intruder hiding in the crawl space. Who might have taken her designs. Although nothing looked pilfered.

He didn't believe me. I don't know if he thought I knew something I wasn't telling, or if he thought I had joined Alicia in selling secrets to the Chinese. But he kept at me for so long that I finally pushed my call button. When the nurse arrived, I explained that I was worn out and could she please show my visitor out? He left but promised me that he would return.

Cursing my weakness, I fell asleep again. When I next awoke it was morning, and both my cold and my shoulder were much improved. When the doctors came by on their morning visit, I got their agreement to a discharge. Before I bathed and left, the Warrenville police sent out a man who took a detailed statement.

I called my answering service from a phone in the lobby. Ernesto had been in touch. I reached him at Torfino's.

"Saw about your accident in the papers, Warshawski. How you feeling? . . . About Dauphine. Apparently she's signed a note for seven hundred fifty thousand dollars to Art Smollensk. Can't do anything to help you out. The don sends his best wishes for your recovery."

Art Smollensk, gambling king. When I worked

for the public defender, I'd had to defend some of his small-time employees — people at the level of smashing someone's fingers in a car door. The ones who did hits and arson usually could afford their own attorneys.

Alicia as a gambler made no sense to me — but we hadn't been close for over a decade. There were lots of things I didn't know about her.

At home for a change of clothes I stopped in the basement, where I store useless mementos in a locked stall. After fifteen minutes of shifting boxes around, I was sweating and my left shoulder was throbbing and oozing stickily, but I'd located my high school yearbook. I took it upstairs with me and thumbed through it, trying to gain inspiration on where Alicia might have gone to earth.

None came. I was about to leave again when the phone rang. It was Alicia, talking against a background of noise. "Thank God you're safe, Vic. I saw about the shooting in the paper. Please don't worry about me. I'm okay. Stay away and don't worry."

She hung up before I could ask her anything. I concentrated, not on what she'd said, but what had been in the background. Metal doors banging open and shut. Lots of loud, wild talking. Not an airport — the talking was too loud for that, and there weren't any intercom announcements in the background. I knew what it was. If I'd just let my mind relax, it would come to me.

Idly flipping through the yearbook, I looked

for faces Alicia might trust. I found my own staring from a group photo of the girls' basketball team. I'd been a guard — Victoria the protectress from way back. On the next page, Alicia smiled fiercely, holding a swimming trophy. Her coach, who also taught Latin, had desperately wanted Alicia to train for the Olympics, but Alicia had had her heart set on the U of I and engineering.

Suddenly I knew what the clanking was, where Alicia was. No other sound like that exists anywhere on earth.

V

Alicia and I grew up under the shadow of the steel mills in South Chicago. Nowhere else has the deterioration of American industry shown up more clearly. Wisconsin Steel is padlocked shut. The South Works are a fragment of their former monstrous grandeur. Unemployment is over 30 percent, and the number of jobless youths lounging in the bars and on the streets had grown from the days when I hurried past them to the safety of my mother's house.

The high school was more derelict than I remembered. Many windows were boarded over. The asphalt playground was cracked and covered with litter, and the bleachers around the football field were badly weathered.

The guard at the doorway demanded my business. I showed her my P.I. license and said I needed to talk to the women's gym teacher on confidential business. After some dickering — hostile on her side, snuffly on mine — she gave me a pass. I didn't need directions down the scuffed corridors, past the battered lockers, past the smell of rancid oil coming from the cafeteria, to the noise and life of the gym.

Teenage girls in gold shirts and black shorts — the school colors — were shrieking, jumping, wailing in pursuit of volleyballs. I watched the pandemonium until the buzzer ended the period, then walked up to the instructor.

She was panting and sweating and gave me an incurious glance, looking only briefly at the pass I held out for her. "Yes?"

"You have a new swimming coach, don't you?"

"Just a volunteer. Are you from the union? She isn't drawing a paycheck. But Miss Finley, the head coach, is desperately shorthanded — she teaches Latin, you know — and this woman is a big help."

"I'm not from the union. I'm her trainer. I need to talk to her — find out why she's dropped out and whether she plans to compete in any of her meets this fall."

The teacher gave me the hard look of someone used to sizing up fabricated excuses. I didn't think she believed me, but she told me I could go into the pool area and talk to the swim coach.

The pool dated to the time when this high school served an affluent neighborhood. It was twenty-five yards long, built with skylights along the outer wall. You reached it through the changing rooms, separate ones with showers for girls and boys. It didn't have an outside hallway entrance.

Alicia was perched alone on the high dive. A few students, boys and girls, were splashing about in the pool, but no organized training was in progress. Alicia was staring at nothing.

I cupped my hands and called up to her, "You're not working very hard at your new job."

At that she turned and recognized me. "Vic!" Her cry was enough to stop the splashing in the pool. "How — Are you alone?"

"I'm alone. Come down. I took a slug in the shoulder — I'd rather not climb up after you."

She shot off the board in a perfect arc, barely rippling the surface of the water. The kids watched with envy. I was pretty jealous, myself — nothing I do is done with that much grace.

She surfaced near me but looked at the students. "I want you guys swimming laps," she said sharply. "What do you think this is — summer camp?"

They left us reluctantly and began swimming. "How did you find me?"

"It was easy. I was looking through the yearbook, trying to think of someone you would trust. Miss Finley was the simple answer — I remembered how you practically lived in her house for two years. You liked to read *Jane Eyre* together, and she adored you.

"You are in deep trouble. Smollensk is after you, and so is the FBI. You can't hide here forever. You'd better talk to the bureau guys. They won't love you, but at least they're not going to shoot you."

"The FBI? Whatever for?"

"Your designs, sweetie pie. Your designs and the Chinese. The FBI are the people who look into that kind of thing."

"Vic. I don't know what you're talking about." The words were said with such slow deliberateness that I was almost persuaded.

"The seven hundred fifty thousand dollars you owe Art Smollensk."

She shook her head, then said, "Oh. Yes. That."

"Yes, that. I guess it seems like more money to me than it does to you. Or had you forgotten Louise Carmody getting shot? . . . Anyway, a known Chinese spy left Fermilab yesterday or the day before, and you're gone, and some of your wing designs are gone, and the FBI thinks you've sold them overseas and maybe gone East yourself. I didn't tell them about Art, but they'll probably get to him before too long."

"How sure are they that the designs are gone?"

"Your boss can't find them. Maybe you have a duplicate set at home nobody knows about."

She shook her head again. "I don't leave that kind of thing at home. I had them last Saturday, working, but I took the diskettes back . . ." Her voice trailed off as a look of horror washed across her face. "Oh, no. This is worse than I thought."

She hoisted herself out of the pool. "I've got to go. Got to get away before someone else figures out I'm here."

"Alicia, for Christ's sake. What has happened?"

She stopped and looked at me, tears swimming in her black eyes. "If I could tell anyone, it would be you, Vic." Then she was jogging into the girls' changing room, leaving the students in the pool swimming laps.

I stuck with her. "Where are you going? The Feds have a hook on any place you have friends or relations. Smollensk does, too."

That stopped her. "Tom, too?"

"Tom first, last, and foremost. He's the only relative you have in Chicago." She was starting to shiver in the bare corridor. I grabbed her and shook her. "Tell me the truth, Alicia. I can't fly blind. I already took a bullet in the shoulder."

Suddenly she was sobbing on my chest. "Oh, Vic. It's been so awful. You can't know . . . you can't understand . . . you won't believe . . ." She was hiccuping.

I led her into the shower room and found a towel. Rubbing her down, I got the story in choking bits and pieces.

Tom was the gambler. He'd gotten into it in a small way in high school and college. After he went into business for himself, the habit grew. He'd mortgaged his insurance agency assets, taken out a second mortgage on the house, but couldn't stop.

"He came to me two weeks ago. Told me he

was going to start filing false claims with his companies, collect the money." She gave a twisted smile. "He didn't have to put that kind of pressure on — I can't help helping him."

"But Alicia, why? And how does Art Smollensk have your name?"

"Is that the man Tom owes money to? I think he uses my name — Alonso, my middle name — I know he does; I just don't like to think about it. Someone came around threatening me three years ago. I told Tom never to use my name again, and he didn't for a long time, but now I guess he was desperate — seven hundred fifty thousand dollars, you know. . . ."

"As to why I help him . . . You never had any brothers or sisters, so maybe you can't understand. When Mom died, I was thirteen, he was six. I looked after him. Got him out of trouble. All kinds of stuff. It gets to be a habit, I guess. Or an obligation. That's why I've never married, you know, never had any children of my own. I don't want any more responsibilities like this one."

"And the designs?"

She looked horrified again. "He came over for dinner on Saturday. I'd been working all day on the things, and he came into the study when I was logging off. I didn't tell him it was Defense Department work, but it's not too hard to figure out what I do is defense-related — after all, that's all Berman does; we don't make commercial aircraft. I haven't had a chance to look at the designs since — I worked out all day Sunday getting ready for that damned meet Monday. Tom must have taken my diskettes and swapped the labels with some others — I've got tons of them lying around."

She gave a twisted smile. "It was a gamble: a gamble that there'd be something valuable on them and a gamble I wouldn't discover the switch before he got rid of them. But he's a gambler."

"I see. . . . Look, Alicia. You can only be responsible for Tom so far. Even if you could bail him out this time — and I don't see how you possibly can — there'll be a next time. And you may not survive this one to help him again. Let's call the FBI."

She squeezed her eyes shut. "You don't understand, Vic. You can't possibly understand."

While I was trying to reason her into phoning the bureau, Miss Finley, swim coach-cum-romantic-Latin-teacher, came briskly into the locker room. "Allie! One of the girls came to get me. Are you all —" She did a double take. "Victoria! Good to see you. Have you come to help Allie? I told her she could count on you."

"Have you told her what's going on?" I demanded of Alicia.

Yes, Miss Finley knew most of the story. Agreed that it was very worrying but said Allie could not possibly turn in her own brother. She had given Allie a gym mat and some bedding to sleep on — she could just stay at the gym until the furor died down and they could think of something else to do.

I sat helplessly as Miss Finley led Alicia off to get some dry clothes. At last, when they didn't rejoin me, I sought them out, poking through half-remembered halls and doors until I found the staff coaching office. Alicia was alone, looking about fifteen in an old cheerleader's uniform Miss Finley had dug up for her.

"Miss Finley teaching?" I asked sharply.

Alicia looked guilty but defiant. "Yes. Two-thirty class. Look. The critical thing is to get those diskettes back. I called Tom, explained it to him. Told him I'd try to help him raise the money but that we couldn't let the Chinese have those things. He agreed, so he's bringing them out here."

The room rocked slightly around me. "No. I know you don't have much of a sense of humor, but this is a joke, isn't it?"

She didn't understand. Wouldn't understand that if the Chinese had already left the country, Tom no longer had the material. That if Tom was coming here, she was the scapegoat. At last, despairing, I said, "Where is he meeting you? Here?"

"I told him I'd be at the pool."

"Will you do one thing my way? Will you go to Miss Finley's class and conjugate verbs for forty-five minutes and let me meet him at the pool? Please?"

At last, her jaw set stubbornly, she agreed. She still wouldn't let me call the bureau, though. "Not until I've talked to Tom myself. It may all be a mistake, you know."

We both knew it wasn't, but I saw her into the Latin class without making the phone call I knew it was my duty to make and returned to the pool. Driving out the two students still splashing around in the water, I put signs on the locker room doors saying the water was contaminated and there would be no swimming until further notice.

I turned out the lights and settled in a corner of the room remote from the outside windows to wait. And go over and over the story in my mind. I believed it. Was I fooling myself? Was that why she wouldn't call the Feds?

At last Tom came in through the boys' locker room entrance. "Allie? Allie?" His voice bounced off the high rafters and echoed around me. I was well back in the shadows, my Smith & Wesson in hand; he didn't see me.

After half a minute or so another man joined him. I didn't recognize the stranger, but his baggy clothes marked him as part of Smollensk's group, not the bureau. He talked softly to Tom for a minute. Then they went into the girls' locker room together.

When they returned, I had moved part way up the side of the pool, ready to follow them if they went back into the main part of the high school looking for Alicia.

"Tom!" I called. "It's V. I. Warshawski. I know the whole story. Give me the diskettes."

"Warshawski!" he yelled. "What the hell are you doing here?"

I sensed rather than saw the movement his friend made. I shot at him and dived into the water. His bullet zipped as it hit the tiles where I'd been standing. My wet clothes and my sore shoulder made it hard to move. Another bullet hit the water by my head, and I went under again, fumbling with my heavy jacket, getting it free, surfacing, hearing Alicia's sharp, "Tom, why are you shooting at Vic? Stop it now. Stop it and give me back the diskettes."

Another flurry of shots, this time away from me, giving me a chance to get to the side of the pool, to climb out. Alicia lay on the floor near the door to the girls' locker room. Tom stood silently by. The gunman was jamming more bullets into his gun.

As fast as I could in my sodden clothes I lumbered to the hit man, grabbing his arm, squeezing, feeling blood start to seep from my shoulder, stepping on his instep, putting all the force of my body into my leg. Tom, though, Tom was taking the gun from him. Tom was going to shoot me.

"Drop that gun, Tom Dauphine." It was Miss Finley. Years of teaching in a tough school gave creditable authority to her; Tom dropped the gun.

VI

Alicia lived long enough to tell the truth to the FBI. It was small comfort to me. Small consolation to see Tom's statement. He hoped he could get Smollensk to kill his sister before she said anything. If that happened, he had a good gamble on her dying a traitor in everyone's eyes — after all, her designs were gone, and her name was in Smollensk's files. Maybe the truth never would have come out. Worth a gamble to a betting man.

The Feds arrived about five minutes after the shooting stopped. They'd been watching Tom, just not closely enough. They were sore that they'd let Alicia get shot. So they dumped some charges on me — obstructing federal authorities, not telling them where Alicia was, not calling as soon as I had the truth from her, God knows what else. I spent several days in jail. It seemed like a suitable penance, just not enough of one.

The Maltese Cat

I

HER VOICE ON the phone had been soft and husky, with just a whiff of the South laid across it like a rare perfume. "I'd rather come to your office; I don't want people in mine to know I've hired a detective."

I'd offered to see her at her home in the evening — my Spartan office doesn't invite client confidences. But she didn't want to wait until tonight, she wanted to come today, almost at once, and no, she wouldn't meet me in a restaurant. Far too hard to talk, and this was extremely personal.

"You know my specialty is financial crime, don't you?" I asked sharply.

"Yes, that's how I got your name. One o'clock, fourth floor of the Pulteney, right?" And she'd hung up without telling me who she was.

An errand at the County building took me longer than I'd expected; it was close to one-thirty by the time I got back to the Pulteney. My caller's problem apparently was urgent: she was waiting outside my office door, tapping one high heel impatiently on the floor as I trudged down the

200

hall in my running shoes.

"Ms. Warshawski! I thought you were standing me up."

"No such luck," I grunted, opening my office door for her.

In the dimly lit hall she'd just been a slender silhouette. Under the office lights the set of the shoulders and signature buttons told me her suit had come from the hands of someone at Chanel. Its blue enhanced the cobalt of her eyes. Soft makeup hid her natural skin tones — I couldn't tell if that dark red hair was natural, or merely expertly painted.

She scanned the spare furnishings and picked the cleaner of my two visitor chairs. "My time is valuable, Ms. Warshawski. If I'd known you were going to keep me waiting without a place to sit I would have finished some phone calls before walking over here."

I'd dressed in jeans and a work shirt for a day at the Recorder of Deeds office. Feeling dirty and outclassed made me grumpy. "You hung up without giving me your name or number, so there wasn't much I could do to let you know you'd have to stand around in your pointy little shoes. My time's valuable, too. Why don't you tell me where the fire is so I can start putting it out."

She flushed. When I turn red I look blotchy, but in her it only enhanced her makeup. "It's my sister." The whiff of Southern increased. "Corinne. She's run off to Ja— my ex-husband, and

I need someone to tell her to come back."

I made a disgusted face. "I can't believe I raced back from the County building to listen to this. It's not 1890, you know. She may be making a mistake but presumably she can sort it out for herself."

Her flush darkened. "I'm not being very clear. I'm sorry. I'm not used to having to ask for things. My sister — Corinne — she's only fourteen. She's my ward. I'm sixteen years older than she is. Our parents died three years ago and she's been living with me since then. It's not easy, not easy for either of us. Moving from Mobile to here was just the beginning. When she got here she wanted to run around, do all the things you can't do in Mobile."

She waved a hand to indicate what kinds of things those might be. "She thinks I'm a tough bitch and that I was too hard on my ex-husband. She's known him since she was three and he was a big hero. She couldn't see he'd changed. Or not changed, just not had the chance to be heroic anymore in public. So when she took off two days ago I assumed she went there. He's not answering his phone or the doorbell. I don't know if they've left town or he's just playing possum or what. I need someone who knows how to get people to open their doors and knows how to talk to people. At least if I could see Corinne I might — I don't know."

She broke off with a helpless gesture that didn't match her sophisticated looks. Nothing like responsibility for a minor to deflate even the most urbane.

I grimaced more ferociously. "Why don't we start with your name, and your husband's name and address, and then move on to her friends."

"Her friends?" The deep blue eyes widened. "I'd just as soon this didn't get around. People talk, and even though it's not 1890, it could be hard on her when she gets back to school."

I suppressed a howl. "You can't come around demanding my expertise and then tell me what or what not to do. What if she's not with your husband? What if I can't get in touch with you when I've found that out and she's in terrible trouble and her life depends on my turning up some new leads? If you can't bring yourself to divulge a few names — starting with your own — you'd better go find yourself a more pliant detective. I can recommend a couple who have waiting rooms."

She set her lips tightly: whatever she did she was in command — people didn't talk to her that way and get away with it. For a few seconds it looked as though I might be free to get back to the Recorder of Deeds that afternoon, but then she shook her head and forced a smile to her lips.

"I was told not to mind your abrasiveness because you were the best. I'm Brigitte LeBlanc. My sister's name is Corinne, also LeBlanc. And my ex-husband is Charles Pierce." She scooted her chair up to the desk so she could scribble his address on a sheet of paper torn from a memo pad in her bag. She scrawled busily for several minutes, then handed me a list that included Corinne's three closest school friends, along with Pierce's address.

"I'm late for a meeting. I'll call you tonight to see if you've made any progress." She got up.

"Not so fast," I said. "I get a retainer. You have to sign a contract. And I need a number where I can reach you."

"I really am late."

"And I'm really too busy to hunt for your sister. If you have a sister. You can't be that worried if your meeting is more important than she is."

Her scowl would have terrified me if I'd been alone with her in an alley after dark. "I do have a sister. And I spent two days trying to get into my ex-husband's place, and then in tracking down people who could recommend a private detective to me. I can't do anything else to help her except go earn the money to pay your fee."

I pulled a contract from my desk drawer and stuck it in the manual Olivetti that had belonged to my mother — a typewriter so old that I had to order special ribbons for it from Italy. A word processor would be cheaper and more impressive but the wrist action keeps my forearms strong. I got Ms. LeBlanc to give me her address, to sign on the dotted line for $400 a day plus expenses, to write in the name of a guaranteeing financial institution and to hand over a check for two hundred.

When she'd left I wrestled with my office windows, hoping to let some air in to blow her pricey perfume away. Carbon flakes from the el would be better than the lingering scent, but the windows, painted over several hundred times, wouldn't budge. I turned on a desktop fan and frowned sourly at her bold black signature.

What was her ex-husband's real name? She'd bitten off "Ja—" Could be James or Jake, but it sure wasn't Charles. Did she really have a sister? Was this just a ploy to get back at a guy late on his alimony? Although Pierce's address on North Winthrop didn't sound like the place for a man who could afford alimony. Maybe everything went to keep her in Chanel suits while he lived on Skid Row.

She wasn't in the phone book, so I couldn't check her own address on Belden. The operator told me the number was unlisted. I called a friend at the Ft. Dearborn Trust, the bank Brigitte had drawn her check on, and was assured that there was plenty more where that came from. My friend told me Brigitte had parlayed the proceeds of a high-priced modeling career into a successful media consulting firm.

"And if you ever read the fashion pages you'd know these things. Get your nose out of the sports section from time to time, Vic — it'll help with your career."

"Thanks, Eva." I hung up with a snap. At

least my client wouldn't turn out to be named something else, always a good beginning to a tawdry case.

I looked in the little mirror perched over my filing cabinet. A dust smudge on my right cheek instead of peach blush was the only distinction between me and Ms. LeBlanc. Since I was dressed appropriately for North Winthrop, I shut up my office and went to retrieve my car.

II

Charles Pierce lived in a dismal ten-flat built flush onto the Uptown sidewalk. Ragged sheets made haphazard curtains in those windows that weren't boarded over. Empty bottles lined the entryway, but the smell of stale Ripple couldn't begin to mask the stench of fresh urine. If Corinne LeBlanc had run away to this place, life with Brigitte must be unmitigated hell.

My client's ex-husband lived in 3E. I knew that because she'd told me. Those few mailboxes whose doors still shut wisely didn't trumpet their owners' identities. The filthy brass nameplate next to the doorbells was empty and the doorbells didn't work. Pushing open the rickety door to the hall, I wondered again about my client's truthfulness: she told me Ja— hadn't answered his phone or his bell.

A rheumy-eyed woman was sprawled across the

bottom of the stairs, sucking at a half-pint. She stared at me malevolently when I asked her to move, but she didn't actively try to trip me when I stepped over her. It was only my foot catching in the folds of her overcoat.

The original building probably held two apartments per floor. At least, on the third floor only two doors at either end looked as though they went back to the massive, elegant construction of the building's beginnings. The other seven were flimsy newcomers that had been hastily installed when an apartment was subdivided. Peering in the dark I found one labeled B and counted off three more to the right to get to E. After knocking on the peeling veneer several times I noticed a button imbedded in the grime on the jamb. When I pushed it I heard a buzz resonate inside. No one came to the door. With my ear against the filthy panel I could hear the faint hum of a television.

I held the buzzer down for five minutes. It's hard on the finger but harder on the ear. If someone was really in there he should have come boiling to the door by now.

I could go away and come back, but if Pierce was lying doggo to avoid Brigitte, that wouldn't buy me anything. She said she'd tried off and on for two days. The television might be running as a decoy, or — I pushed more lurid ideas from my mind and took out a collection of skeleton keys. The second worked easily in the insubstantial lock. In two minutes I was inside the apartment, looking at an illustration from *House Beautiful in Hell.*

It was a single room with a countertop kitchen on the left side. A tidy person could pull a corrugated screen to shield the room from signs of cooking, but Pierce wasn't tidy. Ten or fifteen stacked pots, festooned with rotting food and roaches, trembled precariously when I shut the door.

Dominating the place was a Murphy bed with a grotesquely fat man sprawled in at an ominous angle. He'd been watching TV when he died. He was wearing frayed, shiny pants with the fly lying carelessly open and a lumberjack shirt that didn't quite cover his enormous belly.

His monstrous size and the horrible angle at which his bald head was tilted made me gag. I forced it down and walked through a pile of stale clothes to the bed. Lifting an arm the size of a tree trunk, I felt for a pulse. Nothing moved in the heavy arm, but the skin, while clammy, was firm. I couldn't bring myself to touch any more of him but stumbled around the perimeter to peer at him from several angles. I didn't see any obvious wounds. Let the medical examiner hunt out the obscure ones.

By the time I was back in the stairwell I was close to fainting. Only the thought of falling into someone else's urine or vomit kept me on my feet. On the way down I tripped in earnest over the rheumy-eyed woman's coat. Sprawled on the floor at the bottom, I couldn't keep from throwing up myself. It didn't make me feel any better.

I dug a water bottle out of the detritus in my trunk and sponged myself off before calling the police. They asked me to stay near the body. I thought the front seat of my car on Winthrop would be close enough.

While I waited for a meat wagon I wondered about my client. Could Brigitte have come here after leaving me, killed him and taken off while I was phoning around checking up on her? If she had, the rheumy-eyed woman in the stairwell would have seen her. Would the bond forged by my tripping over her and vomiting in the hall be enough to get her to talk to me?

I got out of the car, but before I could get back to the entrance the police arrived. When we pushed open the rickety door my friend had evaporated. I didn't bother mentioning her to the boys — and girl — in blue: her description wouldn't stand out in Uptown, and even if they could find her she wouldn't be likely to say much.

We plodded up the stairs in silence. There were four of them. The woman and the youngest of the three men seemed in good shape. The two older men were running sadly to flab. I didn't think they'd be able to budge my client's ex-husband's right leg, let alone his mammoth red-wood torso.

"I got a feeling about this," the oldest officer muttered, more to himself than the rest of us. "I got a feeling."

When we got to 3E and he looked across at

the mass on the bed he shook his head a couple of times. "Yup. I kind of knew as soon as I heard the call."

"Knew what, Tom?" the woman demanded sharply.

"Jade Pierce," he said. "Knew he lived around here. Been a lot of complaints about him. Thought it might be him when I heard we was due to visit a real big guy."

The woman stopped her brisk march to the bed. The rest of us looked at the behemoth in shared sorrow. Jade. Not James or Jake but Jade. Once the most famous down lineman the Bears had ever fielded. Now . . . I shuddered.

When he played for Alabama some reporter said his bald head was as smooth and cold as a piece of jade, and went on to spin some tiresome simile relating it to his play. When he signed with the Bears, I was as happy as any other Chicago fan, even though his reputation for off-field violence was pretty unappetizing. No wonder Brigitte LeBlanc hadn't stayed with him, but why hadn't she wanted to tell me who he really was? I wrestled with that while Tom called for reinforcements over his lapel mike.

"So what were you doing here?" he asked me.

"His ex-wife hired me to check up on him." I don't usually tell the cops my clients' business, but I didn't feel like protecting Brigitte. "She wanted to talk to him and he wasn't answering his phone or his door."

"She wanted to check up on him?" the fit younger officer, a man with high cheekbones and a well-tended mustache, echoed me derisively. "What I hear, that split up was the biggest fight Jade was ever in. Only big fight he ever lost, too."

I smiled. "She's doing well, he isn't. Wasn't. Maybe her conscience pricked her. Or maybe she wanted to rub his nose in it hard. You'd have to ask her. All I can say is she asked me to try to get in, I did, and I called you guys."

While Tom mulled this over I pulled out a card and handed it to him. "You can find me at this number if you want to talk to me."

He called out after me but I went on down the hall, my footsteps echoing hollowly off the bare walls and ceiling.

III

Brigitte LeBlanc was with a client and couldn't be interrupted. The news that her ex-husband had died couldn't pry her loose. Not even the idea that the cops would be around before long could move her. After a combination of cajoling and heckling, the receptionist leaned across her blond desk and whispered at me confidentially: "The Vice President of the United States had come in for some private media coaching." Brigitte had said no interruptions unless it was the President or the pope — two people I wouldn't

211

even leave a dental appointment to see.

When they made me unwelcome on the forty-third floor I rode downstairs and hung around the lobby. At five-thirty a bevy of Secret Service agents swept me out to the street with the other loiterers. Fifteen minutes later the Vice President came out, his boyish face set in purposeful lines. Even though this was a private visit the vigilant television crews were waiting for him. He grinned and waved but didn't say anything before climbing into his limo. Brigitte must be really good if she'd persuaded him to shut up.

At seven I went back to the forty-third floor. The double glass doors were locked and the lights turned off. I found a key in my collection that worked the lock, but when I'd prowled through the miles of thick gray plush, explored the secured studios, looked in all the offices, I had to realize my client was smarter than me. She'd left by some back exit.

I gave a high-pitched snarl. I didn't lock the door behind me. Let someone come in and steal all the video equipment. I didn't care.

I swung by Brigitte's three-story brownstone on Belden. She wasn't in. The housekeeper didn't know when to expect her. She was eating out and had said not to wait up for her.

"How about Corinne?" I asked, sure that the woman would say "Corinne who?"

"She's not here, either."

I slipped inside before she could shut the door on me. "I'm V. I. Warshawski. Brigitte hired me to find her sister, said she'd run off to Jade. I went to his apartment. Corinne wasn't there and Jade was dead. I've been trying to talk to Brigitte ever since but she's avoiding me. I want to know a few things, like if Corinne really exists, and did she really run away, and could either she or Brigitte have killed Jade."

The housekeeper stared at me for a few minutes, then made a sour face. "You got some I.D.?"

I showed her my P.I. license and the contract signed by Brigitte. Her sour look deepened but she gave me a few spare details. Corinne was a fat, unhappy teenager who didn't know how good she had it. Brigitte gave her everything, taught her how to dress, sent her to St. Scholastica, even tried to get her to special diet clinics, but she was never satisfied, always whining about her friends back home in Mobile, trashy friends to whom she shouldn't be giving the time of day. And yes, she had run away, three days ago now, and she, the housekeeper, said good riddance, but Brigitte felt responsible. And she was sorry that Jade was dead, but he was a violent man, Corinne had over-idealized him, she didn't realize what a monster he really was.

"They can't turn it off when they come off the field, you know. As for who killed him, he probably killed himself, drinking too much. I always said it would happen that way. Corinne couldn't have done it, she doesn't have enough oomph to her. And Brigitte doesn't have any call to — she already got him beat six ways from Sunday."

"Maybe she thought he'd molested her sister."

"She'd have taken him to court and enjoyed seeing him humiliated all over again."

What a lovely cast of characters; it filled me with satisfaction to think I'd allied myself to their fates. I persuaded the housekeeper to give me a picture of Corinne before going home. She was indeed an overweight, unhappy-looking child. It must be hard having a picture-perfect older sister trying to turn her into a junior deb. I also got the housekeeper to give me Brigitte's unlisted home phone number by telling her if she didn't, I'd be back every hour all night long ringing the bell.

I didn't turn on the radio going home. I didn't want to hear the ghoulish excitement lying behind the unctuousness the reporters would bring to discussing Jade Pierce's catastrophic fall from grace. A rehashing of his nine seasons with the Bears, from the glory years to the last two where nagging knee and back injuries grew too great even for the painkillers. And then to his harsh retirement, putting seventy or eighty pounds of fat over his playing weight of 310, the barroom fights, the guns fired at other drivers from the front seat of his Ferrari Daytona, then the sale of the Ferrari to pay his legal bills, and finally the three-ring circus that was his divorce. Ending on a Murphy bed in a squalid Uptown apartment.

I shut the Trans Am's door with a viciousness

it didn't deserve and stomped up the three flights to my apartment. Fatigue mixed with bitterness dulled the sixth sense that usually warns me of danger. The man had me pinned against my front door with a gun at my throat before I knew he was there.

I held my shoulder bag out to him. "Be my guest. Then leave. I've had a long day and I don't want to spend too much of it with you."

He spat. "I don't want your stupid little wallet."

"You're not going to rape me, so you might as well take my stupid little wallet."

"I'm not interested in your body. Open your apartment. I want to search it."

"Go to hell." I kneed him in the stomach and swept my right arm up to knock his gun hand away. He gagged and bent over. I used my handbag as a clumsy bolas and whacked him on the back of the head. He slumped to the floor, unconscious.

I grabbed the gun from his flaccid hand. Feeling gingerly inside his coat, I found a wallet. His driver's license identified him as Joel Sirop, living at a pricey address on Dearborn Parkway. He sported a high-end assortment of credit cards — Bonwit, Neiman Marcus, an American Express platinum — and a card that said he was a member in good standing of the Feline Breeders Association of North America. I slid the papers back into his billfold and returned it to his breast pocket.

He groaned and opened his eyes. After a few

diffuse seconds he focused on me in outrage. "My head. You've broken my head. I'll sue you."

"Go ahead. I'll hang on to your pistol for use in evidence at the trial. I've got your name and address, so if I see you near my place again I'll know where to send the cops. Now leave."

"Not until I've searched your apartment." He was unarmed and sickly but stubborn.

I leaned against my door, out of reach but poised to stomp on him if he got cute. "What are you looking for, Mr. Sirop?"

"It was on the news, how you found Jade. If the cat was there, you must have taken it."

"Rest your soul, there were no cats in that apartment when I got there. Had he stolen yours?"

He shut his eyes, apparently to commune with himself. When he opened them again he said he had no choice but to trust me. I smiled brightly and told him he could always leave so I could have dinner, but he insisted on confiding in me.

"Do you know cats, Ms. Warshawski?"

"Only in a manner of speaking. I have a dog and she knows cats."

He scowled. "This is not a laughing matter. Have you heard of the Maltese?"

"Cat? I guess I've heard of them. They're the ones without tails, right?"

He shuddered. "No. You are thinking of the Manx. The Maltese — they are usually a bluish gray. Very rarely will you see one that is almost blue. Brigitte LeBlanc has — or had — such a cat. Lady Iva of Cairo."

"Great. I presume she got it to match her eyes."

He waved aside my comment as another frivolity. "Her motives do not matter. What matters is that the cat has been very difficult to breed. She has now come into season for only the third time in her four-year life. Brigitte agreed to let me try to mate Lady Iva with my sire, Casper of Valletta. It is imperative that she be sent to stay with him, and soon. But she has disappeared."

It was my turn to look disgusted. "I took a step down from my usual practice to look for a runaway teenager today. I'm damned if I'm going to hunt a missing cat through the streets of Chicago. Your sire will find her faster than I will. Matter of fact, that's my advice. Drive around listening for the yowling of mighty sires and eventually you'll find your Maltese."

"This runaway teenager, this Corinne, it is probable that she took Lady Iva with her. The kittens, if they are born, if they are purebred, could fetch a thousand or more each. She is not ignorant of that fact. But if Lady Iva is out on the streets and some other sire finds her first, they would be half-breeds, not worth the price of their veterinary care."

He spoke with the intense passion I usually reserve for discussing Cubs or Bears trades. Keeping myself turned toward him, I unlocked my front door. He flung himself at the opening with a ferocity that proved his long years with felines had rubbed off on him. I grabbed his jacket as he hurtled past me but he tore himself free.

"I am not leaving until I have searched your premises," he panted.

I rubbed my head tiredly. "Go ahead, then."

I could have called the cops while he hunted around for Lady Iva. Instead I poured myself a whiskey and watched him crawl on his hands and knees, making little whistling sounds — perhaps the mating call of the Maltese. He went through my cupboards, my stove, the refrigerator, even insisted, his eyes wide with fear, that I open the safe in my bedroom closet. I removed the Smith & Wesson I keep there before letting him look.

When he'd inspected the back landing he had to agree that no cats were on the premises. He tried to argue me into going downtown to check my office. At that point my patience ran out.

"I could have you arrested for attempted assault and criminal trespass. So get out now while the going's good. Take your guy down to my office. If she's in there and in heat, he'll start carrying on and you can call the cops. Just don't bother me." I hustled him out the front door, ignoring his protests.

I carefully did up all the locks. I didn't want some other deranged cat breeder sneaking up on me in the middle of the night.

IV

It was after midnight when I finally reached Brigitte. Yes, she'd gotten my message about Jade. She was terribly sorry, but since she couldn't do anything to help him now that he was dead, she hadn't bothered to try to reach me.

"We're about to part company, Brigitte. If you didn't know the guy was dead when you sent me up to Winthrop, you're going to have to prove it. Not to me, but to the cops. I'm talking to Lieutenant Mallory at the Central District in the morning to tell him the rigmarole you spun me. They'll also be able to figure out if you were more interested in finding Corinne or your cat."

There was a long silence at the other end. When she finally spoke, the hint of Southern was pronounced. "Can we talk in the morning before you call the police? Maybe I haven't been as frank as I should have. I'd like you to hear the whole story before you do anything rash."

Just say no, just say no, I chanted to myself. "You be at the Belmont Diner at eight, Brigitte. You can lay it out for me but I'm not making any promises."

I got up at seven, ran the dog over to Belmont Harbor and back and took a long shower. I figured even if I put a half hour into grooming myself I wasn't going to look as good as Brigitte, so I just scrambled into jeans and a cotton sweater.

It was almost ten minutes after eight when I got to the diner, but Brigitte hadn't arrived yet. I picked up a *Herald-Star* from the counter and took it over to a booth to read with a cup of coffee. The headline shook me to the bottom of my stomach.

FOOTBALL HERO SURVIVES
FATE WORSE THAN DEATH

Charles "Jade" Pierce, once the smoothest man on the Bears' fearsome defense, eluded offensive blockers once again. This time the stakes were higher than a touchdown, though: the offensive lineman was Death.

I thought Jeremy Logan was overdoing it by a wide margin but I read the story to the end. The standard procedure with a body is to take it to a hospital for a death certificate before it goes to the morgue. The patrol team hauled Jade to Beth Israel for a perfunctory exam. There the intern, noticing a slight sweat on Jade's neck and hands, dug deeper for a pulse than I'd been willing to go. She'd found faint but unmistakable signs of life buried deep in the mountain of flesh and had brought him back to consciousness.

Jade, who's had substance abuse problems since leaving the Bears, had mainlined a potent mixture of ether and hydrochloric acid before drinking a quart of bourbon. When he came to his first words were characteristic: "Get the f—— out of my face."

Logan then concluded with the obligatory rundown on Jade's career and its demise, with a pious sniff about the use and abuse of sports heroes left to die in the gutter when they could no longer please the crowd. I read it through twice, including the fulsome last line, before Brigitte arrived.

"You see, Jade's still alive, so I couldn't have killed him," she announced, sweeping into the booth in a cloud of Chanel.

"Did you know he was in a coma when you came to see me yesterday?"

She raised plucked eyebrows in hauteur. "Are you questioning my word?"

One of the waitresses chugged over to take our order. "You want your fruit and yogurt, right, Vic? And what else?"

"Green pepper and cheese omelet with rye toast. Thanks, Barbara. What'll yours be, Brigitte?" Dry toast and black coffee, no doubt.

"Is your fruit *really* fresh?" she demanded.

Barbara rolled her eyes. "Honey, the melon pinched me so hard I'm black-and-blue. Better not take a chance if you're sensitive."

Brigitte set her shoulder — covered today in green broadcloth with black piping — and got ready to do battle. I cut her off before the first "How dare you" rolled to its ugly conclusion.

221

"This isn't the kind of place where the maître d' wilts at your frown and races over to make sure madam is happy. They don't care if you come back or not. In fact, about now they'd be happier if you'd leave. You can check out my fruit when it comes and order some if it tastes right to you."

"I'll just have wheat toast and black coffee," she said icily. "And make sure they don't put any butter on it."

"Right," Barbara said. "Wheat toast, margarine instead of butter. Just kidding, hon," she added as Brigitte started to tear into her again. "You gotta learn to take it if you want to dish it out."

"Did you bring me here to be insulted?" Brigitte demanded when Barbara had left.

"I brought you here to talk. It didn't occur to me that you wouldn't know diner etiquette. We can fight if you want to. Or you can tell me about Jade and Corinne. And your cat. I had a visit from Joel Sirop last night."

She swallowed some coffee and made a face. "They should rinse the pots with vinegar."

"Well, keep it to yourself. They won't pay you a consulting fee for telling them about it. Joel tell you he'd come around hunting Lady Iva?"

She frowned at me over the rim of the coffee cup, then nodded fractionally.

"Why didn't you tell me about the damned cat when you were in my office yesterday?"

Her poise deserted her for a moment; she looked briefly ashamed. "I thought you'd look for Corinne. I didn't think I could persuade you to hunt down my cat. Anyway, Corinne must have taken Iva with her, so I thought if you found her you'd find the cat, too."

"Which one do you really want back?"

She started to bristle again, then suddenly laughed. It took ten years from her face. "You wouldn't ask that if you'd ever lived with a teen-ager. And Corinne's always been a stranger to me. She was eighteen months old when I left for college and I only saw her a week or two at a time on vacations. She used to worship me. When she moved in with me I thought it would be a piece of cake: I'd get her fixed up with the right crowd and the right school, she'd do her best to be like me, and the system would run itself. Instead, she put on a lot of weight, won't listen to me about her eating, slouches around with the kids in the neighborhood when my back is turned, the whole nine yards. Jade's influence. It creeps through every now and then when I'm not thinking."

She looked at my blueberries. I offered them to her and she helped herself to a generous spoon-ful.

"And that was the other thing. Jade. We got together when I was an Alabama cheerleader and he was the biggest hero in town. I thought I'd really caught me a prize, my yes, a big prize. But the first, last, and only thing in a marriage with a football player is football. And him, of course, how many sacks he made, how many yards he allowed, all that boring crap. And if he has to sit out a game, or he gives up a touchdown, or he doesn't get the glory, watch out. Jade was mean. He was mean on the field, he was mean off it. He broke my arm once."

Her voice was level but her hand shook a little as she lifted the coffee cup to her mouth. "I got me a gun and shot him in the leg the next time he came at me. They put it down as a hunting accident in the papers, but he never tried anything on me after that — not physical, I mean. Until his career ended. Then he got real, real ugly. The papers crucified me for abandoning him when his career was over. They never had to live with him."

She was panting with emotion by the time she finished. "And Corinne shared the papers' views?" I asked gently.

She nodded. "We had a bad fight on Sunday. She wanted to go to a sleepover at one of the girls' in the neighborhood. I don't like that girl and I said no. We had a gale-force battle after that. When I got home from work on Monday she'd taken off. First I figured she'd gone to this girl's place. They hadn't seen her, though, and she hadn't shown up at school. So I figured she'd run off to Jade. Now . . . I don't know. I would truly appreciate it if you'd keep looking, though."

Just say no, Vic, I chanted to myself. "I'll need a thousand up front. And more names and addresses of friends, including people in Mobile.

I'll check in with Jade at the hospital. She might have gone to him, you know, and he sent her on someplace else."

"I stopped by there this morning. They said no visitors."

I grinned. "I've got friends in high places." I signaled Barbara for the check. "Speaking of which, how was the Vice President?"

She looked as though she were going to give me one of her stiff rebuttals, but then she curled her lip and drawled, "Just like every other good old boy, honey, just like every other good old boy."

V

Lotty Herschel, an obstetrician associated with Beth Israel, arranged for me to see Jade Pierce. "They tell me he's been difficult. Don't stand next to the bed unless you're wearing a padded jacket."

"You want him, you can have him," the floor head told me. "He's going home tomorrow morning. Frankly, since he won't let anyone near him, they ought to release him right now."

My palms felt sweaty when I pushed open the door to Jade's room. He didn't throw anything when I came in, didn't even turn his head to stare through the restraining rails surrounding the bed. His mountain of flesh poured through them,

225

ebbing away from a rounded summit in the middle. The back of his head, smooth and shiny as a piece of polished jade, reflected the ceiling light into my eyes.

"I don't need any goddamned ministering angels, so get the fuck out of here," he growled to the window.

"That's a relief. My angel act never really got going."

He turned his head at that. His black eyes were mean, narrow slits. If I were a quarterback I'd hand him the ball and head for the showers.

"What are you, the goddamned social worker?"

"Nope. I'm the goddamned detective who found you yesterday before you slipped off to the great huddle in the sky."

"Come on over then, so I can kiss your ass," he spat venomously.

I leaned against the wall and crossed my arms. "I didn't mean to save your life: I tried getting them to send you to the morgue. The meat wagon crew double-crossed me."

The mountain shook and rumbled. It took me a few seconds to realize he was laughing. "You're right, detective: you ain't no angel. So what do you want? True confessions on why I was such a bad boy? The name of the guy who got me the stuff?"

"As long as you're not hurting anyone but yourself I don't care what you do or where you get your shit. I'm here because Brigitte hired me to find Corinne."

His face set in ugly lines again. "Get out."
I didn't move.

"I said get out!" He raised his voice to a bellow.

"Just because I mentioned Brigitte's name?"

"Just because if you're pally with that broad, you're a snake by definition."

"I'm not pally with her. I met her yesterday. She's paying me to find her sister." It took an effort not to yell back at him.

"Corinne's better off without her," he growled, turning the back of his head to me again.

I didn't say anything, just stood there. Five minutes passed. Finally he jeered, without looking at me. "Did the sweet little martyr tell you I broke her arm?"

"She mentioned it, yes."

"She tell you how that happened?"

"Please don't tell me how badly she misunderstood you. I don't want to throw up my breakfast."

At that he swung his gigantic face around toward me again. "Com'ere."

When I didn't move, he sighed and patted the bed rail. "I'm not going to slug you, honest. If we're going to talk, you gotta get close enough for me to see your face."

I went over to the bed and straddled the chair, resting my arms on its back. Jade studied me in silence, then grunted as if to say I'd passed some minimal test.

"I won't tell you Brigitte didn't understand me. Broad had my number from day one. I didn't break her arm, though: that was B. B. Wilder. Old Gunshot. Thought he was my best friend on the club, but it turned out he was Brigitte's. And then, when I come home early from a hunting trip and found her in bed with him, we all got carried away. She loved the excitement of big men fighting. It's what made her a football groupie to begin with down in Alabama."

I tried to imagine ice-cold Brigitte flushed with excitement while the Bears' right tackle and defensive end fought over her. It didn't seem impossible.

"So B. B. broke her arm but I agreed to take the rap. Her little old modeling career was just getting off the ground and she didn't want her good name sullied. And besides that, she kept hoping for a reconciliation with her folks, at least with their wad, and they'd never fork over if she got herself some ugly publicity committing violent adultery. And me, I was just the baddest boy the Bears ever fielded; one more mark didn't make that much difference to me." The jeering note returned to his voice.

"She told me it was when you retired that things deteriorated between you."

"Things deteriorated — what a way to put it. Look, detective what did you say your name was? V. I., that's a hell of a name for a girl. What did your mamma call you?"

"Victoria," I said grudgingly. "And no one calls me Vicki, so don't even think about it." I prefer not to be called a girl, either, much less a broad, but Jade didn't seem like the person to discuss that particular issue with.

"Victoria, huh? Things deteriorated, yeah, like they was a picnic starting out. I was born dumb and I didn't get smarter for making five hundred big ones a year. But I wouldn't hit a broad, even one like Brigitte who could get me going just looking at me. I broke a lot of furniture, though, and that got on her nerves."

I couldn't help laughing. "Yeah, I can see that. It'd bother me, too."

He gave a grudging smile. "See, the trouble is, I grew up poor. I mean, dirt poor. I used to go to the projects here with some of the black guys on the squad, you know, Christmas appearances, shit like that. Those kids live in squalor, but I didn't own a pair of shorts to cover my ass until the county social worker come 'round to see why I wasn't in school."

"So you broke furniture because you grew up without it and didn't know what else to do with it?"

"Don't be a wiseass, Victoria. I'm sure your mamma wouldn't like it."

I made a face — he was right about that.

"You know the LeBlancs, right? Oh, you're a Yankee, Yankees don't know shit if they haven't stepped in it themselves. LeBlanc Gas, they're one of the biggest names on the Gulf Coast. They're a long, *long* way from the Pierces of Florette.

"I muscled my way into college, played football

for Old Bear Bryant, met Brigitte. She liked raw meat, and mine was just about the rawest in the South, so she latched on to me. When she decided to marry me she took me down to Mobile for Christmas. There I was, the Hulk, in Miz Effie's lace and crystal palace. They hated me, knew I was trash, told Brigitte they'd cut her out of everything if she married me. She figured she could sweet-talk her daddy into anything. We got married and it didn't work, not even when I was a national superstar. To them I was still the dirt I used to wipe my ass with."

"So she divorced you to get back in their will?"

He shrugged, a movement that set a tidal wave going down the mountain. "Oh, that had something to do with it, sure, it had something. But I was a wreck and I was hell to live with. Even if she'd been halfway normal to begin with, it would have gone bust, 'cause I didn't know how to live with losing football. I just didn't care about anyone or anything."

"Not even the Daytona," I couldn't help saying.

His black eyes disappeared into tiny dots. "Don't you go lecturing me just when we're starting to get on. I'm not asking you to cry over my sad jock story. I'm just trying to give you a little different look at sweet, beautiful Brigitte."

"Sorry. It's just . . . I'll never do anything to be able to afford a Ferrari Daytona. It pisses me to see someone throw one away."

He snorted. "If I'd known you five years ago I'd of given it to you. Too late now. Anyway,

Brigitte waited too long to jump ship. She was still in negotiations with old man LeBlanc when he and Miz Effie dropped into the Gulf of Mexico with the remains of their little Cessna. Everything that wasn't tied down went to Corinne. Brigitte, being her guardian, gets a chunk for looking after her, but you ask me, if Corinne's gone missing it's the best thing she could do. I'll bet you . . . well, I don't have anything left to bet. I'll hack off my big toe and give it to you if Brigitte's after anything but the money."

He thought for a minute. "No. She probably likes Corinne some. Or would like her if she'd lose thirty pounds, dress like a Mobile debutante and hang around with a crowd of snot-noses. I'll hack off my toe if the money ain't number one in her heart, that's all."

I eyed him steadily, wondering how much of his story to believe. It's why I stay away from domestic crime: everyone has a story, and it wears you out trying to match all the different pieces together. I could check the LeBlancs' will to see if they'd left their fortune the way Jade reported it. Or if they had a fortune at all. Maybe he was making it all up.

"Did Corinne talk to you before she took off on Monday?"

His black eyes darted around the room. "I haven't laid eyes on her in months. She used to come around, but Brigitte got a peace bond on me, I get arrested if I'm within thirty feet of Corinne."

"I believe you, Jade," I said steadily. "I believe you haven't seen her. But did she talk to you? Like on the phone, maybe."

The ugly look returned to his face, then the mountain shook again as he laughed. "You don't miss many signals, do you, Victoria? You oughta run a training camp. Yeah, Corinne calls me Monday morning. 'Why don't you have your cute little ass in school?' I says. 'Even with all your family dough that's the only way to get ahead — they'll ream you six ways from Sunday if you don't get your education so you can check out what all your advisers are up to.' "

He shook his head broodingly. "I know what I'm talking about, believe me. The lawyers and agents and financial advisers, they all made out like hogs at feeding time when I was in the money, but come trouble, it wasn't them, it was me hung out like a slab of pork belly to dry on my own."

"So what did Corinne say to your good advice?" I prompted him, trying not to sound impatient: I could well be the first sober person to listen to him in a decade.

"Oh, she's crying, she can't stand it, why can't she just run home to Mobile? And I tell her 'cause she's underage and rich, the cops will all be looking for her and just haul her butt back to Chicago. And when she keeps talking wilder and wilder I tell her they'll be bound to blame me if something happens to her and does she really need to run away so bad that I go to jail or something. So I thought that calmed her down. 'Think of

232

it like rookie camp,' I told her. 'They put you through the worst shit but if you survive it you own them.' I thought she figured it out and was staying."

He shut his eyes. "I'm tired, detective. I can't tell you nothing else. You go away and detect."

"If she went back to Mobile who would she stay with?"

"Wouldn't nobody down there keep her without calling Brigitte. Too many of them owe their jobs to LeBlanc Gas." He didn't open his eyes.

"And up here?"

He shrugged, a movement like an earthquake that rattled the bed rails. "You might try the neighbors. Seems to me Corinne mentioned a Miz Hellman who had a bit of a soft spot for her." He opened his eyes. "Maybe Corinne'll talk to you. You got a good ear."

"Thanks." I got up. "What about this famous Maltese cat?"

"What about it?"

"It went missing along with Corinne. Think she'd hurt it to get back at Brigitte?"

"How the hell should I know? Those LeBlancs would do anything to anyone. Even Corinne. Now get the fuck out so I can get my beauty rest." He shut his eyes again.

"Yeah, you're beautiful all right, Jade. Why don't you use some of your old connections and get yourself going at something? It's really pathetic seeing you like this."

"You wanna save me along with the Daytona?"

The ugly jeer returned to his voice. "Don't go all do-gooder on me now, Victoria. My daddy died at forty from too much moonshine. They tell me I'm his spitting image. I know where I'm going."

"It's trite, Jade. Lots of people have done it. They'll make a movie about you and little kids will cry over your sad story. But if they make it honest they'll show that you're just plain selfish."

I wanted to slam the door but the hydraulic stop took the impact out of the gesture. "God-damned motherfucking waste," I snapped as I stomped down the corridor.

The floor head heard me. "Jade Pierce? You're right about that."

VI

The Hellmans lived in an apartment above the TV repair shop they ran on Halsted. Mrs. Hellman greeted me with some relief.

"I promised Corinne I wouldn't tell her sister as long as she stayed here instead of trying to hitchhike back to Mobile. But I've been pretty worried. It's just that . . . to Brigitte LeBlanc I don't exist. My daughter Lily is trash that she doesn't want Corinne associated with, so it never even occurred to her that Corinne might be here."

She took me through the back of the shop and

up the stairs to the apartment. "It's only five rooms, but we're glad to have her as long as she wants to stay. I'm more worried about the cat: she doesn't like being cooped up in here. She got out Tuesday night and we had a terrible time hunting her down."

I grinned to myself: So much for the thoroughbred descendants pined for by Joel Sirop.

Mrs. Hellman took me into the living room where they had a sofa bed that Corinne was using. "This here is a detective, Corinne. I think you'd better talk to her."

Corinne was hunched in front of the television, an outsize console model far too large for the tiny room. In her man's white shirt and tattered blue jeans she didn't look at all like her svelte sister. Her complexion was a muddy color that matched her lank, straight hair. She clutched Lady Iva of Cairo close in her arms. Both of them looked at me angrily.

"If you think you can make me go back to that cold-assed bitch, you'd better think again."

Mrs. Hellman tried to protest her language.

"It's okay," I said. "She learned it from Jade. But Jade lost every fight he ever was in with Brigitte, Corinne. Maybe you ought to try a different method."

"Brigitte hated Jade. She hates anyone who doesn't do stuff just the way she wants it. So if you're working for Brigitte you don't know shit about anything."

I responded to the first part of her comments.

235

"Is that why you took the cat? So you could keep her from having purebred kittens like Brigitte wants her to?"

A ghost of a smile twitched around her unhappy mouth. All she said was "They wouldn't let me bring my dogs or my horse up north. Iva's kind of a snoot but she's better than nothing."

"Jade thinks Brigitte's jealous because you got the LeBlanc fortune and she didn't."

She made a disgusted noise. "Jade worries too much about all that shit. Yeah, Daddy left me a big fat wad. But the company went to Daddy's cousin Miles. You can't inherit LeBlanc Gas if you're a girl and Brigitte knew that, same as me. I mean, they told both of us growing up so we wouldn't have our hearts set on it. The money they left me, Brigitte makes that amount every year in her business. She doesn't care about the money."

"And you? Does it bother you that the company went to your cousin?"

She gave a long ugly sniff — no doubt another of Jade's expressions. "Who wants a company that doesn't do anything but pollute the Gulf and ream the people who work for them?"

I considered that. At fourteen it was probably genuine bravado. "So what do you care about?"

She looked at me with sulky dark eyes. For a minute I thought she was going to tell me to mind my own goddamned business and go to hell, but she suddenly blurted out, "It's my horse. They left the house to Miles along with my horse.

236

They didn't think about it, just said the house and all the stuff that wasn't left special to someone else went to him and they didn't even think to leave me my own horse."

The last sentence came out as a wail and her angry young face dissolved into sobs. I didn't think she'd welcome a friendly pat on the shoulder. I just let the tears run their course. She finally wiped her nose on a frayed cuff and shot me a fierce look to see if I cared.

"If I could persuade Brigitte to buy your horse from Miles and stable him up here, would you be willing to go back to her until you're of age?"

"You never would. Nobody ever could make that bitch change her mind."

"But if I could?"

Her lower lip was hanging out. "Maybe. If I could have my horse and go to school with Lily instead of fucking St. Scholastica."

"I'll do my best." I got to my feet. "In return maybe you could work on Jade to stop drugging himself to death. It isn't romantic, you know: it's horrible, painful, about the ugliest thing in the world."

She only glowered at me. It's hard work being an angel. No one takes at all kindly to it.

VII

Brigitte was furious. Her cheeks flamed with natural color and her cobalt eyes glittered. I couldn't help wondering if this was how she looked when Jade and B. B. Wilder were fighting over her.

"So he knew all along where she was! I ought to have him sent over for that. Can't I charge him with contributing to her delinquency?"

"Not if you're planning on using me as a witness you can't," I snapped.

She ignored me. "And her, too. Taking Lady Iva off like that. Mating her with some alley cat."

As if on cue, Casper of Valletta squawked loudly and started clawing the deep silver plush covering Brigitte's living room floor. Joel Sirop picked up the tom and spoke soothingly to him.

"It is bad, Brigitte, very bad. Maybe you should let the girl go back to Mobile if she wants to so badly. After three days, you know, it's too late to give Lady Iva a shot. And Corinne is so wild, so uncontrollable — what would stop her the next time Lady Iva comes into season?"

Brigitte's nostrils flared. "I should send her to reform school. Show her what discipline is really like."

"Why in hell do you even want custody over

Corinne if all you can think about is revenge?"
I interrupted.

She stopped swirling around her living room
and turned to frown at me. "Why, I love her,
of course. She is my sister, you know."

"Concentrate on that. Keep saying it to yourself.
She's not a cat that you can breed and mold to
suit your fancy."

"I just want her to be happy when she's older.
She won't be if she can't learn to control herself.
Look at what happened when she started hanging
around trash like that Lily Hellman. She would
never have let Lady Iva breed with an alley cat
if she hadn't made that kind of friend."

I ground my teeth. "Just because Lily lives
in five rooms over a store doesn't make her trash.
Look, Brigitte. You wanted to lead your own
life. I expect your parents tried keeping you on
a short leash. Hell, maybe they even threatened
you with reform school. So you started fucking
every hulk you could get your hands on. Are
you so angry about that that you have to treat
Corinne the same way?"

She gaped at me. Her jaw worked but she
couldn't find any words. Finally she went over
to a burled oak cabinet that concealed a bar. She
pulled out a chilled bottle of Sancerre and poured
herself a glass. When she'd gulped it down she
sat at her desk.

"Is it that obvious? Why I went after Jade and
B. B. and all those boys?"

I hunched a shoulder. "It was just a guess,

Brigitte. A guess based on what I've learned about you and your sister and Jade the last two days. He's not such an awful guy, you know, but he clearly was an awful guy for you. And Corinne's lonely and miserable and needs someone to love her. She figures her horse for the job."

"And me?" Her cobalt eyes glittered again. "What do I need? The embraces of my cat?"

"To shed some of those porcupine quills so someone can love you, too. You could've offered me a glass of wine, for example."

She started an ugly retort, then went over to the liquor cabinet and got out a glass for me. "So I bring Flitcraft up to Chicago and stable her. I put Corinne into the filthy public high school. And then we'll all live happily ever after."

"She might graduate." I swallowed some of the wine. It was cold and crisp and eased some of the tension the LeBlancs and Pierces were putting into my throat. "And in another year she won't run away to Lily's, but she'll go off to Mobile or hit the streets. Now's your chance."

"Oh, all right," she snapped. "You're some kind of saint, I know, who never said a bad word to anyone. You can tell Corinne I'll cut a deal with her. But if it goes wrong you can be the one to stay up at night worrying about her."

I rubbed my head. "Send her back to Mobile, Brigitte. There must be a grandmother or aunt or nanny or someone who really cares about her. With your attitude, life with Corinne is just going to be a bomb waiting for the fuse to blow."

"You can say that again, detective." It was Jade, his bulk filling the double doors to the living room.

Behind him we could hear the housekeeper without being able to see her. "I tried to keep him out, Brigitte, but Corinne let him in. You want me to call the cops, get them to exercise that peace bond?"

"I have a right to ask whoever I want into my own house," came Corinne's muffled shriek.

Squawking and yowling, Casper broke from Joel Sirop's hold. He hurtled himself at the doorway and stuffed his body through the gap between Jade's feet. On the other side of the barricade we could hear Lady Iva's answering yodel and a scream from Corinne — presumably she'd been clawed.

"Why don't you move, Jade, so we can see the action?" I suggested.

He lumbered into the living room and perched his bulk on the edge of a pale gray sofa. Corinne stumbled in behind him and sat next to him. Her muddy skin and lank hair looked worse against the sleek modern lines of Brigitte's furniture than they had in Mrs. Hellman's crowded sitting room.

Brigitte watched the blood drip from Corinne's right hand to the rug and jerked her head at the housekeeper hovering in the doorway. "Can you clean that up for me, Grace?"

When the housekeeper left, she turned to her

sister. "Next time you're that angry at me take it out on me, not the cat. Did you really have to let her breed in a back alley?"

"It's all one to Iva," Corinne muttered sulkily. "Just as long as she's getting some she don't care who's giving it to her. Just like you."

Brigitte marched to the couch. Jade caught her hand as she was preparing to smack Corinne.

"Now look here, Brigitte," he said. "You two girls don't belong together. You know that as well as I do. Maybe you think you owe it to your public image to be a mamma to Corinne, but you're not the mamma type. Never have been. Why should you try now?"

Brigitte glared at him. "And you're Mister Wonderful who can sit in judgment on everyone else?"

He shook his massive jade dome. "Nope. I won't claim that. But maybe Corinne here would like to come live with me." He held up a massive palm as Brigitte started to protest. "Not in Uptown. I can get me a place close to here. Corinne can have her horse and see you when you feel calm enough. And when your pure little old cat has her half-breed kittens they can come live with us."

"On Corinne's money," Brigitte spat.

Jade nodded. "She'd have to put up the stake. But I know some guys who'd back me to get started in somethin'. Commodities, somethin' like that."

"You'd be drunk or doped up all the time.

And then you'd rape her —" She broke off as he did his ugly-black-slit number with his eyes.

"You'd better not say anything else, Brigitte LeBlanc. Damned well better not say anything. You want me to get up in the congregation and yell that I never touched a piece of ass that shoved itself in my nose, I ain't going to. But you know better'n anyone that I never in my life laid hands on a girl to hurt her. As for the rest . . ." His eyes returned to normal and he put a redwood branch around Corinne's shoulders. "First time I'm drunk or shooting somethin' Corinne comes right back here. We can try it for six months, Brigitte. Just a trial. Rookie camp, you know how it goes."

The football analogy brought her own mean look to Brigitte's face. Before she could say anything Joel bleated in the background, "It sounds like a good idea to me, Brigitte. Really. You ought to give it a try. Lady Iva's nerves will never be stable with the fighting that goes on around her when Corinne is here."

"No one asked you," Brigitte snapped.

"And no one asked me, either," Corinne said. "If you don't agree, I — I'm going to take Lady Iva and run away to New York. And send you pictures of her with litter after litter of alley cats."

The threat, uttered with all the venom she could muster, made me choke with laughter. I swallowed some Sancerre to try to control myself, but I couldn't stop laughing. Jade's mountain rumbled and shook as he joined in. Joel gasped

243

in horror. Only the two LeBlanc women remained unmoved, glaring at each other.

"What I ought to do, I ought to send you to reform school, Corinne Alton LeBlanc."

"What you ought to do is cool out," I advised, putting my glass down on a chrome table. "It's a good offer. Take it. If you don't, she'll only run away."

Brigitte tightened her mouth in a narrow line. "I didn't hire you to have you turn on me, you know."

"Yeah, well, you hired me. You didn't buy me. My job is to help you resolve a difficult problem. And this looks like the best solution you're going to be offered."

"Oh, very well," she snapped pettishly, pouring herself another drink. "For six months. And if her grades start slipping, or I hear she's drinking or doping or anything like that, she comes back here."

I got up to go. Corinne followed me to the door.

"I'm sorry I was rude to you over at Lily's," she muttered shyly. "When the kittens are born you can have the one you like best."

I gulped and tried to smile. "That's very generous of you, Corinne. But I don't think my dog would take too well to a kitten."

"Don't you like cats?" The big brown eyes stared at me poignantly. "Really, cats and dogs get along very well unless their owners expect them not to."

"Like LeBlancs and Pierces, huh?"

She bit her lip and turned her head, then said in a startled voice, "You're teasing me, aren't you?"

"Just teasing you, Corinne. You take it easy. Things are going to work out for you. And if they don't, give me a call before you do anything too rash, okay?"

"And you will take a kitten?"

Just say no, Vic, just say no, I chanted to myself. "Let me think about it. I've got to run now." I fled the house before she could break my resolve any further.

Settled Score

I

"IT'S SUCH A difficult concept to deal with. I just don't like to use that word." Paul Servino turned to me, his mobile mouth pursed consideringly. "I put it to you, Victoria: you're a lawyer. Would you not agree?"

"I agree that the law defines responsibility differently than we do when we're talking about social or moral relations," I said carefully. "No state's attorney is going to try to get Mrs. Hampton arrested, but does that —"

"You see," Servino interrupted. "That's just my point."

"But it's not mine," Lotty said fiercely, her thick dark brows forming a forbidding line across her forehead. "And if you had seen Claudia with her guts torn out by lye, perhaps you would think a little differently."

The table was silenced for a moment: we were surprised by the violent edge to Lotty's anger. Penelope Herschel shook her head slightly at Servino.

He caught her eye and nodded. "Sorry, Lotty.

I didn't mean to upset you so much."

Lotty forced herself to smile. "Paul, you think you develop a veneer after thirty years as a doctor. You think you see people in all their pain and that your professionalism protects you from too much feeling. But that girl was fifteen. She had her life in front of her. She didn't want to have a baby. And her mother wanted her to. Not for religious reasons, even — she's English with all their contempt for Catholicism. But because she hoped to continue to control her daughter's life. Claudia felt overwhelmed by her mother's pressure and swallowed a jar of oven cleaner. Now don't tell me the mother is not responsible. I do not give one damn if no court would try her: to me, she caused her daughter's death as surely as if she had poured the poison into her."

Servino ignored another slight headshake from Lotty's niece. "It is a tragedy. But a tragedy for the mother, too. You don't think she meant her daughter to kill herself, do you, Lotty?"

Lotty gave a tense smile. "What goes on in the unconscious is surely your department, Paul. But perhaps that was Mrs. Hampton's wish. Of course, if she didn't *intend* for Claudia to die, the courts would find her responsibility diminished. Am I not right, Vic?"

I moved uneasily in my chair. I didn't want to referee this argument: it had all the earmarks of the kind of domestic fight where both contestants attack the police. Besides, while the rest of the dinner party was interested in the case

247

and sympathetic to Lotty's feelings, none of them cared about the question of legal versus moral responsibility.

The dinner was in honor of Lotty Herschel's niece Penelope, making one of her periodic scouting forays into Chicago's fashion scene. Her father — Lotty's only brother — owned a chain of high-priced women's dress shops in Montreal, Quebec, and Toronto. He was thinking of making Chicago his U.S. beachhead, and Penelope was out looking at locations as well as previewing the Chicago designers' spring ideas.

Lotty usually gave a dinner for Penelope when she was in town. Servino was always invited. An analyst friend of Lotty's, he and Penelope had met on one of her first buying trips to Chicago. Since then, they'd seen as much of each other as two busy professionals half a continent apart could manage. Although their affair now had five years of history to it, Penelope continued to stay with Lotty when she was in town.

The rest of the small party included Max Loewenthal, the executive director of Beth Israel, where Lotty treated perinatal patients, and Chaim Lemke, a clarinetist with the Aeolus Woodwind Quintet. A slight, melancholy man, he had met Lotty and Max in London, where they'd all been refugees. Chaim's wife, Greta, who played harpsichord and piano for an early music group, didn't come along. Lotty said not to invite her because she was seeing Paul professionally, but anyway, since she was currently living with Aeolus oboist

248

Rudolph Strayarn, she probably wouldn't have accepted.

We were eating at my apartment. Lotty had called earlier in the day, rattled by the young girl's death and needing help putting the evening together. She was so clearly beside herself that I'd felt compelled to offer my own place. With cheese and fruit after dinner Lotty had begun discussing the case with the whole group, chiefly expressing her outrage with a legal system that let Mrs. Hampton off without so much as a warning.

For some reason Servino continued to argue the point despite Penelope's warning frowns. Perhaps the fact that we were on our third bottle of Barolo explained the lapse from Paul's usual sensitive courtesy.

"Mrs. Hampton did not point a gun at the girl's head and force her to become pregnant," he said. "The daughter was responsible, too, if you want to use that word. And the boy — the father, whoever that was."

Lotty, normally abstemious, had drunk her share of the wine. Her black eyes glittered and her Viennese accent became pronounced.

"I know the argument, believe you me, Paul: it's the old 'who pulled the trigger?' — the person who fired the gun, the person who manufactured it, the person who created the situation, the parents who created the shooter. To me, that is Scholastic hairsplitting — you know, all that crap they used to teach us a thousand years ago in Europe.

Who is the ultimate cause, the immediate cause, the sufficient cause, and on and on.

"It's dry theory, not life. It takes people off the hook for their own actions. You can quote Heinz Kohut and the rest of the self-psychologists to me all night, but you will never convince me that people are unable to make conscious choices for their actions or that parents are not responsible for how they treat their children. It's the same thing as saying the Nazis were not responsible for how they treated Europe."

Penelope gave a strained smile. She loved both Lotty and Servino and didn't want either of them to make fools of themselves. Max, on the other hand, watched Lotty affectionately — he liked to see her passionate. Chaim was staring into space, his lips moving. I assumed he was reading a score in his head.

"I would say that," Servino snapped, his own Italian accent strong. "And don't look at me as though I were Joseph Goebbels. Chaim and I are ten years younger than you and Max, but we share your story in great extent. I do not condone or excuse the horrors our families suffered, or our own dispossession. But I can look at Himmler, or Mussolini, or even Hitler and say, they behaved in such and such a way because of weaknesses accentuated in them by history, by their parents, by their culture. You could as easily say the French were responsible, the French because their need for — for — *rappresaglia* — what am I trying to say, Victoria?"

"Reprisal," I supplied.

"Now you see, Lotty, now I, too, am angry: I forget my English. . . . But if they and the English had not stretched Germany with reparations, the situation might have been different. So how can you claim responsibility — for one person, or one nation? You just have to do the best you can with what is going on around you."

Lotty's face was set. "Yes, Paul. I know what you are saying. Yes, the French created a situation. And the English wished to accommodate Hitler. And the Americans would not take in the Jews. All these things are true. But the Germans chose, nonetheless. They could have acted differently. I will not take them off the hook just because other people should have acted differently."

I took her hand and squeezed it. "At the risk of being the Neville Chamberlain in the case, could I suggest some appeasement? Chaim brought his clarinet and Max his violin. Paul, if you'll play the piano, Penelope and I will sing."

Chaim smiled, relaxing the sadness in his thin face. He loved making music, whether with friends or professionals. "Gladly, Vic. But only a few songs. It's late and we go to California for a two-week tour tomorrow."

The atmosphere lightened. We went into the living room, where Chaim flipped through my music, pulling out Wolf's *Spanisches Liederbuch*.

251

In the end, he and Max stayed with Lotty, playing and talking until three in the morning, long after Servino and Penelope's departure.

II

The detective business is not as much fun in January as at other times of the year. I spent the next two days forcing my little Chevy through unplowed side streets trying to find a missing witness who was the key to an eighteen-million-dollar fraud case. I finally succeeded Tuesday evening a little before five. By the time I'd convinced the terrified woman, who was hiding with a niece at Sixty-seventh and Honore, that no one would shoot her if she testified, gotten her to the state's attorney, and seen her safely home again, it was close to ten o'clock.

I fumbled with the outer locks on the apartment building with my mind fixed on a hot bath, lots of whiskey, and a toasted cheese sandwich. When the ground-floor door opened and Mr. Contreras popped out to meet me, I ground my teeth. He's a retired machinist with more energy than Navratilova. I didn't have the stamina to deal with him tonight.

I mumbled a greeting and headed for the stairs.

"There you are, doll." The relief in his voice was marked. I stopped wearily. Some crisis with the dog. Something involving lugging a sixty-pound retriever to the vet through snow-packed streets.

"I thought I ought to let her in, you know. I told her there was no saying when you'd be home, sometimes you're gone all night on a case" — a delicate reference to my love life — "but she was all set she had to wait and she'd'a been sitting on the stairs all this time. She won't say what the problem is, but you'd probably better talk to her. You wanna come in here or should I send her up in a few minutes?"

Not the dog, then. "Uh, who is it?"

"Aren't I trying to tell you? That beautiful girl. You know, the doc's niece."

"Penelope?" I echoed foolishly.

She came out into the hall just then, ducking under the old man's gesticulating arms. "Vic! Thank God you're back. I've got to talk to you. Before the police do anything stupid."

She was huddled in an ankle-length silver fur. Ordinarily elegant, with exquisite makeup and jewelry and the most modern of hairstyles, she didn't much resemble her aunt. But shock had stripped the sophistication from her, making her dark eyes the focus of her face; she looked so much like Lotty that I went to her instinctively.

"Come on up with me and tell me what's wrong." I put an arm around her.

Mr. Contreras closed his door in disappointment as we disappeared up the stairs. Penelope waited until we were inside my place before saying anything else. I slung my jacket and down vest on the hooks in the hallway and went into the living room to undo my heavy walking shoes.

Penelope kept her fur wrapped around her. Her high-heeled kid boots were not meant for street wear: they were rimmed with salt stains. She shivered slightly despite the coat.

"Have — have you heard anything?"

I shook my head, rubbing my right foot, stiff from driving all day.

"It's Paul. He's dead."

"But — he's not that old. And I thought he was very healthy." Because of his sedentary job, Servino always ran the two miles from his Loop office to his apartment in the evening.

Penelope gave a little gulp of hysterical laughter. "Oh, he was very fit. But not healthy enough to overcome a blow to the head."

"Could you tell the story from the beginning instead of letting it out in little dramatic bursts?"

As I'd hoped, my rudeness got her angry enough to overcome her incipient hysteria. After flashing me a Lotty-like look of royal disdain, she told me what she knew.

Paul's office was in a building where a number of analysts had their practices. A sign posted on his door this morning baldly announced that he had canceled all his day's appointments because of a personal emergency. When a janitor went in at three to change a lightbulb, he'd found the doctor dead on the floor of his consulting room.

Colleagues agreed they'd seen Servino arrive around a quarter of eight, as he usually did.

They'd seen the notice and assumed he'd left when everyone else was tied up with appointments. No one thought any more about it.

Penelope had learned of her lover's death from the police, who picked her up as she was leaving a realtor's office where she'd been discussing shop leases. Two of the doctors with offices near Servino's had mentioned seeing a dark-haired woman in a long fur coat near his consulting room.

Penelope's dark eyes were drenched with tears. "It's not enough that Paul is dead, that I learn of it in such an unspeakable way. They think I killed him — because I have dark hair and wear a fur coat. They don't know what killed him — some dreary blunt instrument — it sounds stupid and banal, like an old Agatha Christie. They've pawed through my luggage looking for it."

They'd questioned her for three hours while they searched and finally, reluctantly, let her go, with a warning not to leave Chicago. She'd called Lotty at the clinic and then come over to find me.

I went into the dining room for some whiskey. She shook her head at the bottle. I poured myself an extra slug to make up for missing my bath. "And?"

"And I want you to find who killed him. The police aren't looking very hard because they think it's me."

"Do they have a reason for this?"

She blushed unexpectedly. "They think he was

refusing to marry me."

"Not much motive in these times, one would have thought. And you with a successful career to boot. Was he refusing?"

"No. It was the other way around, actually. I felt — felt unsettled about what I wanted to do — come to Chicago to stay, you know. I have — friends in Montreal, too, you know. And I've always thought marriage meant monogamy."

"I see." My focus on the affair between Penelope and Paul shifted slightly. "You didn't kill him, did you — perhaps for some other reason?"

She forced a smile. "Because he didn't agree with Lotty about responsibility? No. And for no other reason. Are you going to ask Lotty if she killed him?"

"Lotty would have mangled him Sunday night with whatever was lying on the dining room table — she wouldn't wait to sneak into his office with a club." I eyed her thoughtfully. "Just out of vulgar curiosity, what were you doing around eight this morning?"

Her black eyes scorched me. "I came to you because I thought you would be sympathetic. Not to get the same damned questions I had all afternoon from the police!"

"And what were you doing at eight this morning?"

She swept across the room to the door, then thought better of it and affected to study a Nell Blaine poster on the nearby wall. With her back to me she said curtly, "I was having a second cup of coffee. And no, there are no witnesses. As you know, by that time of day Lotty is long gone. Perhaps someone saw me leave the building at eight-thirty — I asked the detectives to question the neighbors, but they didn't seem much interested in doing so."

"Don't sell them short. If you're not under arrest, they're still asking questions."

"But you could ask questions to clear me. They're just trying to implicate me."

I pinched the bridge of my nose, trying to ease the dull ache behind my eyes. "You do realize the likeliest person to have killed him is an angry patient, don't you? Despite your fears the police have probably been questioning them all day."

Nothing I said could convince her that she wasn't in imminent danger of a speedy trial before a kangaroo court, with execution probable by the next morning. She stayed until past midnight, alternating pleas to hide her with commands to join the police in hunting down Paul's killer. She wouldn't call Lotty to tell her she was with me because she was afraid Lotty's home phone had been tapped.

"Look, Penelope," I finally said, exasperated. "I can't hide you. If the police really suspect you, you were tailed here. Even if I could figure out a way to smuggle you out and conceal you someplace, I wouldn't do it — I'd lose my license on obstruction charges and I'd deserve to."

I tried explaining how hard it was to get a court order for a wiretap and finally gave up.

I was about ready to start screaming with frustration when Lotty herself called, devastated by Servino's death and worried about Penelope. The police had been by with a search warrant and had taken away an array of household objects, including her umbrella. Such an intrusion would normally have made her spitting mad, but she was too upset to give it her full emotional attention. I turned the phone over to Penelope. Whatever Lotty said to her stained her cheeks red, but did make her agree to let me drive her home.

When I got back to my place, exhausted enough to sleep round the clock, I found John McGonnigal waiting for me in a blue-and-white outside my building. He came up the walk behind me and opened the door with a flourish.

I looked at him sourly. "Thanks, Sergeant. It's been a long day — I'm glad to have a doorman at the end of it."

"It's kind of cold down here for talking, Vic. How about inviting me up for coffee?"

"Because I want to go to bed. If you've got something you want to say, or even ask, spit it out down here."

I was just ventilating and I knew it — if a police sergeant wanted to talk to me at one in the morning, we'd talk. Mr. Contreras's coming out in a magenta bathrobe to see what the trouble was merely speeded my decision to cooperate.

While I assembled cheese sandwiches, McGonnigal asked me what I'd learned from Penelope.

"She didn't throw her arms around me and howl, 'Vic, I killed him, you've got to help me.' " I put the sandwiches in a skillet with a little olive oil. "What've you guys got on her?"

The receptionist and two of the other analysts who'd been in the hall had seen a small, dark-haired woman hovering in the alcove near Servino's office around twenty of eight. Neither of them had paid too much attention to her; when they saw Penelope they agreed it might have been she, but they couldn't be certain. If they'd made a positive I.D., she'd already have been arrested, even though they couldn't find the weapon.

"They had a shouting match at the Filigree last night. The maître d' was quite upset. Servino was a regular and he didn't want to offend him, but a number of diners complained. The Herschel girl" — McGonnigal eyed me warily — "woman, I mean, stormed off on her own and spent the night with her aunt. One of the neighbors saw her leave around seven the next morning, not at eight-thirty as she says."

I didn't like the sound of that. I asked him about the cause of death.

"Someone gave him a good crack across the side of the neck, close enough to the back to fracture a cervical vertebra and sever one of the main arteries. It would have killed him pretty fast. And as you know, Servino wasn't very tall — the Herschel woman could easily have done it."

"With what?" I demanded.

That was the stumbling block. It could have been anything from a baseball bat to a steel pipe. The forensic pathologist who'd looked at the body favored the latter, since the skin had been broken in places. They'd taken away anything in Lotty's apartment and Penelope's luggage that might have done the job and were having them examined for traces of blood and skin.

I snorted. "If you searched Lotty's place, you must have come away with quite an earful."

McGonnigal grimaced. "She spoke her mind, yes. . . . Any ideas? On what the weapon might have been?"

I shook my head, too nauseated by the thought of Paul's death to muster intellectual curiosity over the choice of weapon. When McGonnigal left around two-thirty, I lay in bed staring at the dark, unable to sleep despite my fatigue. I didn't know Penelope all that well. Just because she was Lotty's niece didn't mean she was incapable of murder. To be honest, I hadn't been totally convinced by her histrionics tonight. Who but a lover could get close enough to you to snap your neck? I thrashed around for hours, finally dropping into an uneasy sleep around six.

Lotty woke me at eight to implore me to look for Servino's killer; the police had been back at seven-thirty to ask Penelope why she'd forgotten to mention she'd been at Paul's apartment early yesterday morning.

"Why was she there?" I asked reasonably.

"She says she wanted to patch things up after their quarrel, but he'd already left for the office. When the police started questioning her, she was too frightened to tell the truth. Vic, I'm terrified they're going to arrest her."

I mumbled something. It looked to me like they had a pretty good case, but I valued my life too much to say that to Lotty. Even so the conversation deteriorated rapidly.

"I come out in any wind or weather to patch you up. With never a word of complaint." That wasn't exactly true, but I let it pass. "Now, when I beg you for help you turn a deaf ear to me. I shall remember this, Victoria."

Giant black spots formed and re-formed in front of my tired eyes. "Great, Lotty."

Her receiver banged in my ear.

III

I spent the day doggedly going about my own business, turning on WBBM whenever I was in the car to see if any news had come in about Penelope's arrest. Despite all the damaging eye-witness reports, the state's attorney apparently didn't want to move without a weapon.

I trudged up the stairs to my apartment a little after six, my mind fixed on a bath and a rare steak followed immediately by bed. When I got to the top landing, I ground my teeth in futile rage: a fur-coated woman was sitting in front of the door.

When she got to her feet I realized it wasn't Penelope but Greta Schipauer, Chaim Lemke's wife. The dark hallway had swallowed the gold of her hair.

"Vic! Thank God you've come back. I've been here since four and I have a concert in two hours."

I fumbled with the three stiff locks. "I have an office downtown just so that people won't have to sit on the floor outside my home," I said pointedly.

"You do? Oh — it never occurred to me you didn't just work out of your living room."

She followed me in and headed over to the piano, where she picked out a series of fifths. "You really should get this tuned, Vic."

"Is that why you've been here for two hours? To tell me to tune my piano?" I slung my coat onto a hook in the entryway and sat on the couch to pull off my boots.

"No, no." She sat down hastily. "It's because of Paul, of course. I spoke to Lotty today and she says you're refusing to stir yourself to look for his murderer. Why, Vic? We all need you very badly. You can't let us down now. The police were questioning me for two hours yesterday. It utterly destroyed my concentration. I couldn't practice at all; I know the recital tonight will be a disaster. Even Chaim has been affected, and he's out on the West Coast."

I was too tired to be tactful. "How do you

know that? I thought you've been living with Rudolph Strayarn."

She looked surprised. "What does that have to do with anything? I'm still interested in Chaim's music. And it's been terrible. Rudolph called this morning to tell me and I bought an L.A. paper downtown."

She thrust a copy of the *L.A. Times* in front of me. It was folded back to the arts section where the headline read AEOLUS JUST BLOWING IN THE WIND. They'd used Chaim's publicity photo as an inset.

I scanned the story:

Chaim Lemke, one of the nation's most brilliant musicians, must have left his own clarinet at home because he played as though he'd never handled the instrument before. Aeolus manager Claudia Laurents says the group was shattered by the murder of a friend in Chicago; the rest of the quintet managed to pull a semblance of a concert together, but the performance by America's top woodwind group was definitely off-key.

I handed the paper back to Greta. "Chaim's reputation is too strong — an adverse review like this will be forgotten in two days. Don't worry about it — go to your concert and concentrate on your own music."

Her slightly protuberant blue eyes stared at me. "I didn't believe Lotty when she told me. I don't

263

believe I'm hearing you now. Vic, we need you. If it's money, name your figure. But put aside this coldness and help us out."

"Greta, the only thing standing between the police and an arrest right now is the fact that they can't find the murder weapon. I'm not going to join them in hunting for it. The best we can hope for is that they never find it. After a while they'll let Penelope go back to Montreal and your lives will return to normal."

"No, no. You're thinking Penelope committed this crime. Never, Vic, never. I've known her since she was a small child — you know I grew up in Montreal — it's where I met Chaim. Believe me, I know her. She never committed this murder."

She was still arguing stubbornly when she looked at her watch, gave a gasp, and said she had to run or she'd never make the auditorium in time. When I'd locked the door thankfully behind her, I saw she'd dropped her paper. I looked at Chaim's delicate face again, sad as though he knew he would have to portray mourning in it when the picture was taken.

IV

When the police charged Penelope late on Thursday, I finally succumbed to the alternating pleas and commands of her friends to undertake an independent investigation. The police had never found a weapon, but the state's attorney was willing to believe it was in the Chicago River.

I got the names of the two analysts and the receptionist who'd seen Servino's presumed assailant outside his office on Tuesday. They were too used to seeing nervous people shrinking behind partitions to pay much attention to this woman; neither of them was prepared to make a positive I.D. in court. That would be a help to Freeman Carter, handling Penelope's defense, but it couldn't undo the damage caused by Penelope's original lies about her Tuesday morning activities.

She was free on $100,000 bond. Swinging between depression and a kind of manic rage, she didn't tell a very convincing story. Still, I was committed to proving her innocence; I did my best with her and trusted that Freeman was too savvy to let her take the witness stand herself.

I got a list of Paul's patients, both current and former, from a contact at the police. Lotty, Max, and Greta were bankrolling both Freeman and me to any amount we needed, so I hired the Streeter brothers to check up on patient alibis.

I talked to all of them myself, trying to ferret out any sense of betrayal or rage urgent enough to drive one of them to murder. With a sense of shameful voyeurism, I even read Paul's notes. I was fascinated by his descriptions of Greta. Her total self-absorption had always rubbed me the wrong way. Paul, while much more empathic, seemed to be debating whether she would ever be willing to participate in her own analysis.

"How did Paul feel about your affair with Rudolph?" I asked Greta one afternoon when she had made one of her frequent stops for a progress report.

"Oh, you know Paul: he had a great respect for the artistic temperament and what someone like me needs to survive in my work. Besides, he convinced me that I didn't have to feel responsible — you know, that my own parents' cold narcissism makes me crave affection. And Rudolph is a much more relaxing lover than poor Chaim, with his endless parade of guilt and self-doubt."

I felt my skin crawl slightly. I didn't know any psychoanalytic theory, but I couldn't believe Paul meant his remarks on personal responsibility to be understood in quite this way.

Meanwhile, Chaim's performance had deteriorated so badly that he decided to cancel the rest of the West Coast tour. The Aeolus found a backup, the second clarinet in the Chicago Symphony, but their concert series got mediocre reviews in Seattle and played to half-full houses in Vancouver and Denver.

Greta rushed to the airport to meet Chaim on his return. I knew because she'd notified the local stations and I found her staring at me on the ten o'clock news, escorting Chaim from the baggage area with a maternal solicitude. She shed the cameras before decamping for Rudolph's —

she called me from there at ten-thirty to make sure I'd seen her wifely heroics.

I wasn't convinced by Greta's claims that Chaim would recover faster on his own than with some-one to look after him. The next day I went to check on him for myself. Even though it was past noon, he was still in his dressing gown. I apologized for waking him, but he gave a sweet sad smile and assured me he'd been up for some time. When I followed him into the living room, a light, bright room facing Lake Michigan, I was shocked to see how ill he looked. His black eyes had become giant holes in his thin face; he ap-parently hadn't slept in some time.

"Chaim, have you seen a doctor?"

"No, no." He shook his head. "It's just that since Paul's death I can't make music. I try to play and I sound worse than I did at age five. I don't know which is harder — losing Paul or having them arrest Penelope. Such a sweet girl. I've known her since she was born. I'm sure she didn't kill him. Lotty says you're investigating?"

"Yeah, but not too successfully. The evidence against her is very sketchy — it's hard for me to believe they'll get a conviction. If the weapon turns up . . ." I let the sentence trail away. If the weapon turned up, it might provide the final caisson to shore up the state's platform. I was trying hard to work for Penelope, but I kept having disloyal thoughts.

"You yourself are hunting for the weapon? Do you know what it is?"

I shook my head. "The state's attorney gave me photos of the wound. I had enlargements made and I took them to a pathologist I know to see if he could come up with any ideas. Some kind of pipe or stick with spikes or something on it — like a caveman's club — I'm so out of ideas I even went to the Field Museum to see if they could suggest something, or were missing some old-fashioned lethal weapon."

Chaim had turned green. I felt contrite — he had such an active imagination I should have watched my tongue. Now he'd have nightmares for weeks and would wait even longer to get his music back. I changed the subject and persuaded him to let me cook some lunch from the meager supplies in the kitchen. He didn't eat much, but he was looking less feverish when I left.

V

Chaim's cleaning woman found him close to death the morning Penelope's trial started. Lotty, Max, and I had spent the day in court with Lotty's brother Hugo and his wife. We didn't get any of Greta's frantic messages until Lotty checked in at the clinic before dinner.

Chaim had gone to an Aeolus rehearsal the night before, his first appearance at the group in some weeks. He had bought a new clarinet, thinking perhaps the problem lay with the old one. Wind instruments aren't like violins — they deteriorate over time, and an active clarinetist has to buy a new one every ten years or so. Despite the new instrument, a Buffet he had flown to Toronto to buy, the rehearsal had gone badly.

He left early, going home to turn on the gas in the kitchen stove. He left a note which simply said: "I have destroyed my music." The cleaning woman knew enough about their life to call Greta at Rudolph's apartment. Since Greta had been at the rehearsal — waiting for the oboist — she knew how badly Chaim had played.

"I'm not surprised," she told Lotty over the phone. "His music was all he had after I left him. With both of us gone from his life he must have felt he had no reason to live. Thank God I learned so much from Paul about why we aren't responsible for our actions, or I would feel terribly guilty now."

Lotty called the attending physician at the University of Chicago Hospital and came away with the news that Chaim would live, but he'd ruined his lungs — he could hardly talk and would probably never be able to play again.

She reported her conversation with Greta with a blazing rage while we waited for dinner in her brother's suite at the Drake. "The wrong person's career is over," she said furiously. "It's the one thing I could never understand about Chaim — why he felt so much passion for that self-centered whore!"

Marcella Herschel gave a grimace of distaste

— she didn't deal well with Lotty at the best of times and could barely tolerate her when she was angry. Penelope, pale and drawn from the day's ordeal, summoned a smile and patted Lotty's shoulder soothingly while Max tried to persuade her to drink a little wine.

Freeman Carter stopped by after dinner to discuss strategy for the next day's session. The evening broke up soon after, all of us too tired and depressed to want even a pretense of conversation.

The trial lasted four days. Freeman did a brilliant job with the state's sketchy evidence; the jury was out for only two hours before returning a "not guilty" verdict. Penelope left for Montreal with Hugo and Marcella the next morning. Lotty, much shaken by the winter's events, found a locum for her clinic and took off with Max for two weeks in Portugal.

I went to Michigan for a long weekend with the dog, but didn't have time or money for more vacation than that. Monday night, when I got home, I found Hugo Wolf's *Spanisches Liederbuch* still open on the piano from January's dinner party with Chaim and Paul. Between Paul's murder and preparing for Penelope's trial I hadn't sung since then. I tried picking out "In dem Schatten meiner Locken," but Greta was right: the piano needed tuning badly.

I called Mr. Fortieri the next morning to see if he could come by to look at it. He was an old man who repaired instruments for groups like the Aeolus Quintet and their ilk; he also tuned

270

pianos for them. He only helped me because he'd known my mother and admired her singing.

He arranged to come the next afternoon. I was surprised — usually you had to wait four to six weeks for time on his schedule — but quickly reshuffled my own Tuesday appointments to accommodate him. When he arrived, I realized that he had come so soon because Chaim's suicide attempt had shaken him. I didn't have much stomach for rehashing it, but I could see the old man was troubled and needed someone to talk to.

"What bothers me, Victoria, is what I should do with his clarinet. I've been able to repair it, but they tell me he'll never play again — surely it would be too cruel to return it to him, even if I didn't submit a bill."

"His clarinet?" I asked blankly. "When did he give it to you?"

"After that disastrous West Coast tour. He said he had dropped it in some mud — I still don't understand how that happened, why he was carrying it outside without the case. But he said it was clogged with mud and he'd tried cleaning it, only he'd bent the keys and it didn't play properly. It was a wonderful instrument, only a few years old, and costing perhaps six thousand dollars, so I agreed to work on it. He'd had to use his old one in California and I always thought that was why the tour went so badly. That and Paul's death weighing on him, of course."

"So you repaired it and got it thoroughly clean," I said foolishly.

"Oh, yes. Of course, the sound will never be as good as it was originally, but it would still be a fine instrument for informal use. Only — I hate having to give him a clarinet he can no longer play."

"Leave it with me," I said gently. "I'll take care of it."

Mr. Fortieri seemed relieved to pass the responsibility on to me. He went to work on the piano and tuned it back to perfection without any of his usual criticisms on my failure to keep to my mother's high musical standard.

As soon as he'd gone, I drove down to the University of Chicago Hospital. Chaim was being kept in the psychiatric wing for observation, but he was allowed visitors. I found him sitting in the lounge, staring into space while *People's Court* blared meaninglessly on the screen overhead.

He gave his sad sweet smile when he saw me and croaked out my name in the hoarse parody of a voice.

"Can we go to your room, Chaim? I want to talk to you privately."

He flicked a glance at the vacant faces around us but got up obediently and led me down the hall to a Spartan room with bars on the window.

"Mr. Fortieri was by this afternoon to tune my piano. He told me about your clarinet."

Chaim said nothing, but he seemed to relax a little.

"How did you do it, Chaim? I mean, you left for California Monday morning. What did you do — come back on the red-eye?"

"Red-eye?" he croaked hoarsely.

Even in the small space I had to lean forward to hear him. "The night flight."

"Oh. The red-eye. Yes. Yes, I got to O'Hare at six, came to Paul's office on the el, and was back at the airport in time for the ten o'clock flight. No one even knew I'd left L.A. — we had a rehearsal at two and I was there easily."

His voice was so strained it made my throat ache to listen to him.

"I thought I hated Paul. You know, all those remarks of his about responsibility. I thought he'd encouraged Greta to leave me." He stopped to catch his breath. After a few gasping minutes he went on.

"I blamed him for her idea that she didn't have to feel any obligation to our marriage. Then, after I got back, I saw Lotty had been right. Greta was just totally involved in herself. She should have been named Narcissus. She used Paul's words without understanding them."

"But Penelope," I said. "Would you really have let Penelope go to jail for you?"

He gave a twisted smile. "I didn't mean them to arrest Penelope. I just thought — I've always had trouble with cold weather, with Chicago winters. I've worn a long fur for years. Because I'm so small people often think I'm a woman when I'm wrapped up in it. I just thought, if anyone saw me they would think it was a woman. I never meant them to arrest Penelope."

He sat panting for a few minutes. "What are you going to do now, Vic? Send for the police?"

I shook my head sadly. "You'll never play again — you'd have been happier doing life in Joliet than you will now that you can't play. I want you to write it all down, though, the name you used on your night flight and everything. I have the clarinet; even though Mr. Fortieri cleaned it, a good lab might still find blood traces. The clarinet and your statement will go to the papers after you die. Penelope deserves that much — to have the cloud of suspicion taken away from her. And I'll have to tell her and Lotty."

His eyes were shiny. "You don't know how awful it's been, Vic. I was so mad with rage that it was like nothing to break Paul's neck. But then, after that, I couldn't play anymore. So you are wrong: even if I had gone to Joliet I would still never have played."

I couldn't bear the naked anguish in his face. I left without saying anything, but it was weeks before I slept without seeing his black eyes weeping onto me.

Skin Deep

I

THE WARNING BELL clangs angrily and the submarine dives sharply. Everyone to battle stations. The Nazis pursuing closely, the bell keeps up its insistent clamor, loud, urgent, filling my head. My hands are wet: I can't remember what my job is in this cramped, tiny boat. If only someone would turn off the alarm bell. I fumble with some switches, pick up an intercom. The noise mercifully stops.

"Vic! Vic, is that you?"

"What?"

"I know it's late. I'm sorry to call so late, but I just got home from work. It's Sal, Sal Barthele."

"Oh, Sal. Sure." I looked at the orange clock readout. It was four-thirty. Sal owns the Golden Glow, a bar in the south Loop I patronize.

"It's my sister, Vic. They've arrested her. She didn't do it. I know she didn't do it."

"Of course not, Sal — Didn't do what?"

"They're trying to frame her. Maybe the manager . . . I don't know."

I swung my legs over the side of the bed. "Where are you?"

She was at her mother's house, 95th and Vincennes. Her sister had been arrested three hours earlier. They needed a lawyer, a good lawyer. And they needed a detective, a good detective. Whatever my fee was, she wanted me to know they could pay my fee.

"I'm sure you can pay the fee, but I don't know what you want me to do," I said as patiently as I could.

"She — they think she murdered that man. She didn't even know him. She was just giving him a facial. And he dies on her."

"Sal, give me your mother's address. I'll be there in forty minutes."

The little house on Vincennes was filled with neighbors and relatives murmuring encouragement to Mrs. Barthele. Sal is very black, and statuesque. Close to six feet tall, with a majestic carriage, she can break up a crowd in her bar with a look and a gesture. Mrs. Barthele was slight, frail, and light-skinned. It was hard to picture her as Sal's mother.

Sal dispersed the gathering with characteristic firmness, telling the group that I was here to save Evangeline and that I needed to see her mother alone.

Mrs. Barthele sniffed over every sentence. "Why did they do that to my baby?" she demanded of me. "You know the police, you know their ways. Why did they come and take my baby, who never did a wrong thing in her life?"

As a white woman, I could be expected to understand the machinations of the white man's law. And to share responsibility for it. After more of this meandering, Sal took the narrative firmly in hand.

Evangeline worked at La Cygnette, a high-prestige beauty salon on North Michigan. In addition to providing facials and their own brand-name cosmetics at an exorbitant cost, they massaged the bodies and feet of their wealthy clients, stuffed them into steam cabinets, ran them through a Bataan-inspired exercise routine, and fed them herbal teas. Signor Giuseppe would style their hair for an additional charge.

Evangeline gave facials. The previous day she had one client booked after lunch, a Mr. Darnell.

"Men go there a lot?" I interrupted.

Sal made a face. "That's what I asked Evangeline. I guess it's part of being a yuppie — go spend a lot of money getting cream rubbed into your face."

Anyway, Darnell was to have had his hair styled before his facial, but the hairdresser fell behind schedule and asked Evangeline to do the guy's face first.

Sal struggled to describe how a La Cygnette facial worked — neither of us had ever checked out her sister's job. You sit in something like a dentist's chair, lean back, relax — you're naked from the waist up, lying under a big down comforter. The facial expert — cosmetician was

Evangeline's official title — puts cream on your hands and sticks them into little electrically heated mitts, so your hands are out of commission if you need to protect yourself. Then she puts stuff on your face, covers your eyes with heavy pads, and goes away for twenty minutes while the face goo sinks into your hidden pores.

Apparently while this Darnell lay back deeply relaxed, someone had rubbed some kind of poison into his skin. "When Evangeline came back in to clean his face, he was sick — heaving, throwing up, it was awful. She screamed for help and started trying to clean his face — it was terrible, he kept vomiting on her. They took him to the hospital, but he died around ten tonight.

"They came to get Baby at midnight — you've got to help her, V. I. — even if the guy tried something on her, she never did a thing like that — she'd haul off and slug him, maybe, but rubbing poison into his face? You go help her."

II

Evangeline Barthele was a younger, darker edition of her mother. At most times, she probably had Sal's energy — sparks of it flared now and then during our talk — but a night in the holding cells had worn her down.

I brought a clean suit and makeup for her: justice may be blind but her administrators aren't.

We talked while she changed.

"This Darnell — you sure of the name? — had he ever been to the salon before?"

She shook her head. "I never saw him. And I don't think the other girls knew him either. You know, if a client's a good tipper or a bad one they'll comment on it, be glad or whatever that he's come in. Nobody said anything about this man."

"Where did he live?"

She shook her head. "I never talked to the guy, V. I."

"What about the PestFree?" I'd read the arrest report and talked briefly to an old friend in the M.E.'s office. To keep roaches and other vermin out of their posh Michigan Avenue offices, La Cygnette used a potent product containing a wonder chemical called chorpyrifos. My informant had been awestruck — "Only an operation that didn't know shit about chemicals would leave chorpyrifos lying around. It's got a toxicity rating of five — it gets you through the skin — you only need a couple of tablespoons to kill a big man if you know where to put it."

Whoever killed Darnell had either known a lot of chemistry or been lucky — into his nostrils and mouth, with some rubbed into the face for good measure, the pesticide had made him convulsive so quickly that even if he knew who killed him he'd have been unable to talk, or even reason.

Evangeline said she knew where the poison was kept — everyone who worked there knew, knew it was lethal and not to touch it, but it was easy to get at. Just in a little supply room that wasn't kept locked.

"So why you? They have to have more of a reason than just that you were there."

She shrugged bitterly. "I'm the only black professional at La Cygnette — the other blacks working there sweep rooms and haul trash. I'm trying hard not to be paranoid, but I gotta wonder."

She insisted Darnell hadn't made a pass at her, or done anything to provoke an attack — she hadn't hurt the guy. As for anyone else who might have had opportunity, salon employees were always passing through the halls, going in and out of the little cubicles where they treated clients — she'd seen any number of people, all with legitimate business in the halls, but she hadn't seen anyone emerging from the room where Darnell was sitting.

When we finally got to bond court later that morning, I tried to argue circumstantial evidence — any of La Cygnette's fifty or so employees could have committed the crime, since all had access and no one had motive. The prosecutor hit me with a very unpleasant surprise: the police had uncovered evidence linking my client to the dead man. He was a furniture buyer from Kansas City who came to Chicago six times a year, and the doorman and the maids at his hotel had identified Evangeline without any trouble as the woman who accompanied him on his visits.

Bail was denied. I had a furious talk with Evangeline in one of the interrogation rooms before she went back to the holding cells.

"Why the hell didn't you tell me? I walked into the courtroom and got blindsided."

"They're lying," she insisted.

"Three people identified you. If you don't start with the truth right now, you're going to have to find a new lawyer and a new detective. Your mother may not understand, but for sure Sal will."

"You can't tell my mother. You can't tell Sal!"

"I'm going to have to give them some reason for dropping your case, and knowing Sal it's going to have to be the truth."

For the first time she looked really upset. "You're my lawyer. You should believe my story before you believe a bunch of strangers you never saw before."

"I'm telling you, Evangeline, I'm going to drop your case. I can't represent you when I know you're lying. If you killed Darnell we can work out a defense. Or if you didn't kill him and knew him we can work something out, and I can try to find the real killer. But when I know you've been seen with the guy any number of times, I can't go into court telling people you never met him before."

Tears appeared on the ends of her lashes. "The whole reason I didn't say anything was so Mama wouldn't know. If I tell you the truth, you've got to promise me you aren't running back to Vincennes Avenue talking to her."

I agreed. Whatever the story was, I couldn't

believe Mrs. Barthele hadn't heard hundreds like it before. But we each make our own separate peace with our mothers.

Evangeline met Darnell at a party two years earlier. She liked him, he liked her — not the romance of the century, but they enjoyed spending time together. She'd gone on a two-week trip to Europe with him last year, telling her mother she was going with a girlfriend.

"First of all, she has very strict morals. No sex outside marriage. I'm thirty, mind you, but that doesn't count with her. Second, he's white, and she'd murder me. She really would. I think that's why I never fell in love with him — if we wanted to get married I'd never be able to explain it to Mama."

This latest trip to Chicago, Darnell thought it would be fun to see what Evangeline did for a living, so he booked an appointment at La Cygnette. She hadn't told anyone there she knew him. And when she found him sick and dying she'd panicked and lied.

"And if you tell my mother of this, V. I. — I'll put a curse on you. My father was from Haiti and he knew a lot of good ones."

"I won't tell your mother. But unless they nuked Lebanon this morning or murdered the mayor, you're going to get a lot of lines in the paper. It's bound to be in print."

She wept at that, wringing her hands. So after watching her go off with the sheriff's deputies, I called Murray Ryerson at the *Herald-Star* to plead with him not to put Evangeline's liaison in the paper. "If you do she'll wither your testicles. Honest."

"I don't know, Vic. You know the *Sun-Times* is bound to have some kind of screamer headline like DEAD MAN FOUND IN FACE-LICKING SEX ORGY. I can't sit on a story like this when all the other papers are running it."

I knew he was right, so I didn't push my case very hard.

He surprised me by saying, "Tell you what: you find the real killer before my deadline for tomorrow's morning edition and I'll keep your client's personal life out of it. The sex scoop came in too late for today's paper. The *Trib* prints on our schedule and they don't have it, and the *Sun-Times* runs older, slower presses, so they have to print earlier."

I reckoned I had about eighteen hours. Sherlock Holmes had solved tougher problems in less time.

III

Roland Darnell had been the chief buyer of living-room furnishings for Alexander Dumas, a high-class Kansas City department store. He used to own his own furniture store in the nearby town of Lawrence, but lost both it and his wife when he was arrested for drug smuggling ten years earlier. Because of some confusion about his guilt — he claimed his partner, who disappeared the night he was arrested, was really responsible — he'd only served two years. When he got out, he moved to Kansas City to start a new life.

I learned this much from my friends at the Chicago police. At least, my acquaintances. I wondered how much of the story Evangeline had known. Or her mother. If her mother didn't want her child having a white lover, how about a white ex-con, ex- (presumably) drug-smuggling lover?

I sat biting my knuckles for a minute. It was eleven now. Say they started printing the morning edition at two the next morning, I'd have to have my story by one at the latest. I could follow one line, and one line only — I couldn't afford to speculate about Mrs. Barthele — and anyway, doing so would only get me killed. By Sal. So I looked up the area code for Lawrence, Kansas, and found their daily newspaper.

The *Lawrence Daily Journal-World* had set up a special number for handling press inquiries. A friendly woman with a strong drawl told me Darnell's age (forty-four); place of birth (Eudora, Kansas); ex-wife's name (Ronna Perkins); and ex-partner's name (John Crenshaw). Ronna Perkins was living elsewhere in the country and the *Journal-World* was protecting her privacy. John Crenshaw had disappeared when the police arrested Darnell.

Crenshaw had done an army stint in Southeast Asia in the late sixties. Since much of the bamboo furniture the store specialized in came from the Far East, some people speculated that Crenshaw had set up the smuggling route when he was out there in the service. Especially since Kansas City immigration officials discovered heroin in the hollow tubes making up chair backs. If Darnell knew anything about the smuggling, he had never revealed it.

"That's all we know here, honey. Of course, you could come on down and try to talk to some people. And we can wire you photos if you want."

I thanked her politely — my paper didn't run too many photographs. Or even have wire equipment to accept them. A pity — I could have used a look at Crenshaw and Ronna Perkins.

La Cygnette was on an upper floor of one of the new marble skyscrapers at the top end of the Magnificent Mile. Tall, white doors opened onto a hushed waiting room reminiscent of a high-class funeral parlor. The undertaker, a middle-aged highly made-up woman seated at a table that was supposed to be French provincial, smiled at me condescendingly.

"What can we do for you?"

"I'd like to see Angela Carlson. I'm a detective."

She looked nervously at two clients seated in a far corner. I lowered my voice. "I've come about the murder."

"But — but they made an arrest."

I smiled enigmatically. At least I hoped it looked enigmatic. "The police never close the door on all options until after the trial." If she knew anything about the police she'd know that was a lie — once they've made an arrest you have to get a presidential order to get them to look at new evidence.

The undertaker nodded nervously and called Angela Carlson in a whisper on the house phone. Evangeline had given me the names of the key players at La Cygnette; Carlson was the manager.

She met me in the doorway leading from the reception area into the main body of the salon. We walked on thick, silver pile through a white maze with little doors opening onto it. Every now and then we'd pass a white-coated attendant who gave the manager a subdued hello. When we went by a door with a police order slapped to it, Carlson winced nervously.

"When can we take that off? Everybody's on edge and that sealed door doesn't help. Our bookings are down as it is."

"I'm not on the evidence team, Ms. Carlson. You'll have to ask the lieutenant in charge when they've got what they need."

I poked into a neighboring cubicle. It contained a large white dentist's chair and a tray covered with crimson pots and bottles, all with the cutaway swans which were the salon's trademark. While the manager fidgeted angrily I looked into a tiny closet where clients changed — it held a tiny sink and a few coat hangers.

Finally she burst out, "Didn't your people get enough of this yesterday? Don't you read your own reports?"

"I like to form my own impressions, Ms. Carlson. Sorry to have to take your time, but the sooner we get everything cleared up, the faster your customers will forget this ugly episode."

She sighed audibly and led me on angry heels to her office, although the thick carpeting took the intended ferocity out of her stride. The office was another of the small treatment rooms with a desk and a menacing phone console. Photographs of a youthful Mme. de Leon, founder of La Cygnette, covered the walls.

Ms. Carlson looked through a stack of pink phone messages. "I have an incredibly busy schedule, Officer. So if you could get to the point. . . ."

"I want to talk to everyone with whom Darnell had an appointment yesterday. Also the receptionist on duty. And before I do that I want to see their personnel files."

"Really! All these people were interviewed yesterday." Her eyes narrowed suddenly. "Are you really with the police? You're not, are you? You're a reporter. I want you out of here now. Or I'll call the real police."

I took my license photostat from my wallet. "I'm a detective. That's what I told your receptionist. I've been retained by the Barthele family. Ms. Barthele is not the murderer and I want to find out who the real culprit is as fast as possible."

She didn't bother to look at the license. "I can barely tolerate answering police questions. I'm certainly not letting some snoop for hire take up

287

my time. The police have made an arrest on extremely good evidence. I suppose you think you can drum up a fee by getting Evangeline's family excited about her innocence, but you'll have to look elsewhere for your money."

I tried an appeal to her compassionate side, using half-forgotten arguments from my court appearances as a public defender. Outstanding employee, widowed mother, sole support, intense family pride, no prior arrests, no motive. No sale.

"Ms. Carlson, you the owner or the manager here?"

"Why do you want to know?"

"Just curious about your stake in the success of the place and your responsibility for decisions. It's like this: you've got a lot of foreigners working here. The immigration people will want to come by and check out their papers.

"You've got lots and lots of tiny little rooms. Are they sprinklered? Do you have emergency exits? The fire department can make a decision on that.

"And how come your only black professional employee was just arrested and you're not moving an inch to help her out? There are lots of lawyers around who'd be glad to look at a discrimination suit against La Cygnette.

"Now if we could clear up Evangeline's involvement fast, we could avoid having all these regulatory people trampling around upsetting your staff and your customers. How about it?"

She sat in indecisive rage for several minutes:

how much authority did I have, really? Could I offset the munificent fees the salon and the building owners paid to various public officials just to avoid such investigations? Should she call headquarters for instruction? Or her lawyer? She finally decided that even if I didn't have a lot of power I could be enough of a nuisance to affect business. Her expression compounded of rage and defeat, she gave me the files I wanted.

Darnell had been scheduled with a masseuse, the hair expert Signor Giuseppe, and with Evangeline. I read their personnel files, along with that of the receptionist who had welcomed him to La Cygnette, to see if any of them might have hailed from Kansas City or had any unusual traits, such as an arrest record for heroin smuggling. The files were very sparse. Signor Giuseppe Fruttero hailed from Milan. He had no next-of-kin to be notified in the event of an accident. Not even a good friend. Bruna, the masseuse, was Lithuanian, unmarried, living with her mother. Other than the fact that the receptionist had been born as Jean Evans in Hammond but referred to herself as Monique from New Orleans, I saw no evidence of any kind of cover-up.

Angela Carlson denied knowing either Ronna Perkins or John Crenshaw or having any employees by either of those names. She had never been near Lawrence herself. She grew up in Evansville, Indiana, came to Chicago to be a model in 1978, couldn't cut it, and got into the beauty business. Angrily she gave me the names of her

parents in Evansville and summoned the receptionist.

Monique was clearly close to sixty, much too
old to be Roland Darnell's ex-wife. Nor had she
heard of Ronna or Crenshaw.

"How many people knew that Darnell was
going to be in the salon yesterday?"

"Nobody knew." She laughed nervously. "I
mean, of course *I* knew — I made the appointment with him. And Signor Giuseppe knew when
I gave him his schedule yesterday. And Bruna,
the masseuse, of course, and Evangeline."

"Well, who else could have seen their sched-
ules?"

She thought frantically, her heavily mascaraed
eyes rolling in agitation. With another nervous
giggle she finally said, "I suppose anyone could
have known. I mean, the other cosmeticians and
the makeup artists all come out for their appointments at the same time. I mean, if anyone was
curious they could have looked at the other
people's lists."

Carlson was frowning. So was I. "I'm trying
to find a woman who'd be forty now, who doesn't
talk much about her past. She's been divorced
and she won't have been in the business long.
Any candidates?"

Carlson did another mental search, then went
to the file cabinets. Her mood was shifting from
anger to curiosity and she flipped through the
files quickly, pulling five in the end.

"How long has Signor Giuseppe been here?"

"When we opened our Chicago branch in 1980 he came to us from Miranda's — I guess he'd been there for two years. He says he came to the States from Milan in 1970."

"He a citizen? Has he got a green card?"

"Oh, yes. His papers are in good shape. We are very careful about that at La Cygnette." My earlier remark about the immigration department had clearly stung. "And now I really need to get back to my own business. You can look at those files in one of the consulting rooms — Monique, find one that won't be used today."

It didn't take me long to scan the five files, all uninformative. Before returning them to Monique I wandered on through the back of the salon. In the rear a small staircase led to an upper story. At the top was another narrow hall lined with small offices and storerooms. A large mirrored room at the back filled with hanging plants and bright lights housed Signor Giuseppe. A dark-haired man with a pointed beard and a bright smile, he was ministering gaily to a thin, middle-aged woman, talking and laughing while he deftly teased her hair into loose curls.

He looked at me in the mirror when I entered. "You are here for the hair, Signora? You have the appointment?"

"*No, Signor Giuseppe. Sono qui perchè la sua fama se è sparsa di fronte a lei. Milano è una bella città, non è vero?*"

He stopped his work for a moment and held up a deprecating hand. "Signora, it is my policy to speak only English in my adopted country."

"Una vera stupida e ignorante usanza io direi."
I beamed sympathetically and sat down on a high
stool next to an empty customer chair. There
were seats for two clients. Since Signor Giuseppe
reigned alone, I pictured him spinning at high
speed between customers, snipping here, pinning
there.

"Signora, if you do not have the appointment,
will you please leave? Signora Dotson here, she
does not prefer the audience."

"Sorry, Mrs. Dotson," I said to the lady's chin.
"I'm a detective. I need to talk to Signor Giuseppe, but I'll wait."

I strolled back down the hall and entertained
myself by going into one of the storerooms and
opening little pots of La Cygnette creams and
rubbing them into my skin. I looked in a mirror
and could already see an improvement. If I got
Evangeline sprung maybe she'd treat me to a facial.

Signor Giuseppe appeared with a plastically
groomed Mrs. Dotson. He had shed his barber's
costume and was dressed for the street. I followed
them down the stairs. When we got to the bottom
I said, "In case you're thinking of going back
to Milan — or even to Kansas — I have a few
questions."

Mrs. Dotson clung to the hairdresser, ready
to protect him.

"I need to speak to him alone, Mrs. Dotson.
I have to talk to him about bamboo."

"I'll get Miss Carlson, Signor Giuseppe," his guardian offered.

"No, no, Signora. I will deal with this crazed woman myself. A million thanks. *Grazie, grazie.*"

"Remember, no Italian in your adopted America," I reminded him nastily.

Mrs. Dotson looked at us uncertainly.

"I think you should get Ms. Carlson," I said. "Also a police escort. Fast."

She made up her mind to do something, whether to get help or flee I wasn't sure, but she scurried down the corridor. As soon as she had disappeared, he took me by the arm and led me into one of the consulting rooms.

"Now, who are you and what is this?" His accent had improved substantially.

"I'm V. I. Warshawski. Roland Darnell told me you were quite an expert on fitting drugs into bamboo furniture."

I wasn't quite prepared for the speed of his attack. His hands were around my throat. He was squeezing and spots began dancing in front of me. I didn't try to fight his arms, just kicked sharply at his shin, following with my knee to his stomach. The pressure at my neck eased. I turned in a half circle and jammed my left elbow into his rib cage. He let go.

I backed to the door, keeping my arms up in front of my face and backed into Angela Carlson.

"What on earth are you doing with Signor Giuseppe?" she asked.

"Talking to him about furniture." I was out

of breath. "Get the police and don't let him leave the salon."

A small crowd of white-coated cosmeticians had come to the door of the tiny treatment room. I said to them, "This isn't Giuseppe Fruttero. It's John Crenshaw. If you don't believe me, try speaking Italian to him — he doesn't understand it. He's probably never been to Milan. But he's certainly been to Thailand, and he knows an awful lot about heroin."

IV

Sal handed me the bottle of Black Label. "It's yours, Vic. Kill it tonight or save it for some other time. How did you know he was Roland Darnell's ex-partner?"

"I didn't. At least not when I went to La Cygnette. I just knew it had to be someone in the salon who killed him, and it was most likely someone who knew him in Kansas. And that meant either Darnell's ex-wife or his partner. And Giuseppe was the only man on the professional staff. And then I saw he didn't know Italian — after praising Milan and telling him he was stupid in the same tone of voice and getting no response it made me wonder."

"We owe you a lot, Vic. The police would never have dug down to find that. You gotta thank the lady, Mama."

Mrs. Barthele grudgingly gave me her thin hand. "But how come those police said Evangeline knew that Darnell man? My baby wouldn't know some convict, some drug smuggler."

"He wasn't a drug smuggler, Mama. It was his partner. The police have proved all that now. Roland Darnell never did anything wrong." Evangeline, chic in red with long earrings that bounced as she spoke, made the point hotly.

Sal gave her sister a measuring look. "All I can say, Evangeline, is it's a good thing you never had to put your hand on a Bible in court about Mr. Darnell."

I hastily poured a drink and changed the subject.

Three-Dot Po

CINDA GOODRICH AND I were jogging acquaintances. A professional photographer, she kept the same erratic hours as a private investigator; we often met along Belmont Harbor in the late mornings. By then we had the lakefront to ourselves; the hip young professionals run early so they can make their important eight o'clock meetings.

Cinda occasionally ran with her boyfriend, Jonathan Michaels, and always with her golden retriever, Three-Dot Po, or Po. The dog's name meant something private to her and Jonathan; they only laughed and shook their heads when I asked about it.

Jonathan played the piano, often at late-night private parties. He was seldom up before noon and usually left exercise to Cinda and Po. Cinda was a diligent runner, even on the hottest days of summer and the coldest of winter. I do twenty-five miles a week in a grudging fight against age and calories, but Cinda made a ten-mile circuit every morning with religious enthusiasm.

One December I didn't see her out for a week and wondered vaguely if she might be sick. The following Saturday, however, we met on the small promontory abutting Belmont Harbor — she returning from her jaunt three miles farther north, and I just getting ready to turn around for home. As we jogged together, she explained that Eli Burton, the fancy North Michigan Avenue department store, had hired her to photograph children talking to Santa. She made a face. "Not the way Eric Lieberman got his start, but it'll finance January in the Bahamas for Jonathan and me." She called to Po, who was inspecting a dead bird on the rocks by the water, and moved on ahead of me.

The week before Christmas the temperature dropped suddenly and left us with the bitterest December on record. My living room was so cold I couldn't bear to use it; I handled all my business bundled in bed, even moving the television into the bedroom. I didn't go out at all on Christmas Eve.

Christmas Day I was supposed to visit friends in one of the northern suburbs. I wrapped myself in a blanket and went to the living room to scrape a patch of ice on a window. I wanted to see how badly snowed over Halsted Street was, assuming my poor little Omega would even start.

I hadn't run for five days, since the temperature first fell. I was feeling flabby, knew I should force myself outside, but felt too lazy to face the weather. I was about to go back to the bedroom and wrap some presents when I caught sight of a golden retriever moving smartly down the street. It was Po; behind her came Cinda, warm in an orange down vest, face covered with a ski mask.

"Ah, nuts," I muttered. If she could do it, I could do it. Layering on thermal underwear, two pairs of wool socks, sweatshirts, and a down vest, I told myself encouragingly, "Quitters never win and winners never quit," and "It's not the size of the dog in the fight that counts but the size of the fight in the dog."

The slogans got me out the door, but they didn't prepare me for the shock of cold. The wind sucked the air out of my lungs and left me gasping. I staggered back into the entryway and tied a scarf around my face, adjusted earmuffs and a wool cap, and put on sunglasses to protect my eyes.

Even so, it was bitter going. After the first mile the blood was flowing well and my arms and legs were warm, but my feet were cold, and even heavy muffling couldn't keep the wind from scraping the skin on my cheeks. Few cars were on the streets, and no other people. It was like running through a wasteland. This is what it would be like after a nuclear war: no people, freezing cold, snow blowing across in fine pelting particles like a desert sandstorm.

The lake made an even eerier landscape. Steam rose from it as from a giant cauldron. The water was invisible beneath the heavy veils of mist. I paused for a moment in awe, but the wind quickly cut through the layers of clothes.

The lake path curved around as it led to the promontory so that you could only see a few yards ahead of you. I kept expecting to meet Cinda and Po on their way back, but the only person who passed me was a solitary male jogger, anonymous in a blue ski mask and khaki down jacket.

At the far point of the promontory the wind blew unblocked across the lake. It swept snow and frozen mist pellets with it, blowing in a high persistent whine. I was about to turn and go home when I heard a dog barking above the keening wind. I hesitated to go down to the water, but what if it was Po, separated from her mistress?

The rocks leading down to the lake were covered with ice. I slipped and slid down, trying desperately for hand- and toe-holds — even if someone were around to rescue me I wouldn't survive a bath in subzero water.

I found Po on a flat slab of rock. She was standing where its edge hung over the mist-covered water, barking furiously. I called to her. She turned her head briefly but wouldn't come.

By now I had a premonition of what would meet me when I'd picked my way across the slab. I lay flat on the icy rock, gripping my feet around one end, and leaned over it through the mist to peer in the water. As soon as I showed up, Po stopped barking and began an uneasy pacing and whining.

Cinda's body was just visible beneath the surface. It was a four-foot drop to the water from where I lay. I couldn't reach her and I didn't dare get down in the water. I thought furiously and finally unwound a long muffler from around my neck. Tying it to a jagged spur near me I wrapped the other end around my waist and prayed. Leaning over from the waist gave me the length I needed to reach into the water. I took a deep breath and plunged my arms in. The shock of the water was almost more than I could bear; I concentrated on Cinda, on the dog, thought of Christmas in the northern suburbs, of everything possible but the cold which made my arms almost useless. "You only have one chance, Vic. Don't blow it."

The weight of her body nearly dragged me in on top of Cinda. I slithered across the icy rock, scissoring my feet wildly until they caught on the spur where my muffler was tied. Po was no help, either. She planted herself next to me, whimpering with anxiety as I pulled her mistress from the water. With water soaked in every garment, Cinda must have weighed two hundred pounds. I almost lost her several times, almost lost myself, but I got her up. I tried desperately to revive her, Po anxiously licking her face, but there was no hope. I finally realized I was going to die of exposure myself if I didn't get away from there. I tried calling Po to come with me, but she wouldn't leave Cinda. I ran as hard as I could back to the harbor, where I flagged down a car. My teeth were chattering so hard I almost couldn't speak, but I got the strangers to realize there was a dead woman back on the promontory point. They drove me to the Town Hall police station.

I spent most of Christmas Day in bed, layered in blankets, drinking hot soup prepared by my friend Dr. Lotty Herschel. I had some frostbite in two of my fingers, but she thought they would recover. Lotty left at seven to eat dinner with her nurse, Carol Alvarado, and her family.

The police had taken Cinda away, and Jonathan had persuaded Po to go home with him. I guess it had been a fairly tragic scene — Jonathan crying, the dog unwilling to let Cinda's body out of her sight. I hadn't been there myself, but one of my newspaper friends told me about it.

It was only eight o'clock when the phone next to my bed began ringing, but I was deep in sleep, buried in blankets. It must have rung nine or ten times before I even woke up, and another several before I could bring myself to stick one of my sore arms out to answer it.

"Hello?" I said groggily.

"Vic. Vic, I hate to bother you, but I need help."

"Who is this?" I started coming to.

"Jonathan Michaels. They've arrested me for killing Cinda. I only get the one phone call." He was trying to speak jauntily, but his voice cracked.

"Killing Cinda?" I echoed. "I thought she slipped and fell."

"Apparently someone strangled her and pushed her in after she was dead. Don't ask me how they know. Don't ask me why they thought I did it. The problem is — the problem is — Po. I don't have anyone to leave her with."

"Where are you now?" I swung my legs over the bed and began pulling on longjohns. He was at their apartment, four buildings up the street from me, on his way downtown for booking and then to Cook County jail. The arresting officer, not inhuman on Christmas Day, would let him wait for me if I could get there fast.

I was half dressed by the time I hung up and quickly finished pulling on jeans, boots, and a heavy sweater. Jonathan and two policemen were standing in the entryway of his building when I ran up. He handed me his apartment keys. In the distance I could hear Po's muffled barking.

"Do you have a lawyer?" I demanded.

Ordinarily a cheerful, bearded young man with long golden hair, Jonathan now looked rather bedraggled. He shook his head dismally.

"You need one. I can find someone for you, or I can represent you myself until we come up with someone better. I don't practice anymore, so you need someone who's active, but I can get you through the formalities."

He accepted gratefully, and I followed him into the waiting police car. The arresting officers wouldn't answer any of my questions. When we got down to the Eleventh Street police headquarters, I insisted on seeing the officer in charge, and was taken in to Sergeant John McGonnigal.

McGonnigal and I had met frequently. He was a stocky young man, very able, and I had a lot of respect for him. I'm not sure he reciprocated it. "Merry Christmas, Sergeant. It's a terrible day to be working, isn't it?"

"Merry Christmas, Miss Warshawski. What are you doing here?"

"I represent Jonathan Michaels. Seems someone got a little confused and thinks he pushed Ms. Goodrich into Lake Michigan this morning."

"We're not confused. She was strangled and pushed into the lake. She was dead before she went into the water. He has no alibi for the relevant time."

"No alibi! Who in this city does have an alibi?"

There was more to it than that, he explained stiffly. Michaels and Cinda had been heard quarreling late at night by their neighbors across the hall and underneath. They had resumed their fight in the morning. Cinda had finally slammed out of the house with the dog around nine-thirty.

"He didn't follow her, Sergeant."

"How do you know?"

I explained that I had watched Cinda from my living room. "And I didn't run into Mr. Michaels out on the point. I only met one person."

He pounced on that. How could I be sure it wasn't Jonathan? Finally agreeing to get a description of his clothes to see if he owned a navy ski mask or a khaki jacket, McGonnigal also pointed out that there were two ways to leave the lakefront — Jonathan could have gone north instead of south.

"Maybe. But you're spinning a very thin thread, Sergeant. It's not going to hold up. Now I need some time alone with my client."

He was most unhappy to let me represent Jonathan, but there wasn't much he could do about it. He left us alone in a small interrogation room.

"I'm taking it on faith that you didn't kill Cinda," I said briskly. "But for the record, did you?"

He shook his head. "No way. Even if I had stopped loving her, which I hadn't, I don't solve my problems that way." He ran a hand through his long hair. "I can't believe this. I can't even really believe Cinda is dead. It's all happened too fast. And now they're arresting me." His hands were beautiful, with long, strong fingers. Strong enough to strangle someone, certainly.

"What were you fighting about this morning?"

"Fighting?"

"Don't play dumb with me, Jonathan; I'm the only help you've got. Your neighbors heard you — that's why the police arrested you."

He smiled a little foolishly. "It all seems so stupid now. I keep thinking, if I hadn't gotten her mad, she wouldn't have gone out there. She'd be alive now."

"Maybe. Maybe not. What were you fighting about?"

He hesitated. "Those damned Santa Claus pictures she took. I never wanted her to do it, any-

way. She's too good — she was too good a photographer to be wasting her time on that kind
of stuff. Then she got mad and started accusing
me of being Lawrence Welk, and who was I to
talk. It all started because someone phoned her
at one this morning. I'd just gotten back from
a gig —" he grinned suddenly, painfully "— a
Lawrence Welk gig, and this call came in. Someone who had been in one of her Santa shots.
Said he was very shy, and wanted to make sure
he wasn't in the picture with his kid, so would
she bring him the negatives?"

"She had the negatives? Not Burton's?"

"Yeah. Stupid idiot. She was developing the
film herself. Apparently this guy called Burton's
first. Anyway, to make a long story short, she
agreed to meet him today and give him the negatives, and I was furious. First of all, why should
she go out on Christmas to satisfy some moron's
whim? And why was she taking those dumb-assed
pictures anyway?"

Suddenly his face cracked and he started sobbing. "She was so beautiful and I loved her so
much. Why did I have to fight with her?"

I patted his shoulder and held his hand until
the tears stopped. "You know, if that was her
caller she was going to meet, that's probably the
person who killed her."

"I thought of that. And that's what I told the
police. But they say it's the kind of thing I'd
be bound to make up under the circumstances."

I pushed him through another half hour of ques-

305

tions. What had she said about her caller? Had he given his name? She didn't know his name. Then how had she known which negatives were his? She didn't — just the day and the time he'd been there, so she was taking over the negatives for that morning. That's all he knew; she'd been too angry to tell him what she was taking with her. Yes, she had taken negatives with her.

He gave me detailed instructions on how to look after Po. Just dry dog food. No table scraps. As many walks as I felt like giving her — she was an outdoor dog and loved snow and water. She was very well trained; they never walked her with a leash. Before I left, I talked to McGonnigal. He told me he was going to follow up on the story about the man in the photograph at Burton's the next day but he wasn't taking it too seriously. He told me they hadn't found any film on Cinda's body, but that was because she hadn't taken any with her — Jonathan was making up that, too. He did agree, though, to hold Jonathan at Eleventh Street overnight. He could get a bail hearing in the morning and maybe not have to put his life at risk among the gang members who run Cook County jail disguised as prisoners.

I took a taxi back to the north side. The streets were clear and we moved quickly. Every mile or so we passed a car abandoned on the roadside, making the Arctic landscape appear more desolate than ever.

Once at Jonathan's apartment it took a major

effort of will to get back outside with the dog. Po went with me eagerly enough, but kept turning around, looking at me searchingly as though hoping I might be transformed into Cinda.

Back in the apartment, I had no strength left to go home. I found the bedroom, let my clothes drop where they would on the floor and tumbled into bed.

Holy Innocents' Day, lavishly celebrated by my Polish Catholic relatives, was well advanced before I woke up again. I found Po staring at me with reproachful brown eyes, panting slightly. "All right, all right," I grumbled, pulling the covers back and staggering to my feet.

I'd been too tired the night before even to locate the bathroom. Now I found it, part of a large darkroom. Cinda apparently had knocked down a wall connecting it to the dining room; she had a sink and built-in shelves all in one handy location. Prints were strung around the room, and chemicals and lingerie jostled one another incongruously. I borrowed a toothbrush, cautiously smelling the toothpaste tube to make sure it really held Crest, not developing chemicals.

I put my clothes back on and took Po around the block. The weather had moderated considerably; a bank thermometer on the corner stood at 9 degrees. Po wanted to run to the lake, but I didn't feel up to going that far this morning, and called her back with difficulty. After lunch, if I could get my car started, we might see whether any clues lay hidden in the snow.

I called Lotty from Cinda's apartment, explaining where I was and why. She told me I was an idiot to have gotten out of bed the night before, but if I wasn't dead of exposure by now I would probably survive until someone shot me. Somehow that didn't cheer me up.

While I helped myself to coffee and toast in Cinda's kitchen I started calling various attorneys to see if I could find someone to represent Jonathan. Tim Oldham, who'd gone to law school with me, handled a good-sized criminal practice. He wasn't too enthusiastic about taking a client without much money, but I put on some not very subtle pressure about a lady I'd seen him with on the Gold Coast a few weeks ago who bore little resemblance to his wife. He promised me Jonathan would be home by supper time, called me some unflattering names and hung up.

Besides the kitchen, bedroom, and darkroom, the apartment had one other room, mostly filled by a grand piano. Stacks of music stood on the floor — Jonathan either couldn't afford shelves or didn't think he needed them. The walls were hung with poster-sized photographs of Jonathan playing, taken by Cinda. They were very good.

I went back into the darkroom and poked around at the pictures. Cinda had put all her Santa Claus photographs in neatly marked envelopes. She'd carefully written the name of each child next to the number of the exposure on that role of film. I switched on a light table and started looking at them. She'd taken pictures every day for three weeks, which amounted to thousands of shots. It looked like a needle-in-the-haystack type task. But most of the pictures were of children. The only others were ones Cinda had taken for her own amusement, panning the crowd, or artsy shots through glass at reflecting lights. Presumably her caller was one of the adults in the crowd.

After lunch I took Po down to my car. She had no hesitation about going with me and leaped eagerly into the backseat. "You have too trusting a nature," I told her. She grinned at me and panted heavily. The Omega started, after a few grumbling moments, and I drove north to Bryn Mawr and back to get the battery well charged before turning into the lot at Belmont Harbor. Po was almost beside herself with excitement, banging her tail against the rear window until I got the door open and let her out. She raced ahead of me on the lake path. I didn't try to call her back; I figured I'd find her at Cinda's rock.

I moved slowly, carefully scanning the ground for traces of — what? Film? A business card? The wind was so much calmer today and the air enough warmer that visibility was good, but I didn't see anything.

At the lake the mist had cleared away, leaving the water steely gray, moving uneasily under its iron bands of cold. Po stood as I expected, on the rock where I'd found her yesterday. She was the picture of dejection. She clearly had expected to find her mistress there.

I combed the area carefully and at last found one of those gray plastic tubes that film comes in. It was empty. I pocketed it, deciding I could at least show it to McGonnigal and hope he would think it important. Po left the rocks with utmost reluctance. Back on the lake path, she kept turning around to look for Cinda. I had to lift her into the car. During the drive to police headquarters, she kept turning restlessly in the back of the car, a trying maneuver since she was bigger than the seat.

McGonnigal didn't seem too impressed with the tube I'd found, but he took it and sent it to the forensics department. I asked him what he'd learned from Burton's; they didn't have copies of the photographs. Cinda had all those. If someone ordered one, they sent the name to Cinda and she supplied the picture. They gave McGonnigal a copy of the list of the seven hundred people requesting pictures and he had someone going through to see if any of them were known criminals, but he obviously believed it was a waste of time. If it weren't for the fact that his boss, Lieutenant Robert Mallory, had been a friend of my father's, he probably wouldn't even have made this much of an effort.

I stopped to see Jonathan, who seemed to be in fairly good spirits. He told me Tim Oldham had been by. "He thinks I'm a hippy and not very interesting compared to some of the mob figures he represents, but I can tell he's doing his best." He was working out the fingering to a Schubert score, using the side of the bed as a keyboard. I told him Po was well, but waiting for me in the car outside, so I'd best be on my way.

I spent the rest of the afternoon going through Cinda's Santa photographs. I'd finished about a third of them at five when Tim Oldham phoned to say that Jonathan would have to spend another night in jail: because of the Christmas holidays he hadn't been able to arrange for bail.

"You owe me, Vic; this has been one of the more thankless ways I've spent a holiday."

"You're serving justice, Tim," I said brightly. "What more could you ask for? Think of the oath you swore when you became a member of the bar."

"I'm thinking of the oaths I'd like to swear at you," he grumbled.

I laughed and hung up. I took Po for one last walk, gave her her evening food and drink and prepared to leave for my own place. As soon as the dog saw me putting my coat back on, she abandoned her dinner and started dancing around my feet, wagging her tail, to show that she was always ready to play. I kept yelling "No" to her with no effect. She grinned happily at me as if to say this was a game she often played — she knew humans liked to pretend they didn't want her along, but they always took her in the end.

She was very upset when I shoved her back

into the apartment behind me. As I locked the door, she began barking. Retrievers are quiet dogs; they seldom bark and never whine. But their voices are deep and full-bodied, coming straight from their huge chests. Good diaphragm support, the kind singers seldom achieve.

Cinda's apartment was on the second floor. When I got to the ground floor, I could still hear Po from the entryway. She was clearly audible outside the front door. "Ah, nuts!" I muttered. How long could she keep this up? Were dogs like babies? Did you just ignore them for a while and discipline them into going to sleep? Did that really work with babies? After standing five minutes in the icy wind I could still hear Po. I swore under my breath and let myself back into the building.

She was totally ecstatic at seeing me, jumping up on my chest and licking my face to show there were no hard feelings. "You're shameless and a fraud," I told her severely. She wagged her tail with delight. "Still, you're an orphan; I can't treat you too harshly."

She agreed and followed me down the stairs and back to my apartment with unabated eagerness. I took a bath and changed my clothes, made dinner and took care of my mail, then walked Po around the block to a little park, and back up the street to her own quarters. I brought my own toothbrush with me this time; there didn't seem much point in trying to leave the dog until Jonathan got out of jail.

Cinda and Jonathan had few furnishings, but they owned a magnificent stereo system and a large record collection. I put some Britten quartets on, found a novel buried in the stack of technical books next to Cinda's side of the bed, and purloined a bottle of burgundy. I curled up on a beanbag chair with the book and the wine. Po lay at my feet, panting happily. Altogether a delightful domestic scene. Maybe I should get a dog.

I finished the book and the bottle of wine a little after midnight and went to bed. Po padded into the bedroom after me and curled up on a rug next to the bed. I went to sleep quickly.

A single sharp bark from the dog woke me about two hours later. "What is it, girl? Nightmares?" I started to turn over to go back to sleep when she barked again. "Quiet, now!" I commanded.

I heard her get to her feet and start toward the door. And then I heard the sound that her sharper ears had caught first. Someone was trying to get into the apartment. It couldn't be Jonathan; I had his keys, and this was someone fumbling, trying different keys, trying to pick the lock. In about thirty seconds I pulled on jeans, boots, and a sweatshirt, ignoring underwear. My intruder had managed the lower lock and was starting on the upper.

Po was standing in front of the door, hackles raised on her back. Obedient to my whispered command she wasn't barking. She followed me reluctantly into the darkroom-bathroom. I took her into the shower stall and pulled the curtain across as quietly as I could.

We waited there in the dark while our intruder finished with locks. It was an unnerving business listening to the rattling, knowing someone would be on us momentarily. I wondered if I'd made the right choice; maybe I should have dashed down the back stairs with the dog and gotten the police. It was too late now, however; we could hear a pair of boots moving heavily across the living room. Po gave a deep, mean growl in the back of her throat.

"Doggy? Doggy? Are you in here, Doggy?" The man knew about Po, but not whether she was here. He must not have heard her two short barks earlier. He had a high tenor voice with a trace of a Spanish accent.

Po continued to growl, very softly. At last the far door to the darkroom opened and the intruder came in. He had a flashlight which he shone around the room; through the curtain I could see its point of light bobbing.

Satisfied that no one was there, he turned on the overhead switch. This was connected to a ventilating fan, whose noise was loud enough to mask Po's continued soft growling.

I couldn't see him, but apparently he was looking through Cinda's photograph collection. He flipped on the switch at the light table and then spent a long time going through the negatives. I was pleased with Po; I wouldn't have expected such patience from a dog. The intruder must have sat for an hour while my muscles cramped and water dripped on my head, and she stayed next to me quietly the whole time.

At last he apparently found what he needed. He got up and I heard more paper rustling, then the light went out.

"Now!" I shouted at Po. She raced out of the room and found the intruder as he was on his way out the far door. Blue light flashed; a gun barked. Po yelped and stopped momentarily. By that time I was across the room, too. The intruder was on his way out the apartment door.

I pulled my parka from the chair where I'd left it and took off after him. Po was bleeding slightly from her left shoulder, but the bullet must only have grazed her because she ran strongly. We tumbled down the stairs together and out the front door into the icy December night. As we went outside, I grabbed the dog and rolled over with her. I heard the gun go off a few times but we were moving quickly, too quickly to make a good target.

Street lamps showed our man running away from us down Halsted to Belmont. He wore the navy ski mask and khaki parka of the solitary runner I'd seen at the harbor yesterday morning.

Hearing Po and me behind him he put on a burst of speed and made it to a car waiting at the corner. We were near the Omega now; I bundled the dog into the backseat, sent up a prayer to the patron saint of Delco batteries, and turned on the engine.

The streets were deserted. I caught up with the car, a dark Lincoln, where Sheridan Road crossed Lake Shore Drive at Belmont. Instead of turning onto the drive, the Lincoln cut straight across to the harbor.

"This is it, girl," I told Po. "You catch this boy, then we take you in and get that shoulder stitched up. And then you get your favorite dinner — even if it's a whole cow."

The dog was leaning over the front seat, panting, her eyes gleaming. She was a retriever, after all. The Lincoln stopped at the end of the harbor parking lot. I halted the Omega some fifty yards away and got out with the dog. Using a row of parked cars as cover, we ran across the lot, stopping near the Lincoln in the shelter of a van. At that point, Po began her deep, insistent barking.

This was a sound which would attract attention, possibly even the police, so I made no effort to stop her. The man in the Lincoln reached the same conclusion; a window opened and he began firing at us. This was just a waste of ammunition, since we were sheltered behind the van.

The shooting only increased Po's vocal efforts. It also attracted attention from Lake Shore Drive; out of the corner of my eye I saw the flashing blue lights which herald the arrival of Chicago's finest.

Our attacker saw them, too. A door opened

and the man in the ski mask slid out. He took off along the lake path, away from the harbor entrance, out toward the promontory. I clapped my hands at Po and started running after him. She was much faster than me; I lost sight of her in the dark as I picked my way more cautiously along the icy path, shivering in the bitter wind, shivering at the thought of the dark freezing water to my right. I could hear it slapping ominously against the ice-covered rocks, could hear the man pounding ahead of me. No noise from Po. Her tough pads picked their way sure and silent across the frozen gravel.

As I rounded the curve toward the promontory I could hear the man yelling in Spanish at Po, heard a gun go off, heard a loud splash in the water. Rage at him for shooting the dog gave me a last burst of speed. I rounded the end of the point. Saw his dark shape outlined against the rocks and jumped on top of him.

He was completely unprepared for me. We fell heavily, rolling down the rocks. The gun slipped from his hand, banged loudly as it bounced against the ice and fell into the water. We were a foot away from the water, fighting recklessly — the first person to lose a grip would be shoved in to die.

Our parkas weighted our arms and hampered our swings. He lunged clumsily at my throat. I pulled away, grabbed hold of his ski mask and hit his head against the rocks. He grunted and drew back, trying to kick me. As I moved away from his foot I lost my hold on him and slid backwards across the ice. He followed through quickly, giving a mighty shove which pushed me over the edge of the rock. My feet landed in the water. I swung them up with an effort, two icy lumps, and tried to back away.

As I scrabbled for a purchase, a dark shape came out of the water and climbed onto the rock next to me. Po. Not killed after all. She shook herself, spraying water over me and over my assailant. The sudden bath took him by surprise. He stopped long enough for me to get well away and gain my breath and a better position.

The dog, shivering violently, stayed close to me. I ran a hand through her wet fur. "Soon, kid. We'll get you home and dry soon."

Just as the attacker launched himself at us, a searchlight went on overhead. "This is the police," a loudspeaker boomed. "Drop your guns and come up."

The dark shape hit me, knocked me over. Po let out a yelp and sunk her teeth into his leg. His yelling brought the police to our sides.

They carried strong flashlights. I could see a sodden mass of paper, a small manila envelope with teethmarks in it. Po wagged her tail and picked it up again.

"Give me that!" our attacker yelled in his high voice. He fought with the police to try to reach the envelope. "I threw that in the water. How can this be? How did she get it?"

"She's a retriever," I said.

Later, at the police station, we looked at the negatives in the envelope Po had retrieved from the water. They showed a picture of the man in the ski mask looking on with intense, brooding eyes while Santa Claus talked to his little boy. No wonder Cinda found him worth photographing.

"He's a cocaine dealer," Sergeant McGonnigal explained to me. "He jumped a ten-million-dollar bail. No wonder he didn't want any photographs of him circulating around. We're holding him for murder this time."

A uniformed man brought Jonathan into McGonnigal's office. The sergeant cleared his throat uncomfortably. "Looks like your dog saved your hide, Mr. Michaels."

Po, who had been lying at my feet, wrapped in a police horse blanket, gave a bark of pleasure. She staggered to her feet, trailing the blanket, and walked stiffly over to Jonathan, tail wagging.

I explained our adventure to him, and what a heroine the dog had been. "What about that empty film container I gave you this afternoon, Sergeant?"

Apparently Cinda had brought that with her to her rendezvous, not knowing how dangerous her customer was. When he realized it was empty, he'd flung it aside and attacked Cinda. "We got a complete confession," McGonnigal said. "He was so rattled by the sight of the dog with the envelope full of negatives in her mouth that he completely lost his nerve. I know he's

319

got good lawyers — one of them's your friend Oldham — but I hope we have enough to convince a judge not to set bail."

Jonathan was on his knees fondling the dog and talking to her. He looked over his shoulder at McGonnigal. "I'm sure Oldham's relieved that you caught the right man — a murderer who can afford to jump a ten-million-dollar bail is a much better client than one who can hardly keep a retriever in dog food." He turned back to the dog. "But we'll blow our savings on a steak; you get the steak and I'll eat Butcher's Blend tonight, Miss Three-Dot Po of Blackstone, People's Heroine, and winner of the Croix de Chien for valor." Po panted happily and licked his face.

The Takamoku *Joseki*

I

MR. AND MRS. Takamoku were a quiet, hardworking couple. Although they had lived in Chicago since the 1940s, when they were relocated from an Arizona detention camp, they spoke only halting English. Occasionally I ran into Mrs. Takamoku in the foyer of the old three-flat we both lived in on Belmont, or at the corner grocery store. We would exchange a few stilted sentences. She knew I lived alone in my third-floor apartment, and she worried about it, although her manners were too perfect for her to come right out and tell me to get myself a husband.

As time passed, I learned about her son, Akira, and her daughter, Yoshio, both professionals living on the West Coast. I always inquired after them, which pleased her.

With great difficulty I got her to understand that I was a private detective. This troubled her; she often wanted to know if I was doing something dangerous, and would shake her head and frown as she asked. I didn't see Mr. Takamoku often. He worked for a printer and usually left long before me in the morning.

Unlike the De Paul students who formed an ever-changing collage on the second floor, the Takamokus did little entertaining, or at least little noisy entertaining. Every Sunday afternoon a procession of Asians came to their apartment, spent a quiet afternoon, and left. One or more Caucasians would join them, incongruous by their height and color. After a while, I recognized the regulars: a tall, bearded white man, and six or seven Japanese and Koreans.

One Sunday evening in late November I was eating sushi and drinking sake in a storefront restaurant on Halsted. The Takamokus came in as I was finishing my first little pot of sake. I smiled and waved at them, and watched with idle amusement as they conferred earnestly, darting glances at me. While they argued, a waitress brought them bowls of noodles and a plate of sushi; they were clearly regular customers with regular tastes.

At last, Mr. Takamoku came over to my table. I invited him and his wife to join me.

"Thank you, thank you," he said in an agony of embarrassment. "We only have question for you, not to disturb you."

"You're not disturbing me. What do you want to know?"

"You are familiar with American customs." That was a statement, not a question. I nodded, wondering what was coming.

"When a guest behaves badly in the house,

what does an American do?"

I gave him my full attention. I had no idea what he was asking, but he would never have brought it up just to be frivolous.

"It depends," I said carefully. "Did they break up your sofa or spill tea?"

Mr. Takamoku looked at me steadily, fishing for a cigarette. Then he shook his head, slowly. "Not as much as breaking furniture. Not as little as tea on sofa. In between."

"I'd give him a second chance."

A slight crease erased itself from Mr. Takamoku's forehead. "A second chance. A very good idea. A second chance."

He went back to his wife and ate his noodles with the noisy appreciation that showed good Japanese manners. I had another pot of sake and finished about the same time as the Takamokus; we left the restaurant together. I topped them by a good five inches and perhaps twenty pounds, so I slowed my pace to a crawl to keep step with them.

Mrs. Takamoku smiled. "You are familiar with go?" she asked, giggling nervously.

"I'm not sure," I said cautiously, wondering if they wanted me to conjugate an intransitive irregular verb.

"It's a game. You have time to stop and see?"

"Sure," I agreed, just as Mr. Takamoku broke in with vigorous objections.

I couldn't tell whether he didn't want to inconvenience me or didn't want me intruding.

However, Mrs. Takamoku insisted, so I stopped at the first floor and went into the apartment with her.

The living room was almost bare. The lack of furniture drew the eye to a beautiful Japanese doll on a stand in one corner, with a bowl of dried flowers in front of her. The only other furnishings were six little tables in a row. They were quite thick and stood low on carved wooden legs. Their tops, about eighteen inches square, were crisscrossed with black lines which formed dozens of little squares. Two covered wooden bowls stood on each table.

"Go-ban," Mrs. Takamoku said, pointing to one of the tables.

I shook my head in incomprehension.

Mr. Takamoku picked up a covered bowl. It was filled with smooth white disks, the size of nickels but much thicker. I held one up and saw beautiful shades and shadows in it.

"Clamshell," Mr. Takamoku said. "They cut, then polish." He picked up a second bowl, filled with black disks. "Slate."

He knelt on a cushion in front of one of the tables and rapidly placed black and white disks on intersections of the lines. A pattern emerged.

"This is go. Black play, then white, then black, then white. Each try to make territory, to make eyes." He showed me an "eye" — a clear space surrounded by black stones. "White cannot play here. Black safe. Now white must play someplace else."

"I see." I didn't really, but I didn't think it mattered.

"This afternoon, someone knock stones from table, turn upside down, and scrape with knife."

"This table?" I asked, tapping the one he was playing on.

"Yes." He swept the stones off swiftly but carefully, and put them in their little pots. He turned the board over. In the middle was a hole, carved and sanded. The wood was very thick — I suppose the hole gave it resonance.

I knelt beside him and looked. I was probably thirty years younger, but I couldn't tuck my knees under me with his grace and ease: I sat cross-legged. A faint scratch marred the sanded bottom.

"Was he American?"

Mr. and Mrs. Takamoku exchanged a look. "Japanese, but born in America," she said. "Like Akira and Yoshio."

I shook my head. "I don't understand. It's not an American custom." I climbed awkwardly back to my feet. Mr. Takamoku stood with one easy movement. He and Mrs. Takamoku thanked me profusely. I assured them it was nothing and went to bed.

II

The next Sunday was a cold, gray day with a hint of snow. I sat in front of the television,

325

in my living room, drinking coffee, dividing my attention between November's income and watching the Bears. Both were equally feeble. I was trying to decide on something friendlier to do when a knock sounded on my door. The outside buzzer hadn't rung. I got up, stacking loose papers on one arm of the chair and balancing the coffee cup on the other.

Through the peephole I could see Mrs. Takamoku. I opened the door. Her wrinkled ivory face was agitated, her eyes dilated. "Oh, good, good, you here. You must come." She tugged at my hand.

I pulled her gently into the apartment. "What's wrong? Let me get you a drink."

"No, no." She wrung her hands in agitation, repeating that I must come, I must come.

I collected my keys and went down the worn, uncarpeted stairs with her. Her living room was filled with cigarette smoke and a crowd of anxious men. Mr. Takamoku detached himself from the group and hurried over to his wife and me. He clasped my hand and pumped it up and down.

"Good. Good you come. You are a detective, yes? You will see the police do not arrest Naoe and me."

"What's wrong, Mr. Takamoku?"

"He's dead. He's killed. Naoe and I were in camp during World War. They will arrest us."

"Who's dead?"

He shrugged helplessly. "I don't know name."

I pushed through the group. A white man lay

326

sprawled on the floor. His face had contorted in dreadful pain as he died, so it was hard to guess his age. His fair hair was thick and unmarked with gray; he must have been relatively young.

A small dribble of vomit trailed from his clenched teeth. I sniffed at it cautiously. Probably hydrocyanic acid. Not far from his body lay a teacup, a Japanese cup without handles. The contents sprayed out from it like a Rorschach. Without touching it, I sniffed again. The fumes were still discernible.

I got up. "Has anyone left since this happened?"

The tall, bearded Caucasian I'd noticed on previous Sundays looked around and said "No" in an authoritative voice.

"And have you called the police?"

Mrs. Takamoku gave an agitated cry. "No police. No. You are detective. You find murderer yourself."

I shook my head and took her gently by the hand. "If we don't call the police, they will put us all in jail for concealing a murder. You must tell them."

The bearded man said, "I'll do that."

"Who are you?"

"I'm Charles Welland. I'm a physicist at the University of Chicago, but on Sundays I'm a go player."

"I see . . . I'm V. I. Warshawski. I live upstairs. I'm a private investigator. The police look very dimly on all citizens who don't report murders, but especially on P.I.'s."

Welland went into the dining room, where the Takamokus kept their phone. I told the Takamokus and their guests that no one could leave before the police gave them permission, then followed Welland to make sure he didn't call anyone besides the police, or take the opportunity to get rid of a vial of poison.

The go players seemed resigned, albeit very nervous. All of them smoked ferociously; the thick air grew bluer. Four of them stood apart arguing in Korean. A lone man fiddled with the stones on one of the go-bans.

None of them spoke English well enough to give a clear account of how the young man died. When Welland came back, I asked him for a detailed report.

The physicist claimed not to know his name. The dead man had only been coming to the go club the last month or two.

"Did someone bring him? Or did he just show up one day?"

Welland shrugged. "He just showed up. Word gets around among go players. I'm sure he told me his name — it just didn't stick. I think he worked for Hansen Electronic, the big computer firm."

I asked if everyone there was a regular player. Welland knew all of them by sight, if not by name. They didn't all come every Sunday, but none of the others was a newcomer.

"I see. Okay. What happened today?"

Welland scratched his beard. He had bushy, arched eyebrows which jumped up to punctuate his stronger statements kind of like Sean Connery. I found it pretty sexy. I pulled my mind back to what he was saying.

"I got here around one-thirty. I think three games were in progress. This guy" — he jerked his thumb toward the dead man — "arrived a bit later. He and I played a game. Then Mr. Hito arrived and the two of them had a game. Dr. Han showed up, and he and I were playing when the whole thing happened. Mrs. Takamoku sets out tea and snacks. We all wander around and help ourselves. About four, this guy took a swallow of tea, gave a terrible cry, and died."

"Is there anything important about the game they were playing?"

Welland looked at the board. A handful of black-and-white stones stood on the corner points. He shook his head. "They'd just started. It looks like our dead friend was trying one of the Takamoku *joseki*s. That's a complicated one — I've never seen it used in actual play before."

"What's that? Anything to do with Mr. Takamoku?"

"The *joseki* are the beginning moves in the corners. Takamoku is this one" — he pointed at the far side — "where black plays on the five-four point — the point where the fourth and fifth lines intersect. It wasn't named for our host. That's just coincidence."

III

Sergeant McGonnigal didn't find out much more than I did. A thickset young detective, he had a lot of experience and treated his frightened audience gently. He was a little less kind to me, demanding roughly why I was there, what my connection with the dead man was, who my client was. It didn't cheer him up any to hear I was working for the Takamokus, but he let me stay with them while he questioned them. He sent for a young Korean officer to interrogate the Koreans in the group. Welland, who spoke fluent Japanese, translated the Japanese interviews. Dr. Han, the lone Chinese, struggled along on his own.

McGonnigal learned that the dead man's name was Peter Folger. He learned that people were milling around all the time watching each other play. He also learned that no one paid attention to anything but the game they were playing, or watching.

"The Japanese say the go player forgets his father's funeral," Welland explained. "It's a game of tremendous concentration."

No one admitted knowing Folger outside the go club. No one knew how he found out that the Takamokus hosted go every Sunday.

My clients hovered tensely in the background,

convinced that McGonnigal would arrest them at any minute. But they could add nothing to the story. Anyone who wanted to play was welcome at their apartment on Sunday afternoon. Why should he show a credential? If he knew how to play, that was the proof.

McGonnigal pounced on that. Was Folger a good player? Everyone looked around and nodded. Yes, not the best — that was clearly Dr. Han or Mr. Kim, one of the Koreans — but quite good enough. Perhaps first *kyu*, whatever that was.

After two hours of this, McGonnigal decided he was getting nowhere. Someone in the room must have had a connection with Folger, but we weren't going to find it by questioning the group. We'd have to dig into their backgrounds.

A uniformed man started collecting addresses while McGonnigal went to his car to radio for plainclothes reinforcements. He wanted everyone in the room tailed and wanted to phone in the command in privacy. A useless precaution, I thought: the innocent wouldn't know they were being followed, and the guilty would expect it.

McGonnigal returned shortly, his face angry. He had a bland-faced, square-jawed man in tow, Derek Hatfield of the FBI. He did computer fraud for them. Our paths had crossed a few times on white-collar crime. I'd found him smart and knowledgeable, but also humorless and overbearing.

"Hello, Derek," I said, without getting up from the cushion I was sitting on. "What brings you here?"

"He had the place under surveillance," McGonnigal said, biting off the words. "He won't tell me who he was looking for."

Derek walked over to Folger's body, covered now with a sheet, which he pulled back. He looked at Folger's face and nodded. "I'm going to have to phone my office for instructions."

"Just a minute," McGonnigal said. "You know the guy, right? You tell me what you were watching him for."

Derek raised his eyebrows haughtily. "I'll have to make a call first."

"Don't be an ass, Hatfield," I said. "You think you're impressing us with how mysterious the FBI is, but you're not, really. You know your boss will tell you to cooperate with the city if it's murder. And we might be able to clear this thing up right now, glory for everyone. We know Folger worked for Hansen Electronic. He wasn't one of your guys working undercover, was he?"

Hatfield glared at me. "I can't answer that."

"Look," I said reasonably. "Either he worked for you and was investigating problems at Hansen, or he worked for them and you suspected he was involved in some kind of fraud. I know there's a lot of talk about Hansen's new Series J computer — was he passing secrets?"

Hatfield put his hands in his pockets and scowled in thought. At last he said, to Mc-

Gonnigal, "Is there someplace we can go and talk?"

I asked Mrs. Takamoku if we could use her kitchen for a few minutes. Her lips moved nervously, but she took Hatfield and me down the hall. Her apartment was laid out like mine and the kitchens were similar, at least in appliances. Hers was spotless; mine had that lived-in look.

McGonnigal told the uniformed man not to let anyone leave or make any phone calls, and followed us.

Hatfield leaned against the back door. I perched on a bar stool next to a high wooden table. McGonnigal stood in the doorway leading to the hall.

"You got someone here named Miyake?" Hatfield asked.

McGonnigal looked through the sheaf of notes in his hand and shook his head.

"Anyone here work for Kawamoto?"

Kawamoto is a big Japanese electronics firm, one of Mitsubishi's peers and a strong rival of Hansen in the megacomputer market.

"Hatfield, are you trying to tell us that Folger was passing Series J secrets to someone from Kawamoto over the go boards here?"

Hatfield shifted uncomfortably. "We only got onto it three weeks ago. Folger was just a go-between. We offered him immunity if he would finger the guy from Kawamoto. He couldn't describe him well enough for us to make a pickup. He was going to shake hands with him or touch

333

him in some way as they left the building."

"The Judas trick," I remarked.

"Huh?" Hatfield looked puzzled.

McGonnigal smiled for the first time that afternoon. "The man I kiss is the one you want. You should've gone to Catholic school, Hatfield."

"Yeah. Anyway, Folger must've told this guy Miyake we were closing in." Hatfield shook his head disgustedly. "Miyake must be part of that group, just using an assumed name. We got a tail put on all of them." He straightened up and started back toward the hall.

"How was Folger passing the information?" I asked.

"It was on microdots."

"Stay where you are. I might be able to tell you which one is Miyake without leaving the building."

Of course, both Hatfield and McGonnigal started yelling at me at once. Why was I suppressing evidence, what did I know, they'd have me arrested.

"Calm down, boys," I said. "I don't have any evidence. But now that I know the crime, I think I know how it was done. I just need to talk to my clients."

Mr. and Mrs. Takamoku looked at me anxiously when I came back to the living room. I got them to follow me into the hall. "They're not going to arrest you," I assured them. "But I need to know who turned over the go board last week. Is he here today?"

They talked briefly in Japanese, then Mr. Takamoku said, "We should not betray guest. But murder is much worse. Man in orange shirt, named Hamai."

Hamai, or Miyake, as Hatfield called him, resisted valiantly. When the police started to put handcuffs on him, he popped a gelatin capsule into his mouth. He was dead almost before they realized what he had done.

Hatfield, impersonal as always, searched his body for the microdot. Hamai had stuck it to his upper lip, where it looked like a mole against his dark skin.

IV

"How did you know?" McGonnigal grumbled, after the bodies had been carted off and the Takamokus' efforts to turn their life savings over to me successfully averted.

"He turned over a go board here last week. That troubled my clients enough that they asked me about it. Once I knew we were looking for the transfer of information, it was obvious that Folger had stuck the dot in the hole under the board. Hamai couldn't get at it, so he had to turn the whole board over. Today, Folger must have put it in a more accessible spot."

Hatfield left to make his top-secret report. McGonnigal followed his uniformed men out of the apartment. Welland held the door for me.

"Was his name Hamai or Miyake?"

"Oh, I think his real name was Hamai — that's what all his identification said. He must have used a false name with Folger. After all, he knew you guys never pay attention to each other's names — you probably wouldn't even notice what Folger called him. If you could figure out who Folger was."

Welland smiled; his bushy eyebrows danced. "How about a drink? I'd like to salute a lady clever enough to solve the Takamoku *joseki* unaided."

I looked at my watch. Three hours ago I'd been trying to think of something friendlier to do than watch the Bears get pummeled. This sounded like a good bet. I slipped my hand through his arm and went outside with him.